The Red Dirt Hymnbook

THE RED DIRT HYMNBOOK

Roxie Faulkner Kirk

Fine Dog Press

Portions of this text have previously appeared in short stories in *Eclectica Literary Journal* and *Cowboy Jamboree*.

FIRST EDITION
ISBN 978-1-7339795-1-1
19 20 21 22 23 IS 10 9 8 7 6 5 4 3 2 1

FOR DAD,

WHO ALWAYS SUSPECTED THIS WOULD HAPPEN

But when he was yet a great way off, his father saw him, and had compassion, and ran, andfell on his neck, and kissed him.

FROM THE PARABLE OF THE PRODIGAL SON

LUKE 15:20

Chapter One

Baxter County Arkansas, 1979

They loved me. I was hitting the high notes, working the room, looking good. My polyester dress had been carefully chosen to complement the sanctuary carpet and matching upholstered pews. My bare arms were covered with a floaty chiffon shrug, so no one could fault me for inciting impurities amongst the menfolk, and the rhinestone belt around my waist was neither overly flashy nor tightly cinched, so as not to attract any envy from the women, either. My look was exactly right. I reminded them of their granddaughter or sister or the girl next door, if only she would get over that bad boyfriend and get herself back in church where she belongs. Of course they loved me.

I've always been a pretty good singer — better than you'll find in most churches, but by no means the best. I just know how to make people think I am more gifted than

I really am. "Oh, that Ruby Fae," they say, "she lights up the whole church when she sings." Back in high school, the show choir judges all loved me, too. They'd go on and on about my "stage presence" and "energy" and things like that. The other show choir kids wanted to know my secret, but there's no great trick to performing. All you have to do is stand aside and let the song go on without you. A good song is like a half-broke horse with an idea all its own and there's no use trying to wrangle it. All you do is open the gate.

I liked singing *Poor Wayfaring Stranger* as a solo and accompanying myself on my guitar, so I wouldn't have to warn anyone else to get out of the song's way. The last time through the chorus, the guitar dropped out and an older verse, often forgotten, sprang free. *And I'll go singing, home to God.* I shivered. *Singing. Home to God.* The people in their pews did, too. Shivered. We all waited, breathless.

A beat of silence followed and I knew that the audience — I mean, *congregation* — would talk it over later and debate the etiquette of applause in church, but they broke with protocol and clapped anyway. Some of them thought they had clapped for me and disapproved, but others knew different, and those lucky ones would carry the song with them all week. I broke into a smile.

"What was that up there?" JW hissed. "I told you not to try anything unrehearsed." The bouncy gospel music covered his words and the Joy of the Lord that was pasted on his face hid his disapproval from the congregation. He ushered me to my seat on Wife's Row like a devoted husband, even as his vice-grip fingers bit into the flesh of my arm. It would bruise, no doubt. Maybe that's why sleeveless dresses are a sin. They show too much that husbands don't want seen.

"Are you trying to make me look stupid?" JW whispered, still smiling. He settled the Bible on my lap and riffed the pages open to Revelations. On cue, I reached up and tweaked his bow tie against his lapel and smoothed his ruffled shirt front. He looked over my shoulder at the congregation and winked. I heard their soft sounds of polite amusement. In response, he dropped a sweet, chaste kiss on my cheek before bounding up the steps to the pulpit.

That tender little scene was a special new touch of his. Thoroughly discussed, debated, and deliberated by his father, of course, but it was all JW's idea. The elder Reverend Jasper had been against it at first. He'd felt it showed an unseemly amount of passion, and worse, deference to a woman. But JW had held firm, for once, arguing that it showed the opposite; his benevolence in bestowing a kiss upon my cheek and the way that he stooped down to my seated height all drew attention to his ordained headship. My father-in-law agreed we could try it, and so, on a probationary basis, my husband was allowed to kiss me.

Of course it worked.

It was the kind of charming little touch that the churches liked to see. I could almost hear the collective sigh from the women in the congregation. *So attentive to his wife*, the married ones would say, approving. *Please God, send me a Godly Husband like Reverend Jasper — the younger one!* — the single women would pray themselves to sleep that night. *That don't mean nothing*, the married men would think. *Does he take such good care of her when no one's looking? That's what counts.* As for the unmarried men, I don't know what they thought, because they weren't there.

My mother-in-law, who was always introduced as Mrs.

Reverend Lemuel T. Jasper and never by her given name, Merrilee, abandoned her post at the piano and joined me in the front pew. The home preacher's wife sat in the first row, next to the center aisle, in the place of honor. Next came the preacher's kids who would be seated according to age, as well as to each congregation's tolerance for babies and toddlers. I always sat next to the children, with my mother-in-law at the other end of the pew where she could easily leap up in time for the offertory. That particular preacher's kids, the three-year-old with ink doodles on her hands especially, made me miss my Susannah. I couldn't keep her in the pew with me anymore, like I had when she was first born. When she was still tiny, some dear mother-hearted woman would always reach for my sweet-bundled baby, holding her while I sang, returning her to me when I sat back down. Those were the services when I worshipped best. While the Reverends Jasper spent those hours raging and preaching with all the fury of Hell, I would be right there at their feet, at peace, adoring my little bit of Heaven swaddled in my arms.

But at eleven months, Susannah was no longer a good church-baby. She cried at strangers, babbled during prayers, and couldn't sit still no matter how many Cheerios I fed her. That's why she had to spend her evenings holed up in the nursery with some baby-lusting pre-teen. I told JW that Susannah's new behaviors were perfectly age-appropriate and normal and in no way an indication of either poor mothering on my part or moral failure on Susannah's. But Old Reverend still worked on JW constantly, telling him how that first birthday was the time to begin training up a child in the way she should go, that the rod of reproof was the safeguard of her soul.

Old Reverend was preaching the last sermon of our

Five-Session Series, "America, The Beautiful," which was one of our more popular shows. Our little traveling team was available for booking in sessions of two, three, or five-day revivals, depending on our schedule. Local churches paid travel expenses up front, including a per-diem, plus our take of the love offering. Our budget was rounded out by sales of our tapes and records, and from pledges from our regular prayer partners mailed to a PO Box in Iowa City. There they were picked up and deposited by our lone employee, the elderly widowed mother of one of Old Reverend's Bible college buddies. Despite her faltering health, Mrs. Gibley took phone calls, forwarded mail, and handled calendars for four different ministries. Only occasionally did she mix them up. This was no mean feat, because Old Rev was adamant that we schedule on a first-come-first-served basis rather than waste any time worrying about whether we could feasibly squeeze a week in Mercedes, Texas between two weeks in southern Idaho. That was the Lord's problem, not ours. Mrs. Gibley would get cranky with Merrilee and me, but because she was doing The Lord's Work she was utterly trustworthy in handling our money and took only enough to pay one quarter of her rent and phone bill and our ministry's share of the postage. The rest of the money went to Reverend Jasper, to whom she was hopelessly devoted.

"Brothers and Sisters, we have been told that there would be wars, and rumors of wars; this should not take us by surprise. Look at the newspapers! Turn on the television! What do you see? War! From Ireland to Iran, Cambodia to Afghanistan; War! Jesus told us himself this would happen! The end times are upon us, dear ones, have no doubts! Even so, quickly come, can I get an 'amen?'"

The congregation answered with a low murmur, a

doubtful baritone, a stage whisper or two. Our people always liked to see a little drama onstage, but they didn't shout back from the pews. They weren't Holy Rollers or Tongue-Speakers; that wasn't our brand. Old Rev said those denominations were more show than dough. People who followed non-denominational, tent-revival-style evangelists tended to be poorer, more erratic in giving and less reliable on the pledge follow-throughs. Old Rev felt they were more of a gambling man's game.

We stuck to established churches and built a reputation for bringing a decent music show. Besides Merrilee and me on keyboards, JW played a fair trumpet, I could chord a guitar, and we all sang, so we had no trouble booking up on the Holiness Circuit. Holiness Churches are your various Freewills, Little Baptists, Wesleyans, Nazarenes, and, of course, Pilgrim's Holiness types. Conservative, but quiet and earnest, for the most part. Back then, they didn't go in so much for politics, like the Big Baptists did. The distinguishing characteristic of Holiness churches is the belief that you can lose your salvation. That you can, somehow, be minding your own business along the Good Ol' Straight and Narrow with your name safely written down in the Lamb's Book of Life, when all of a sudden, *Whoops! Where'd my Salvation go? I just had it! Now it's gone!* And there you are, frantically turning out your pockets and dumping out your purse, right there on the floor in Hell's Lobby.

Oh, I'm sorry, God. That wasn't right. I shouldn't make fun. For all I know, they may be right. Me, I've been saved three times, and my brother Leland gets saved every chance he gets. But my other brother, Chuck, became a Big Baptist when he married Leslie, so he says his twelve-year-old-salvation is still valid. That kind of Baptist only gets saved the once.

Old Rev's rich voice filled the church. "What is America's role in this Glorious Unfolding? In this, the Grand Finale of Days, the foretold End of Times? Turn with me to the Book of Revelations as we delve into these truths."

Bible pages rustled and whispered as the congregation commenced the delving. I looked up at JW sitting in the big oak deacon's chair behind and stage left of the pulpit. He could have sat in the empty one directly behind it and out of sight, but Old Rev felt it was better for him to set an example of attentiveness and responsiveness where everyone could see.

"How long, oh Sinner, will Jesus contend with thee?" Old Rev lamented.

That was my cue. Old Rev ordered everyone to their feet while Merrilee performed her nightly magic trick of disappearing from her pew and re-appearing at the piano unseen, even though she was sitting right there in front of us. The wisps of her fingers flitted over the keys, not being so bold as to actually play them, but merely suggesting a tune as if she were leaving the outcome, an impossibly soft rendition of *I Surrender All*, entirely up to the Lord. JW edged to the side of the altar in front of the piano with a microphone in his hand. He looked over the congregation with a soulful expression that always provoked a flurry of repentance among women of a certain emotional variety. That was fine by me. Of all JW's faults, a wandering eye was never one of them. He knew that adultery was my one and only get-out-of-jail-free card, and he was not about to hand it to me.

I took my place beside my handsome husband. We were

a perfect pair, my husband's light, sweet tenor soaring over my buttery-rich alto. Our earnest faces full of love and devotion to each other and our shared life mission. His strong arm behind me. His fingertip poking at the exact tender spot on my arm where he'd pinched me earlier, under the cover of my filmy chiffon cover-up.

Oh, yes, I could still sing. I was a professional; a pinch was nothing. One of my all-time best solos was a Sunday morning service at a church in Colorado Springs when I sang *How Great Thou Art*. By the time I got to "Then sings my soul," I could feel every single person there was with me, feasting on the beauty of that perfect, true, sliver of a moment, all full of sunlight and God and sweet clean children and soaring, swelling notes. Even at the very top of my range my breath support was excellent. You'd never have guessed that my second and third ribs were cracked.

It was after nine-thirty. We needed to wrap this thing up. Come on, people, I thought. You can't tell me you have an hour's worth of sins with all of you put together. I could tell by looking there was a little envy, some grumblers, two malcontents passing as wives, a lusting Sunday School Superintendent, and a small pack of disco-loving teenaged girls who would vow to burn their BeeGees albums *tonight*. But there were no fans of alcohol, drugs, or sex at this altar. These were people who liked to keep their accounts short. Probably wouldn't find much more than an overdue library book with this bunch.

JW left me to stand in front with his father and help pray over the sinners. I had sung every verse of Just as I Am, Without One Plea twice and I wanted to get off my feet, so I looked over to Merrilee to see if she needed a break, too. Her eyes said *yes*, so I turned off the mic and slid over to the piano bench. Hovering my hands over hers, I waited for a break in the phrasing, then in one synchronized, nylon-swishing swoop, she slid off the other end of the bench as I slid over. We missed barely half a beat. She vaporized, but I knew she was somewhere nearby, massaging her aching hands in a gesture that was often mistaken for wringing them.

My fingers on the keys were not nearly as subtle as Merrilee's, even when I tried. So the mood in the room shifted slightly and people suddenly remembered that eternal considerations are important and all, but these kids needed to get to bed and the old folks didn't need to be out driving so late, either. So Old Rev dismissed us at a quarter to ten and I sprinted to the nursery. I wanted to spend a little time with Susannah and get her down for the night before my prayer time with JW.

"Ruby Fae?" Someone called as I rushed toward a rear door. Dang. I'd almost made a clean getaway. It was the home preacher's wife, so I had to be polite; we hadn't picked up the love offering yet. After a brief struggle, I came up with her name.

"Lisa! I'm sorry, I didn't see you there. I was in such a hurry to get to Susannah."

She put one arm around my waist and continued walking me toward the nursery.

"Believe me, I understand. I don't want to keep you from her." She glimpsed my dress front and said under her breath. "You're still nursing, aren't you?"

Oh, how good it would have been to have girlfriend-talk again.

"Does it show? I'm only feeding her a little, at bedtime, but I don't want anyone to know. They'll all lecture me, or call me a hippy or something, you know?"

"Don't I! Everyone thinks the preacher's wife can't possibly raise her kids without their helpful advice. Like we can't read a book, or don't have our own moms and sisters to ask. I had one old kook tell me today that Ellie's too old to sit on her daddy's lap. What? She's six!"

"That's terrible. I'd sit on my daddy's lap right now, if I could." I said.

Lisa gave me a quick squeeze. "Oh. I don't know how you do it. I'd be too homesick. But you all are so talented, and Brother Jasper has such a heart to save the lost, you have to get out there on the road, don't you?" I didn't have to answer because we were at the door to the nursery. "I won't keep you, but I wanted to give you the mail. It got here today." She handed me a fat stack of newspapers, magazines and envelopes. Thanking her, I stuffed them under my arm and shouldered my purse. One envelope slid out from the middle of the stack and landed on the floor. "Oh! Here you go," Lisa said, sticking it in the same hand as my Bible. Thanking her again, I glanced down at the envelope. The familiar slant of the handwriting gave me a jolt of that particular mixture of joy and guilt that can only come from a letter from Mom. I was happy to get a letter, sure; but I was also ashamed that I hadn't written to her in a long time. I stuck the letter inside my Bible to read later. Right now, I was in a hurry to see my baby.

When I peeked in over the nursery half-door and Susannah and I both squealed. She dropped a naked, shorn-headed, ink-marked baby doll on the floor and waddled, upright, toward me, her arms outstretched.

"Look at you!" I gushed as I entered, "You're really walking like a big girl tonight!" I squatted down to catch her in my arms and felt a runner in my panty hose split wide open.

"Yeah, we've been practicing all night," the volunteer babysitter (Tara? Kara? Sara?) told me as she picked up toys and tossed them into the little painted wooden doll bed in the corner. She looked at Susannah with undisguised longing. "Susannah's sooooooooo cute," she sighed. "I just love babies."

I plucked a summer-weight sleeper out of the diaper bag and plopped Susannah down on a changing table. "I'm sure you'll have all the babies you want one day, and they will be just as cute." I wiggled Susannah out of her ruffly church dress.

"Oh, I know I will. I have faith." The girl answered confidently. "I've already claimed it. I've even made my list of all the qualities I want in my future husband and asked God for him."

I heard that all the time from those junior nursery-workers. It bothered me, but I couldn't really fault them. I'd made a future-husband list, too, once upon a time; that's what Holiness Girls used to do for fun. I couldn't argue with the system, either, because look how well it had paid off for me. God had blessed me with a handsome, blonde husband who loved The Lord, sang harmony and could support a family. Those were the top five must-haves on my list, so it wouldn't have been right to complain after I had gotten exactly what I'd asked for. Why none of us girls ever made lists of the top five schools we wanted to attend or which European countries we wanted to visit, I have no idea. It never crossed our minds.

I handed Susannah her tiny white patent shoe while I yanked off a lacy sock and wiggled her piggies. I didn't look up at Tara — that was her name, Tara — when I said, "Maybe you should ask God for something...more, instead." I tried to keep the edge out of my voice, but still, she was taken aback.

"Like what?"

"I don't know," I admitted, sounding exasperated. "Just, something...else...different." I flapped my hand helplessly in the air. "Bigger."

There was a stunned pause. Poor kid, I didn't mean to shock her. Besides, I was trying to explain something I didn't really know much about, anyway. When you marry your childhood sweetheart, move in with his parents and start a baby all before your nineteenth birthday, you don't get to act like you know anything about The Great Big World Out There. I softened my tone. "I mean, don't rush it. Do something first, before you have babies and a husband. Like college or travel or a really cool job. Do something yourself, then worry about babies and husbands." I glanced up and saw Tara's look of confusion.

Susannah fussed tiredly, half-heartedly. While I changed her diaper, her giggles slid downward into a dull, whiny, slobbery hum as she teethed on her shoe. I snapped up her jammies and handed her to the sitter. "Hold her a second?' Tara was happier than Susannah about that, but I needed two hands to unzip the back of my dress, wriggle a strap off my shoulder and pull up the bottom of my bra on one side, all under the cover of my ever-handy, peach-colored chiffon drape.

I took Susannah back from the still-confused Tara and settled into a rocking chair. "Look," I told her as Susannah yanked up the chiffon and lunged for my wet breast and we both let out a sigh of relief. "Babies are the most wonderful thing in all creation. Just don't be in such a hurry, is all I'm saying." The sweet, familiar tidal wave of mother-y feelings broke over me as Susannah molded and melted into my body and I relaxed instantly. Better than a drug, feeding her always made me sleepy and mellow. I yawned before I said it, but still, I meant it when I assured Tara, "Whenever it happens, you won't believe how much you'll love your baby."

"And my husband," she added, nodding knowingly, confident that this conversation was back on the path of all that is good and right and universally acknowledged. "I have to love him best of all, because I won't ever submit to a husband I don't love."

"That's how it works," I said, the answer coming as effortlessly as my ABC's.

I asked Tara to turn off the overhead light as she left, then I rocked and sang and fed Susannah until her tiny baby snores were the only sound left in the world that mattered. In the shadowy room, I studied Susannah's face. She had traces of JW in her hairline. Maybe the shape of her ears, too. Her golden coloring was definitely him. If I looked very hard, I could see the rough draft of my husband's chin in her perfect little face, and my heart swelled. That was it. Right there. That feeling I had for my little family. What else could it be but love?

Chapter Two

A shadow appeared in the doorway, backlit by harsh fluorescent light. Without a word, I laid my sleeping angel down on the slick-worn sheets in the cast-off crib, pulled my dress back in place and turned to follow my husband. He was acting all serious and preacherly, but he didn't scare me. I knew how to handle the Reverend Mr. John Wesley Jasper. It had been over a week since we'd had a chance to be alone together, so he would be anxious to get past the sorry-I-sinned routine and get straight to the part where I showed him how grateful I was that he always forgave me. I knew what he wanted. All I had to do was sincerely repent and vow to never, ever again get more applause than my husband.

I followed JW into the sanctuary. Patches of saturated ambers and blues glowed on the carpet where streetlights shone through the jigsaw puzzle of stained glass. The air conditioning had been turned off an hour earlier, so it was already warm and stuffy. And there is no silence on earth that is deeper than an empty church at night.

I knelt on the altar steps, put my elbows on the rail and my face in my hands. JW dropped to his knees beside me and rested his forehead on the rail. I took a slow deep breath and waited.

The silence dragged and I wondered if maybe I was supposed to go first this time. "JW, I confess that—"

"Sh," he cut me off without raising his head. "I'm praying," he said to his forearms.

I nodded, knowing that in this absolute stillness he could hear the whisper of my hair moving. It was so quiet I was surprised he couldn't hear the thoughts in my head. Mostly thoughts about how bored I was. I've always been one to keep The Lord updated regularly throughout the day, rather than save it all up for one long prayer at bedtime when you run the risk of forgetting some sin you might have committed before breakfast. Old Rev, though, would spend hours and hours kneeling in prayer, so JW felt compelled to keep up with him.

I listened to JW breathe beside me. His arm brushed mine as he shifted closer to the altar.

I nudged one shoe off with the other, then dangled the other on my toes until it fell to the carpet with the softest thud. My mind wandered. I thought about Mom's letter, waiting for me. I was anxious to read it. Mom and I had written back and forth like crazy at first, but after Susannah was born I wasn't so good about answering. Then Mom's letters slowed down, too. A wave of homesickness hit me like a sucker-punch, reminding me why I tried to think about home as little as possible.

For the first year or so, every time I got too homesick, JW would make a big deal of it, trying to make me feel better. Which was sweet of him, but it nearly always ended up in an all-out ordeal, with Old Rev calling for an impromptu Full-Jasper Healing Service. I would kneel on the bus floor and Old Rev would put his hand on my head and JW and Merrilee would put their hands on my shoulders and they'd take turns praying over me until I was finally too tired or too bored or too sore from being on my knees, so I'd just give up and say I was feeling better.

But I was doing much better now. It had been over six months since my last bad bout of homesickness. And you couldn't really blame me for that one, anyway, because everybody wants to go home for the holidays. There's a reason they write songs about that.

Last Christmas, I had wheedled and nagged until JW finally agreed to go get a family portrait session done at Sears and they'd turned out great. After all, we have all kinds of color-coordinated clothes. The ones of the whole Jasper family with the fake laser-light background came out so well that Old Rev and Merrilee used them in our newsletter, but the best ones, of course, were of Susannah alone. JW and I bought the deluxe package, so we could get the cute one where she was sitting up by herself, holding a Christmasy teddy bear. I sent a bunch of Susannah's pictures and the one pose of just JW and me to Mom and Dad.

This is what Mom wrote back:

JW and Ruby,

Dad and I loved the pictures. Thank you. There's nothing you could have given us that would have made us happier. Susannah is perfect and beautiful and we are heartsick that we haven't met her yet, but that is for another letter.

I was glad to get the family picture, too, but I have to ask. Ruby, were you feeling well that day? Maybe I'm just being a mom, but I want you to call me. You looked exhausted. Maybe your blood's getting iron-poor. Call home.

Love,

Mom

I was a little bit insulted. After all, I'd picked the pictures out myself and I'd thought we looked pretty good. But then again, Mom was like that. A doctor had once told her she was a touch anemic, and ever since then she fretted about everyone else getting enough iron, too.

"Hi, Mom," I said, "It's me!" She already knew that, of course, because the operator had asked her if she'd accept the collect charges from Ruby Jasper.

"Ruby! Are you alright? Are you eating enough meat? Is JW helping you with the baby? How many services are you doing every week? You looked like you had the flu or something in your picture. No color in your skin and you looked peaked out of your eyes," she peppered me with her worries. No how-do-you-do for me, only anxious mother-fussing.

"I'm fine, Mom," I assured her. "It was just that shade of red I was wearing. You know that's never been my color."

"Hm. You don't sound like yourself right now, either," she said, still skeptical. "You sound weak and far away."

"That's because I'm on a speaker phone. I'm calling from a church office in Wichita Falls."

"Hi, Mom McKeever," JW interrupted cheerfully. "Your girls are fine. I'm taking good care of them."

"You're in Wichita Falls, Texas right now? That's only about six hours from here. Will you still be there Sunday?" Mom asked.

I suddenly got excited. "Oh, you and Dad could come see us! Couldn't you? How long will we be here, JW? Are we here until Sunday? That would be great. I miss you guys so much and I want you to see Susannah so bad."

I'd been so very homesick, wanting to go home for a visit, but I never thought about them coming to see me. And

I'd been too busy with Susannah to keep track of our tour route. Now I wished I'd been paying more attention.

"Awww, no, I'm so sorry, Mom Mac," JW said, "We should have given you more notice that we were this close. We're leaving in the morning for McAllen."

I was crushed. I think Mom was let down, too. All the starch had gone from her voice.

"McAllen. Goodness. That's way down south," she said quietly. "On the border, even."

I was so disappointed, I wanted to cry but that would have worried Mom even more. I didn't talk much for the rest of the call, but Mom didn't seem to notice. She mostly chatted with JW, her voice dreadfully pleasant and polite.

Every phone call after that had been the same way, with Mom talking to JW more than to me. It got to where I felt even more homesick after a call, so I quit calling. Dropping a postcard here and there was a better way to keep in touch without making me feel so blue.

Maybe I should try to call home again, though, I decided as we knelt in the silence of the empty sanctuary. Beside me, JW was motionless. Yes, that's what I should do. At our next church, I would get JW to ask the pastor if there was a phone I could use. I would call Mom and apologize for not writing sooner.

A big ol' lumberjacking snore suddenly exploded beside me.

I couldn't help it. I busted out laughing.

"Wha-?" He jerked upright. "What? Oh."

I cut my laugh short and held my breath. I'd forgotten that I was supposed to ask JW to forgive me for changing up the song during tonight's service. But JW only stretched out his back by leaning away from the rail as hard as he could while holding on to it. He slowly unfolded his legs until he stood upright, rolled his head around and then reached a hand out to me. "Come on," he said. "I'm too tired to do this tonight. I forgive you. Let's get Susannah and go to bed."

I took his hand, allowing him to be a gentleman as he helped me to my feet. He pulled me to him, kissed the top of my head, and leaning on each other, we made our way down the aisle.

See, that wasn't so bad. Not like that time in Colorado Springs. That was the only time I actually got hurt. And even that wouldn't have been nearly as bad if I hadn't stumbled into the corner of the pew. That's what did it, really. Hitting the pew.

Alone in my bunk on our darkened bus, I curled toward my window and held up Mom's letter to read by the light from the church sign.

Dear John Wesley, Ruby Fae, and Susannah,

How are you kids? I only have time for a quick note today, but that's better than nothing, isn't it? It's been so hot and dry here, but we're sure to get some rain soon. Chuck and Leslie and the baby were here for dinner after church, and Leland called to talk to everyone. It was really nice, but oh, it did make me miss you. I know you are busy, though.

I was so happy to get your ministry newsletter. It's very professional-looking, very well done. Did you write it, Ruby? I imagined it sounding like you. That picture of you all was lovely, and Susannah looks so precious. She looks just like you, Ruby. I know it's probably hard to keep up with the mail on the road, but do you have a more recent picture? I've enclosed a little money—maybe you could use it for a Kodak and some film? You could even mail me the film and I'll get it developed. Your newsletter sounds like you have lots of bookings. That's great.

And making your own recordings! When you get that new one done, let me know, I definitely want to buy a cassette.

I've been busy canning the lime pickles for Christmas and your dad is doing some dirt work by the old dugout. There's never been any water on that place, so he's finally building a pond there. I think he and Chuck just like playing with the dozer, though. Leland stayed in Stillwater this summer. I had hoped it was because he'd found himself a nice girl, but Chuck said it wasn't. I'm starting to think that may not happen for Leland.

It's almost time to leave for evening service now, so I'll close. Sweetheart, we love you and pray for you every day. If there's ever anything you need from us, please, let us know. That's all I wanted to say today. I'll write more on my regular Tuesday letter.

Your dad sends his love, too. He does. Even if he's too stubborn to say it. But then again, your Grandma Daisy's right—you can always tell a McKeever, but you can't tell 'em much.

Please write.

Love you,

Mom

I unfolded a piece of typing paper wrapped around three twenty-dollar bills. Sixty dollars! My heart pounded. I quickly folded the letter around the money, kissed it, then tucked it back into my Bible.

Her regular Tuesday letter. What did she mean by that? Was she writing me every week?

If Mom wrote me every Tuesday, then where were those letters? Where was my mail?

A jolt of longing hit my chest like the recoil from a cheap shotgun. Winded by the sudden pain, I only wanted to soothe myself, to curl up and have a good cry. I'd thought I was getting better at controlling this bothersome homesickness business, but I still missed Oklahoma terribly. I missed my own Rose of Sharon church, and I missed my family. I stifled a whimper. I knew I should be stronger than this, more grown-up, but feeling sorry for myself was awful tempting. It was only Mom's last sentence — *you can always tell a McKeever* — that stopped me. Remembering it, I shifted in my bed, straightening out of my tight little ball. That's why I wasn't going to give in to self-pity. I wasn't just the "Little Mrs. Reverend Jasper." I was a McKeever.

McKeevers don't lie around and mope. I didn't come from a long line of sulkers. Why, look at Mattie McKeever. When she found herself in a bad fix, all alone in a strange place in need of help, did she spend the night wallering in misery? No, she did not.

I know Mattie's story well. In fact, I know all kinds of family stories because in our family, we don't keep our stories stashed away in boxes and photo albums under our bed or pressed between pages of dusty old books. We keep our stories handy, in our pockets, on our person. You never know when you might need to fact-check a dust bowl movie, entertain a bored child, or explain the difference between a second cousin and a double cousin, twice removed.

Why am I so short? Where'd my big laugh come from? Anything you want to know about me, pull up a chair because I'd have to tell you a family story to explain it.

Mattie's story is one of my favorites. Dad would tell it to us the night before Land Run Day, September 16th, when Mom would be at the sewing machine whipping up homesteader's clothes for my brothers and me to wear to the re-enactment at school the next day. Dad always told it like this:

Mattie had started digging the second grave when she was interrupted by a whistling Irishman with a fifty-pound sack of seed wheat slung across his shoulders. He came striding across the grassy plain in the full moon's light on her first legal night in the Cherokee Strip. She heard him before he saw her, which gave her enough time to drop her shovel in favor of her shotgun, flop belly-down into the shallow pit, fire a warning and shout, "Already claimed! Move on west!"

She prayed that would be sufficient warning. This was a good claim with good water and she intended to hold it, but digging three graves in one day was too much to ask of any woman, let alone a grieving newlywed widow.

The young Irishman may have been whistling, but he was no fool. He stopped, dropped his sack and held up his hands. "I'll move on! No trouble here; I'm only looking for the nearest town."

"Salt Fork's south and east of here. What do you want with it?" Grandma Mattie was trying to disguise her girlish nineteen-year-old voice, but she was interested in getting to town as well. Solving that problem had been the next item on her list, right after burying the no-good, claim-jumping, Kansas-bred outlaw she'd been forced to kill earlier that day. "Come closer," she shouted. "I need a better look at you. Leave your hands up where I can see them."

The Irishman obliged. He took no offense at this woman's gunfire. He understood how losing your one last hope and the rag you wrapped it in can sour a person's disposition. "My name's Jack McKeever," he told her. "I was looking to file a claim, but I was delayed and missed the race altogether. So I thought I'd head down to a town site instead and look for work there." An idea occurred to him. "If you have any work here to be done," he nodded at the small heap of dirt beside the dead man, a good two-hundred-and-fifty-pounder, at least, to be dragged into it, "I'd be happy to work off one night's lodging and be on my way in the morning."

Mattie was a strong young woman in her prime then, but she must have been exhausted. In the previous four days she had eloped with a drifting cowhand from her daddy's Texas ranch, rode hard with him through the not-yet-opened Oklahoma territory to the starting line at the Kansas border, staked a claim, survived a shoot-out and buried a new husband. She was a little tired, now that you mention it.

"There is no lodging. I haven't even had time to start a fire," she said, trying not to relax her grip on her gun.

The Irishman took a cautious step forward. "I can start a fire for you and if you have maybe a few potatoes left in that saddle bag, you could warm 'em up for us while I finish your job there. As for the lodging, all I want is permission to lay down somewhere by a fire without getting arrested or trampled or shot at."

He must have seemed honest enough because the potatoes got cooked and the last body got buried, right there in the southeast corner of the original homestead. It's unmarked, but I can show you the general vicinity. Most every farm out home has a story like that of near-forgotten old-timers buried by the section corner.

I like to imagine the next part of Mattie's story, the cautious negotiations of two strangers sharing a campfire gradually giving way to an arrangement of trust.

Mattie said, "You held up your end of the deal, Mr. McKeever, and I held up mine. Could we strike another?"

"What do you propose?"

"In the morning, I'll stay here and watch our things, while you go to town to legally file this claim for me."

"I don't have any 'things' for you to watch. That bag of seeds you're sitting on comprises the entire property and holdings of the McKeever Feed and Livestock Corporation. At the present," he hastened to add. "I hope to see some improvements by the end of the next quarter."

"That's not nothing. Russian Hard Red Winter Wheat's good for this country; that'll plant a half acre." Mattie said, "You need to get it in the ground soon. It's planting time."

What Mattie needed was to get that claim filed down at the land office in Salt Fork, but she couldn't leave her plot unguarded. There was a limit to the amount of shooting and burying she was willing to do. She pressed on. "So, Mr. McKeever, I can hold out here while you take one of the horses to town. You can go file the deed for me and look around for work at the same time."

"I could, but I'd have to come all the way back here with the deed and the horse, and that'd put me one more day without paid work. What's in this deal for me?"

"If you get back to me with the papers, I'll give you the claim jumper's horse."

"And saddle?"

"And the saddle. Oh, and I'll need you to bring me a few more supplies."

"So now you're needing a drover, as well as a clerk, are you? That might cost you another night's potato stew."

"Fine, then; I'll feed you when you get back, as well. Is it a deal?"

They bargained and bartered all night long, my dad always said, and so I would always ask, "What about?"

Dad's mouth would twitch and he would say, "Ask your mother." To which she would usually reply without looking up, her teeth clenched tight against the pinheads she held between her lips for safekeeping while she sewed with both hands, "About who would clean up after dinner."

Maybe. We'll never know, but when Jack McKeever got ready to leave in the morning, he asked Mattie if there was anything else she needed from town and she answered, "A preacher."

"Are you sure?" He asked her, "Don't you need a little..." he glanced over at the two fresh mounds of dirt not fifty yards away, one of which covered her newly-departed husband, "...time?"

The way the story goes, Great-Great-Grandma Mattie stuck out her chin, looked at my great-great-grandpa-to-be, Jack McKeever, and snapped, "I cried yesterday."

Grandma Mattie was also about my age when she ran away from home to get married and landed herself in a bit of a tight spot. And what did she do next? Whatever needed doing, even if it meant marrying a stranger to get it did. Did Grandma Mattie ever learn to love her stranger?

I once asked Dad what he thought about that question.

"Nobody ever talked about things like that, you know, when I was a kid," he'd said, scanning the horizon through his dirty pickup windshield, hoping to find that last stray heifer. "But, I remember at Grandpa Jack's funeral, Grandma Mattie grieved so hard that Momma got scared and called the doctor, and, sure enough, she didn't last another two weeks."

"I never heard that part before," I said. "That's sweet, but it must have been kinda sad at the time."

"It was. That's why I never told you that part. I don't much like sad stories."

True. My dad does not like sad. I only saw him cry once, at his stepfather's death bed. Unlike the Reverends Jasper, who cried nightly. Usually Old Reverend started up about seven minutes in, blotting a tear or two and building steadily throughout the service. JW held off until the altar call, when he sobbed brokenly over the more prominent sinners coming forward. Merrilee never cried aloud, but sometimes dainty tears dribbled down her cheeks during the sermon. She couldn't out-and-out cry while she was playing, because somebody had to stay alert at the piano.

As for me, oh, sure, I cried some, at the start of the tour, most of it for real. I felt The Spirit moving then, at first. I, too, wanted to pray through, live above, break open my heart, pour out my life and so forth. But one night at a little Nazarene church fifty miles outside of Friendship, Nebraska, I started crying during the second verse of "Softly and Tenderly." I motioned for the congregation to join me, and the voices of all those farmers' families washing over me, singing, "Come home, come home! Ye who are weary come home!" reminded me so much of my own Rose of Sharon Church back home, I cried even harder — the big hiccuppy, gulping kind of crying that tends to attract attention when it's right up front on stage with a microphone. Fortunately, I was quite pregnant with Susannah then, so people were fairly understanding. Well, not Merrilee or The Reverends, of course, but the home pastor's wife was so sweet to me, trying to smooth things over.

She pulled JW and me aside and said, "There's not

anything wrong here; Ruby Fae just needs her Momma right now. She's young, and away from home, and it's her first baby. Why don't you stay here tonight, Ruby Fae? I'll take you to the bus station tomorrow and you can go home for a little visit. JW, if she had her Momma fuss over her some, I bet she'd be good as new. Then she can hop back on a Greyhound again and meet you in Texas. How about that?"

"Oh, please! JW, can I?"

I can see it plain, now, where I made my mistake. I didn't speak up and say what I wanted. I played like a good little wife and asked permission, like I thought I was supposed to. I think my story would be different now, if I'd stood up for myself that night. I really do.

JW was torn. "Uh, I don't know. I'd hate to be so far away from you, with the baby coming and all."

"Then come with me! Please? It'd be just the two of us on a trip, like a little vacation! It would be fun! Please?"

He liked that idea. I know he did. But he couldn't help it. He couldn't stand to make that big of a decision himself. He had to ask Old Reverend, and you can guess how far that went. There were a whole bunch of Bible verses about leaving and cleaving and I don't know what-all, but the short answer was, no; I could get happy in the same high heels I got sad in.

So back on the bus I went. I curled up on my bunk and cried all through the Dakota Badlands until I fell asleep. I was so exhausted and emotional that I cried and slept for most of two days. The Jaspers let me sleep, even through a Wednesday night service. When I woke up, though, Old Rev told JW he'd had a Word From The Lord for me.

JW came to my bunk.

"Ruby Fae."

His voice was low and his face was tight. "Come here, please," he said.

Holding my big baby-belly, I scrambled out and stood barefoot in the aisle. JW pointed to the front of the bus where Old Reverend stood holding his Bible open. Merrilee stood behind and below him in the stairwell, her face bland as she watched me find my feet. JW nudged me forward two steps, but Old Reverend did not look up from his Bible.

"Repent, therefore, of this, thy wickedness, and pray God, if perhaps the thought of thine heart may be forgiven thee. For I perceive that thou art in the gall of bitterness, and in the bond of iniquity,' the Book of Acts, chapter eight, verses twenty-two through twenty-four. These are the words that have been laid on my heart for you, Ruby Fae," Old Reverend said softly, still not looking up.

I looked at JW for a clue as to how I should respond to this, but his eyes were closed, his head bowed. I hazarded an explanation. "I'm not really bitter, Sir. I'm homesick. And disappointed that we changed our itinerary. I thought we were going to take more time off back home after the baby. I don't think that's a sin, I just miss my folks and my home, that's all."

Alright, fine. I was angry.

JW had promised me that he and I would stay in Oklahoma for a few months after the baby came. But I hadn't given up yet. I was sure that as soon as I had a chance to talk to him alone we could work this out. And yes, I was embarrassed that I'd been such a conspicuous cry-baby back in Nebraska, but I was tired and Old Rev had been working JW and me so hard, booking up extra youth meetings for us, that we hadn't had a chance to be alone to talk things out. A date night for us would surely fix this. I didn't see that it merited my own personal revival service.

"JW," Old Rev said, still softly, still scanning his Bible, "The Lord also gave me a word for you."

"Sir?" JW opened his eyes, but Old Rev didn't meet them. Instead, he closed his Bible and handed it behind him to Merrilee. Looking at me while he addressed his son, he said, "Yes. Jesus said you need to get control of your wife and stop being such a pussy." Then he punched JW in the stomach.

I froze, shocked. JW gagged, caught his breath, straightened up and walked stiffly to the driver's seat, where he settled himself in as though nothing had happened. Old Rev sat down in his recliner, put on his reading glasses and opened a biography of Jim Elliot while I stood stupidly in the aisle, not knowing what to do. Someone began softly humming an altar call song, *The Ninety and the Nine*. I had forgotten Merrilee was even there.

Chapter Three

We were spending the day in the house, and when I say "house," I mean a 40-foot diesel Silver Eagle Motor Touring Coach with custom leather interior. So a day spent in the house meant watching Middle America fly past my living room window in a blur. We would put hundreds of miles behind us before bedtime and I was glad. We'd been in Arkansas for a month, and I wouldn't be sorry to leave. Oh, the people were really friendly, but the humidity, ugh. Summer was so sultry and close in the Ozarks, no wind, no breeze at all. And how are you supposed to look at anything with so many trees in the way? I couldn't wait to get back to the Great Plains, where a person can *see*.

When I gave Merrilee the stack of forwarded letters and papers, she asked if that was all the mail. I started to tell her about my letter from Mom, but a startled gasp from the always-unflappable Old Rev interrupted me. He grabbed one of the newspapers from my hands and pointed to a photo on the front page.

"That's Brother Jim," he said, his voice full of anguish and befuddlement. "It is. It's him. You remember him, Merrilee, we visited his church in Indiana. Several times!

What on earth? It can't be him, but it is. How? Why?" Old Rev continued his babbling as he shoved the paper in front of Merrilee. She gasped and put a trembling hand to her mouth.

"What is it, Dad? Jim Who?" JW asked, trying to keep his eyes on the road while he watched us in the rear-view mirror, but Old Rev was ignoring him. He and Merrilee were asking each other disjointed questions about how long it had been since they had heard from Brother Jim, how long ago did this happen, how old was the paper, and so forth. JW was as mystified as I was. He gave me a questioning look, so I moved around Old Rev and tried to make sense of a black-and-white photo taking up half the news page. It looked like a picture of some church camp, complete with rustic benches, an outdoor tabernacle, a cross, and so on. But oddly, the people were all lying face down. The headline read:

FINAL DEATH TOLL 918 – CULT LEADER ORDERED "CHILDREN FIRST"

I looked up at JW helplessly. I couldn't explain what I didn't understand myself.

Old Rev cleared his throat, scooped up all the newspapers and fled to the little "Master" bedroom at the back of the bus. Merrilee slipped out of her seat at the dinette and followed him.

"What in the world was that about? I've never seen Dad that upset," JW said as soon as the bedroom door clicked behind Merrilee.

I told JW what little I'd been able to read, expecting him to be as confused as I was.

But I was wrong. "Oh, Jonestown. Gee, I can't believe it's still in the papers. That happened months ago."

"What are you talking about? How did you know about it and we didn't?"

JW shrugged. "It was all over the radio, I guess. I forget you guys don't hear the news like I do, driving late at night." He went on to share with me what he knew about the sad, bizarre story of the church who followed a crazy man all the way to their horrible end; fear, cyanide-laced Kool-aid, and a mass suicide in a jungle far from home. "To think that Mom and Dad knew Jim Jones," he shook his head in disbelief.

"Did you ever meet him?" I asked.

"If I did, I was too little to remember it."

Susannah was fussing for my attention, but I had one last question for him. "That must have been a huge news story. Why didn't you tell me about it?'

JW looked surprised. "Why would I? It didn't have anything to do with us," he said, and turned his attention back to the road.

Keeping Susannah occupied and out of everybody else's way was hard when she wanted to practice walking all the time. She also climbed like a monkey and got into *everything*. It was a good thing that every door and cabinet had a special traveling latch. They were meant to keep the doors from flying open if you hit a sharp curve, but they made good baby-proofers, too. I could barely get some of them open myself, so there was no way Susannah could get into them. But she tried and some days I spent my every waking hour scrambling after her, trying to corral her.

For the moment she was on my lap working at a See 'n Say toy. She would turn the knob to different animal pictures, waiting for me to pull the string and hear a deep, serious voice intone "The cow says..." then we would both join in on the sounds. Susannah was quick on moos and meows, but my pig snorts always cracked her up.

The bird tweet, though, threw her. It was a realistic *tweeter-tweet* whistle that she couldn't do and sure enough, when the wheel landed on the bird, Susannah didn't like it. She frowned and looked up at me. I tried a short whistle, but it wasn't close enough for her. She grunted and slapped the toy. "Sorry, Baby," I told her. "That's the best I can do."

JW looked up at us in the rearview mirror. "Hey, Susannah," he said, capturing her attention, "like this." He warbled out a perfect imitation of the toy's bird call.

"Wow! That's good! What kind of bird is that?" I asked.

"The Common Mattel bird." He still had Susannah's attention, so he trilled out a variety of whistles and warbles. Intrigued, she squirmed off my lap and toddled a few feet toward him, holding on to the love seat. If our living room hadn't been barreling down the highway, she would have been able to walk the remaining three feet unassisted. But creeping and scrabbling, she persevered until she reached JW's seat, grabbed onto his armrest and tried to crawl up. "C'mere, you monkey," he said, reaching down for her. "Help Daddy drive this thing."

I scooted to the closer end of the love seat, wanting to stay nearby. Susannah wouldn't last long in his lap because there was too much interesting stuff to get into from that point. Fascinating cup holders that swiveled, an irresistible pair of sunglasses on JW's face, and shiny knobs waiting to be fiddled with, all in Susannah's reach now. A case mounted to the wall by JW's left leg held one-hundred and forty-four of his favorite Christian

Contemporary music cassette tapes, which a smart baby could unwind in a flash. I leaned in even closer.

"What do you say, Susannah? You want to learn to drive, too?" JW asked her as he put her little hands on the steering wheel and she leaned in to bite it. JW and I both laughed. "First driving lesson: don't eat the vehicle," he said.

"Did you have a little trouble with that one?" I asked him. Sometimes I could tease him about his big appetite. He ate like a field hand.

"Yep. Billy Sunday had to wipe my slobber off the steering wheel after me." JW and his brother, Billy Sunday both learned the art of bus driving as soon as they turned eighteen, the legal age for a passenger license in some state or other. Neither one had ever driven a regular vehicle, but Old Rev taught them how to back and park and shift and lane change and everything. That would have been like teaching Susannah to dance the cha-cha before she crawled, but that's the way they did it. Well, maybe not quite that hard. I mean, I was driving a wheat truck at fourteen, but that was after I'd been driving stick for a couple of years already. It wasn't like I was starting from scratch. The Jasper boys never drove underage, though. Old Rev was a stickler for the law

JW became the full-time bus driver once Billy Sunday was gone. And yes, Billy Sunday Jasper was JW's brother's legal name, named after the original Billy Sunday, the world's first super-star evangelist and the spiritual grandfather of "The" Billy, Billy Graham.

I always did like Billy Sunday, with his one crooked eyebrow and toothy grin. Every year when the Jaspers came to Rose of Sharon for our week of revival, Mom would have Merrilee and the boys over to our place for a day. Billy Sunday was closer to Chuck and Leland's age than mine, which automatically made him more interesting than JW. Even better, Billy Sunday wanted us to call him B.S. when the grownups were out of earshot and that seemed really, really wicked and wonderful to our innocent ears. And he always wanted in on whatever we had cooked up, whether it was minnow seining in the Greenleaf Crick or chasing swallows out of the barn with bb-guns or climbing in the belly of the rusted old threshing machine parked in our junk yard, it didn't matter. If it was outside, dirty, and loud, count him in. JW, though, always wanted to stay in and watch television. That disgusted me at the time, but now I know why he always went for the TV. He lived on a bus. All the TV he ever got to watch was in somebody else's living room. I was the same way, now; I'd have loved a chance to flop down on the carpet in my old den and watch M*A*S*H.

I hadn't thought of our family's cozy wood-paneled den for a while. But once I started thinking about home again, I couldn't stop and I had a sudden, fierce longing to talk to my Mom.

Which reminded me of something.

"Hey, funny thing, JW. I just got a letter from Mom. It sounds like I didn't get some letters she wrote me. Have your folks said anything about not getting mail lately?"

Susannah was already bored. She turned to face JW and made a try for his sunglasses. He twisted his head slightly, out of her reach, and put her hand back on the steering wheel.

"I dunno. Could be getting lost somewhere. How'd you get this last letter?" he asked and fended off another grab at his sunglasses.

"The pastor's wife gave it to me last night."

Susannah lunged for his coffee cup and he shifted her to his other leg. "When's the last time you wrote to her?" An irritated edge crept into his voice. I couldn't tell if it was for me or Susannah. I got up and stood right beside him, ready to grab her.

"Uh, not too long ago," I said, not entirely convincing. Maybe it had been a while.

Susannah turned back to JW and made yet another swipe for his sunglasses, then squawked when he dodged her. He made an exasperated huffing sound, so I held out my hands.

"Want me to take her?" I offered.

"Sure." He snapped. "And when we stop, I want to look at that letter from your mom and see what you're talking about."

Shoot. If I let him see the letter, he'd know Mom sent me money, and he'd say he needed to "hold it" for me, for safekeeping, of course, and that would be the last I ever saw of it.

"Okay," I said. I perched Susannah on my hip and tried to sound casual as I added, "If I can find it. I might have left it in the nursery last night."

I asked God to forgive my little lie.

I lightly tossed Susannah onto my bunk, and yes, I said "my" bunk. No, JW and I didn't get to share a bed. He slept on one twin-sized bunk and across the aisle, and I slept in the one that used to belong to Billy Sunday. Susannah's little crib bed was mounted on the wall over the window above my bed. Her bed was a beautiful piece of woodwork that JW had designed and added himself using tools borrowed from a pastor in west Texas. I was surprised and impressed by his handiness with them. Susannah's bed looked like an expensive custom modification. The wooden spindles fit in with the décor beautifully, and the way JW designed the safety rails was so ingenious. When I complimented JW on it, he seemed genuinely pleased. I watched him handle the tools one last time before he returned them to the Texas pastor. "You know," he'd said, not really to us, "Jesus was a carpenter, when he was my age."

Over the foot of my bed was a built-in storage rack where I kept a few of Susannah's toys and board books. She busied herself there while I got my guitar case out from under JW's bunk. I sat cross-legged on my bed and leaned out into the aisle a few inches, double-checking. JW couldn't see me from that angle, Merrilee was turned away from me, and Old Rev was still in back. Good.

I could have closed the curtain that hung from the bottom of Susannah's bed and enclosed my bunk, but I only did that when I absolutely had to because I've always been claustrophobic. Instead, I learned to cope with the lack of privacy in the rack I called my bedroom with all sorts of tricks. I used one of them now, pulling my guitar case onto my lap, opening the lid, and hiding behind that. Slipping my hand under the corner of my mattress, I pulled out Mom's envelope, peeled back an edge of the red velvet lining under my guitar, slid the envelope into it and smoothed the lining back down. Then I picked up my guitar and absently strummed, thinking about all the ways I could use sixty dollars.

My money situation was weird. I ran out of pocket money a few months after I married JW, and somehow, it never occurred to me that I wouldn't have more. I'd never given it much thought. My mother never had a paying job, but she always seemed to have her own checkbooks, her own money. I never thought to ask her how, exactly, she got it. I didn't remember her ever asking Dad for money. As for Old Rev and Merrilee, even though she was the one who counted the offerings, handled the envelopes, filled out the deposits and kept the ledgers, she also waited patiently for Old Rev to count off a roll of bills to her and spent accordingly. If Old Rev didn't think of it, Merrilee wouldn't be buying it. Me? The first and last time I asked JW for money, he made me tell Old Rev and Merrilee exactly what it was for. Not only was it none of my father-in-law's business that I needed bigger underwear for my gigantic pregnant rear-end, it wasn't any of our prayer partners' business, either. But any of them who cared to ask for the itemized expense records could look right there under "clothing budget" and see *Ladies' Briefs, Cotton, X-Large, white, 5-pk for Ruby.*

After that, I learned to check the change slots of pay phones and pop machines for stray dimes. I swore I would never ask JW for money again.

I looked up from my guitar when I heard Old Rev clearing his throat. He stood in the aisle beside my bunk. "Am I interrupting your quiet time?" he asked. I assured him he wasn't. "You might want to go up front for a moment, Ruby Fae. Your husband has A Word for you."

"Oh. Ok, sure," I said, and leaned out into the aisle for a look. I expected JW to look up and catch my eye in the mirror, or motion to me or something, but he stared straight down the road. I put my guitar and case away and reached for Susannah, but Merrilee was already there, offering to sit with her instead.

"What's up?" I asked. JW glanced in the mirror twice, to see if he and I were going to be having this conversation privately and on cue, Old Rev and Merrilee began talking to each other about supper plans. This counted as "alone" for JW and me.

JW looked straight ahead, his face expressionless. He sat like a seated soldier, his hands precisely gripping the wheel at ten and two o'clock.

"Ruby Fae," he said, his words taut and crisp, "I feel that you aren't walking by faith when it comes to your homesickness. We have already laid hands on you and prayed over you, rebuking the spirit of despair and homesickness that abides in you. So if you are still homesick, it's because you aren't allowing the Lord to work in you. You are clinging to your old nature, not living in the new one. You know what it says in Matthew, 'Anyone who loves Mother or Father more than Me is not worthy of Me."

I was dumbfounded.

"But," I sputtered, "I don't think — it's not — that's not what that verse means! That you shouldn't ever get to talk to your family? That's not what Jesus meant!"

JW's head snapped toward me. "Are you arguing scripture with me?" he asked.

"No! No, I'm not," I took a deep breath and modulated my voice down a note, getting the sharpness out of it before I continued. *Slow down, Ruby.* "So, what do you want me to do?"

He faced the highway again.

"We, that is, I, feel that if you want to live in the fullness of God's blessings, then you have to act in faith and live as though your prayers have already been answered, as though you've already been freed from this burden of homesickness."

"Ok," I said slowly, uneasily. I tightened my grip on the handle bar of the stairwell behind me.

"So that means you don't need any mail from home, or letters *to* home, until you can claim a true victory over this battle."

"*What?*" my voice shook with anger. "That's ridiculous! I'm only writing to my Mom, how can that be a sin? That's not fair! We *live with* your parents. You don't know what it's like! You've never been away from them for a day in your life, so how come you get to make a stupid rule like—"

The bus suddenly decelerated. JW flipped the turning signal down, toward the shoulder of the highway.

Oh, man.

I looked back to Old Rev and Merrilee who were pointedly not watching us.

Quickly, I dropped to my knees on the bus floor beside the driver's seat. My head down, I said, "I am so sorry, JW, I am so sorry for disrespecting you." I clasped my hands and brought them to my forehead. "I'm asking God for forgiveness right now."

He flipped the signal off, put his foot back on the accelerator and patted my head.

"All right then, I forgive you. I told Dad you would be, I mean, I knew you would be, obedient to me. And the Lord."

Blood roared in my ears. Anger tasted like sour milk in my mouth.

"Is that all?" I asked quietly.

"Yes," he said. I unfolded my legs, stood and took a step.

"Except," he stopped me, "for a sandwich. Would you make me one, Sweetheart? With extra cheese?"

I had to turn away quickly before he saw my face. Even I knew it had to be a sin to look at your husband that way.

Mom had tried to talk me out of marrying JW.

"This is not the ideal situation to be starting out married life," Mom had said as she pinned up the hem on my wedding dress. "Living jammed up like that, you're going to get awful tired of each other. No privacy, no space..." She shoved a tomato-shaped pin cushion into my hand. "Here. Hold this. Don't move." She plucked a straight pin from it, then whipped her metal seamstress gauge under the edge of the white satin, measured a fold in the cloth, pinned it smooth, then rippled her fingers another inch around the edge and reached for the next pin. "You're used to your own room, even your own bathroom, since the boys moved out. Why, your dorm room has more space than that bus!" She fussed on, picking up steam as she talked, until finally, she exploded. "Ruby Fae! What are you thinking, living on a bus? You can't do that! What about your claustrophobia?"

"But the bus is bigger than the trailer house you and Dad started out in. And you lived in that for five years," I argued.

"Yes, but by ourselves, not with our in-laws! Always in each other's laps like that, you'll get on each other's nerves. Women weren't meant to live together that close. We're like stray cats. One of us will stand it only so long until she runs the other one off. Hold still."

"Mom! Honestly! How could Merrilee get on anybody's nerves? She's such a dear, sweet lady. I'm looking forward to learning from her, how to be a godly wife."

Mom paused and rubbed two fingers between her eyebrows, trying to smooth out the crease that recently appeared.

"I'll give you that; Merrilee is a little saint. If ever a mother-in-law could keep her mouth shut in such close quarters, it would be Merrilee. But if you start having babies right away, then you'll see how meek and Godly you two can be. There's not a grandma alive who isn't dying to run her grand-baby's raising."

Mom tapped the side of my foot, and I rotated forty-five degrees away from her. She absently slapped her own hand once, twice, and again with her seamstress gauge, then squinted up at me. "I'm asking one last time, Ruby Fae. Are you? Having a baby already?"

My face turned beet red, flush with injured dignity. "Mom! Seriously? I already told you! How could you think that about us? About me? About JW?"

Mom studied me for a moment, trying to decide whether or not to believe me. Funny thing is, though, I was telling the truth. I couldn't be pregnant; we hadn't even done it yet. Not for real, anyway. What we had done, though, was scare ourselves half to death making out after every session of a three-day youth rally over Christmas break. We had kept our clothes on, more or less, but we were terrified that the next time, we'd go all the way. That's why, from a phone booth in Idaho two days later, JW proposed to me, and, alone in my dorm room, I accepted. Maybe it wasn't the romantic proposal I'd always dreamed of, but what else could I do? JW had touched my bare skin. I had felt the fire in him. We had seared ourselves to each other. From that moment on, I think I lumped all of my life's greatest moments together; getting saved, singing on stage, and JW's hand up my shirt. All three filled me with the very same savage joy, so it was only logical to marry JW, right? That way, I could have them all, all at once. No guilt necessary.

Of course I got pregnant about ten minutes after we left the church. And, believe it or don't, it doesn't matter now, but Susannah really was three-and-a-half weeks early. She was small, barely six pounds, but I feel bad that Mom will always wonder if I lied.

And Dad?

I cringed, remembering.

He'd been furious.

My gentle, even-tempered, church-going Daddy who'd never raised a hand to me, who could barely stand to scold me, who'd never, ever uttered a cuss word in front of me, had slammed his boot into his pickup, leaving a nasty dent in the door.

"You think I've been busting my ass all my life to see my only daughter live in a damn *school bus?*" he'd yelled, his face red and his veins bulging. "Wandering up and down the countryside like a damn *hobo?* Look here, Ruby Fae, I know JW can smile pretty and talk sweet, and you think he's so sophisticated and shiny because he's traveled all over, but the truth is that little teat-sucker's never really been anywhere outside a churchyard. Do you want your kids to grow up like he did? No place to call home, no neighbor to know you, no patch of your own ground where you can grow a damn *onion,* even?"

If Dad had stopped there, he might have had me. Because as much as I wanted to go with JW, to sing on stage in fancy clothes and live like some Gypsy for Jesus, I also wanted to stay right there in Oklahoma, raising kids as wild as bobcats and living my open-range life. If Dad had stuck to that line, I probably would have caved. But he didn't. He had more to say.

"Oh, yeah, JW told me how you two were 'called' or some-such horseshit. Really? You show me where Jesus says you gotta live like a dad-blamed carnie worker, roaming around, hawking religion like it's nothin' but a rolly-coaster ride. You think that's what God's telling you? Is that how JW is hooking you? Telling you Jesus is *making* you haul off and run away from home?"

Well, that ticked me off. I mean, I was a grown woman, making my own decisions, right? So I said some ugly stuff back at Dad. I even accused him of being a Luke-Warm Presbyterian. And then before you knew it, we both had our heels dug in and weren't about to give an inch. We weren't exactly feuding still, me and Dad, but let's just say I left town on a runaway horse and Dad didn't lift a rope to stop it.

"Fine, then," he'd muttered as he walked me down the aisle. "Run off with the dang-fool Jesus Circus, why don't ya?"

I wrapped a paper towel around the bottom of JW's sandwich so he wouldn't make a mess eating one-handed at the wheel. I wiped the counter. Okay, fine, I thought. I give up. I'll admit it; Mom and Dad were right about some things. A few, maybe.

But it was a little late for horse-changing. I'd thrown in with the Jaspers. My life, my daughter, and my husband were on the bus. My husband, JW, the man I married. The man I made sacred promises with, before God.

You know, vows.

"Thanks," JW said as I handed him the sandwich and I had a swift, wicked fantasy of him choking on his Wonder Bread and dropping, lifelessly, to the bus floor while I heroically grabbed the wheel, saving us all from a fiery death and steering us back to Oklahoma. But even though I was fairly certain God knew I didn't really mean that, I asked for forgiveness before that thought was even finished.

I thanked Merrilee for watching Susannah and crawled back onto my bunk beside my baby. I helped her hammer toy peg-things with a plastic mallet until it cracked.

You might as well simmer down, Ruby, I thought. Getting mad wouldn't change one thing.

After I put Susannah down for her nap, JW called out so nicely, "Ruby Fae? Would you like to sit up here by me and keep me company?" He must have made sure Old Rev was occupied before he asked me, or else he would have used a different tone. But Old Rev and Merrilee had their heads bent over the ledger books and were not going to be distracted. Maybe JW had thought over the mail thing and felt a little bit bad, because he was being extra sweet to me. Oh, he wouldn't admit he was wrong because that could be mistaken for weakness, and good husbands are strong. He needed to think of himself as a good husband, after all.

"Sure," I said, and I sat down on the floor beside him. Maybe there was some wiggle room on this particular Word From The Lord, I decided. Playing nice was a good start. Besides, it wasn't like I had any place else to go. I dangled my legs into the stairwell and leaned back against the rail. As we rolled along, the floorboard over the diesel engine rumbled and shook and warmed the seat of my jeans. It was almost hypnotic. Soothing. JW kept talking to me, trying to be extra-nice. If I weren't so all-fired angry at these Jaspers, this could have been a pleasant moment.

"I've been thinking about what you said," he said, looking back one more time to make sure Old Rev wasn't listening, "You're right. We do need more contemporary songs. Like Andrae Crouch. You would sound fantastic on *My Tribute*." He hummed a little demonstration, so contented with himself and his kindness towards me.

And, dang it, he was right; that song would be a terrific pick for me.

We harmonized on it a little, playing around, which lead us to some more Andrae Crouch songs. Then we sang some from The Imperials, and then a BJ Thomas one, with one song leading to another until, unexpectedly, JW belted out "Joy To The World." But he wasn't singing the Christmas kind of Joy to The World, he was singing the Three Dog Night kind. I glanced back at the Jaspers. We couldn't sing this song! It has that line in it about Making Sweet Love and I am embarrassed enough singing it with JW. But the Jaspers, who were immersed in their business at the table, didn't seem to notice. So I jumped in and sang along with JW until he completely lost his head, slapped a rhythm on his thigh and belted out "Ba-da-DUM!"

He pointed to me, and I sang the next line, using the gear shifter for a microphone.

He slapped his thigh again, "Ba-da-DUM!"

The next line got a full-fledged shimmy as well.

Then JW and I sang it together, but with both of us looking back to make sure we weren't in trouble. We were singing about drinking wine! And not even the communion kind!

We sang that rowdy song over and over, not even trying to hide the fact that we were singing a worldly song. We felt good, we felt dangerous and rebellious. We felt deliciously wrong.

Until, behind us at their little table, still distracted by their receipts and calculations, half-listening to the "Joy to the Worlds" and thinking it was just some new praise song we sang to the youth groups, Old Rev and Merrilee absentmindedly joined in with us on the choruses.

Well, Joy To You, Too, Reverend and Mrs. Jasper.

This was probably the bravest thing I'd ever seen JW do, singing pop music in front of Merrilee and Old Rev. In some silly, secret part of me, I was proud of my husband for that.

Chapter Four

We were on our way to a three-day revival service way up in northern Minnesota, almost to the Canadian line. Old Rev was thrilled about this. Holiness churches are thin on the ground the further north you go. It's mostly Lutheran and Catholic country up there, so Old Rev felt like a real missionary, a regular David Livingstone amongst the savages, every time he got a call for Minnesota. Who knows? Some unsuspecting papist might wander into a service at the only Freewill Church in a two-hundred-mile radius and accidentally get saved. If that happened, Old Rev wanted to be danged sure it was credited to his own heavenly account.

Northbound on I-94, it seemed like we were dragging along slower than a hog on a leash. Which was not much of an exaggeration because no Reverend Jasper would ever speed. In fact, JW and Old Rev never even complained about the national 55-miles-per-hour speed limit like every other normal American driver did. Old Rev didn't care how slow we went, because, you know, God was our co-pilot and all that. The speed limit law was passed a few years before JW got his license, so he'd never driven any faster than 55 and didn't know any better. He would just shake his head at other drivers zooming past us as we plodded lawfully along.

But JW did have a fuzzbuster and he loved to use it and his CB to warn truckers behind him. He felt like he was doing his neighborly duty when he signed on with "Breaker, breaker, must be a bear in the bushes, around yardstick one-eighty on I-75. My bird dog is howlin'! Don't want nobody gettin' a driving award, ya copy?" When JW was on the CB, he sounded like the most red-neck ol' boy you ever heard. He twanged worse than my Uncle Thorpe. But in real life, JW had no accent at all. Where would he pick up an accent? His home town was I-35.

That afternoon I was desperate for a distraction, so I started eavesdropping in on JW as he fiddled with the CB. It wasn't very interesting, mostly just guy stuff with the truckers like cars, gas shortage rumors, sports, things like that. I was about to give up and find a magazine to re-read when a breathy, girlish voice cut through the static. "Breaker one-nine, this is Itty-Bitty Betty from Big Bad City and I'm looking for some good company. Any lonely truckers out there got their ears on?"

JW picked up his mic, "Well, helloooooo, Betty. You got Bible Boy here. What's the good word, come back?"

Oh, good grief. Would he never learn? A faint smirk threatened to show on my face, so I quickly looked down at my magazine. JW was talking to a Hired Skirt again. That's CB talk for a prostitute. So is Lot Lizard, Sleeper Leaper, Chartered Seat Cover, and worse. The first time JW talked to one, I'll confess it worried me some. But like I said, JW was no cheater. He didn't want to meet up with any of the Sweet Thangs in some rain locker — that's more CB talk, it means a meeting in a truck stop shower stall. No, JW had bigger plans than that for all the Rent-a-Hearts out there; he wanted to save them.

Itty-Bitty Betty from the Big Bad City paused a beat before she answered. "Bible Boy? Now that's a handle I've never heard before, over."

"You must be new on the job then, Itty-Bitty Betty. I been crawlin' over this stretch of blacktop for a long time, hauling hallelujahs and truckin' for the Lord. Can I share Jesus with ya today? He's standing by, ready to save, Praise the Lord."

Itty-Bitty Betty's voice lost its breathiness and suddenly she didn't sound quite so young any more. "Throttle down there, preacher man. Tell you what. How about you mind your freight and I'll mind mine?"

"No offense intended, Ma'am. I just can't help myself when it comes to sharing the Good News with those in need," JW answered, his cheeriness maybe a little more forced than before.

"What do you mean by 'in need,' Bible Boy? You think I 'need' anything you got?" she answered. "You're no better 'n me. Same road, different load, that's all. You copy me? We're the same kind."

JW clicked his mic button on and off, wordlessly, about three times before he answered. In CB land, that's like stuttering. "Come again, Betty?" he finally asked. "How are we the same kind?"

A third voice, a rumbling bass, butted into the conversation. "Break one-nine for Itty-Bitty Betty. I'm in the market for your kind of cargo. Let's key up to channel two-oh where we can talk business. Look for me under the handle Red Bull Wrangler, over and out."

"Roger that, Bull. And Bible Boy, you keep it between

the lines and I'll catch you on the flip-flop. Maybe I'll be the one praying for you. Over and out,"

JW gave an indignant huff and spun the dial on the CB to channel twenty just in time to catch Betty's girly voice again. "Follow me to eleven," she said. "10-4," answered Red Bull Wrangler.

"Why are they switching channels like that so fast?" I asked JW.

"Avoiding cops." He twitched the dial again, but the signal was getting weaker. A CB range is only about ten or twelve miles. Faintly, we heard Itty-Bitty Betty's girlie voice say, "Fifteen minutes, then, over and out."

JW keyed his mic, "Break one-one for Itty-Bitty Betty. Itty-Bitty Betty, come on." There was no response. He tried again. "Betty? Betty? What did you mean by that? We're the same kind? Betty! We are not the same kind!"

Static.

JW clutched the mic and yelled into it. "Betty! Do you hear me, Betty? We are not the same! Not. The. Same." JW punctuated each word by slapping the steering wheel. He snarled and slammed the mic down in its cradle while I crept back to my seat. Apparently Itty-Bitty Betty had hit a big ol' nerve.

Before the evening service, we ate supper with a church family who lived nearby. The pastor loaned us his car so that we wouldn't have to drive our bus over the dirt roads, and I sat in the back with Merrilee while Susannah bounced on my lap. Funny, she'd been a passenger all her little life, but riding in a car was a new experience for her. She was so excited! *Look!* I knew she wanted to say as she pointed, *Cows!* She banged on the windows. Since she couldn't say the words yet, I said them for her. *Look, there's a silo! A mailbox! A tractor!*

On the bus, we always looked down from above, rolling along like we were in an army tank. But in a car on a narrow county road, Susannah could be eye level with the world. JW drove slowly, checking against the written directions the pastor had given us, so Susannah had time to really look things over. The late afternoon light hit the country sideways, highlighting its features as if God had adjusted his gooseneck desk lamp especially for Susannah and me so He could point out certain details, like that wild honeysuckle overtaking the corner post right there, that He was especially proud of.

We pulled up to a beautiful farm with a giant red barn, its precise white "Z" painted on the door. A gracious antique of a three-story house surrounded by a full porch where a fat Tabby napped on the rail. A tire swung from a big oak in the yard. Calico-colored chickens roamed loose and horses whinnied from the corral. This was a spread like you'd see back home. That is, if the price of wheat was always high and oil wells never ran dry. There are no showplace farmhouses like this around Rose of Sharon, because all the houses built before statehood have either been blown away by tornadoes or torn down to make way for something decent. A generation ago, my family and all my neighbors were barely crawling out of their dugouts, not building picture-book houses and lovely old barns. Farms like this one must come from older money than I am used to. I didn't think these people were the same kind of farmers I knew.

But I was wrong. Turns out that the Olsons were as nice as could be. Before dinner, their two pre-teen girls took a break from their shy mooning over JW's looks long enough to give Susannah and me a guided tour of the stock show winnings displayed prominently in the living room. They showed us framed photos of their most famous animals and tried to get Susannah to baa and moo at them. Mrs. Olson and I talked about pickles while I helped her in the kitchen. She had put up a big batch of them earlier that day, so I told her about a good family recipe she might like. I have a story to go with it, of course, but it's a little sad so I didn't tell that part.

At the table, Mr. Olson talked lovingly about fishing. His voice was tender and warm when he recalled each individual catch; his face softened as he intimately described a particular spot on a Canadian stream. Merrilee asked if he went often. "Oh, you know, I go every chance I get," he answered and looked down at his pot roast. I interpreted that to mean, "If I'm very, very lucky and the herd is healthy and it's been a good year for the corn, and the wife absolutely insists, I might possibly get away every three or four years."

The part about Canada, though, is what Old Rev heard. He perked up like a hound on point. "Where do you go, in Canada? Do you know many people up there? Any churches?"

Mr. Olson had fishing, not church-going, on his mind when he went north, so he drew a blank. But Mrs. Olson chimed in. "My cousin married a man from up that way. They go to a little church back up in the sticks near the Angle." She shook her head. "Why anyone would want to live in that ice-box of a wilderness is beyond me." This, from a woman who probably used an electric blanket ten months of the year.

But Old Rev's eyes shone. "Those hearty people must be

thirsting for a fresh word from the Lord." JW looked at his dad, and his face went all dreamy, too.

"*Canada?*" That came out like a yelp. I didn't know anything about Canada! I imagined packing Susannah around some foreign place where half the signs were in French. What if she got sick, or we needed help? How did things work up there? I didn't know how to call home from another country, or make change or mail a letter or do anything Canadian. I was distraught.

"But you have to have passports, don't you? Or Visas? Or something?" I asked. Surely, Old Rev couldn't haul off and drag us clear out of the country on one of his missionary whims. We had plenty of American heathens to worry about. Surely God would just as soon have us finish up with them before we tackled the Canadian heathens.

JW shot me a look that meant women should stick to kitchen talk and let the men discuss business.

"Is it any trouble, crossing the border?" JW asked. "Do you need any papers or permission or anything?"

"Well, now, if you cross at the bigger crossings, like in Pembina, there may be a wait. Somebody might ask to see your driver's license, but that's about all," Mr. Olson answered. "I usually cross at Noyes. Sometimes I just show my fishing pole and they wave me on through. You could probably hold up your Bible and they'd let you go right on in."

Old Rev and JW positively glowed, but I was twitchy with panic. Longing for home broke over me like a fever. I did not want to leave the country, I wanted to go back to Oklahoma.

When Mrs. Olson told Old Rev she'd get him the name of her cousin's church in Canada, I got so flustered I almost forgot my own mission for the night. But right before the pineapple-upside-down cake made the rounds, I gave an excuse about cleaning up Susannah. My hostess pointed to a small bathroom off the kitchen. She apologized for it saying, "We haven't remodeled it yet. It's still an eyesore, I'm afraid."

Once inside, I locked the door with an old-fashioned hook and eye, plopped Susannah on the floor and took inventory. Dang. This wouldn't be as good as the pastor's house, where there was only one bathroom for the entire family. This house probably had at least one, maybe two more bathrooms. This one was an afterthought, so it wasn't likely to be fully stocked.

I eased the latch on the mirrored door of the old bead-board cabinet over the pedestal sink. Aspirin, I was good there, so I left it alone. Pepto-Bismol? No, the bottle was almost new, so it might be missed. A half-dozen dentist-office samples of floss. I pocketed three of them. Some Oil of Olay, nope, that breaks me out. Five tampons, yay, the good kind. I took three. And then, jackpot! Yes, thank you, Jesus. A silver card full of pink pills, loose, without the box. Expired this month. Probably forgotten. Capsules, not chewable. Not as good as liquid, but I could make it work.

Closing the cabinet door, I was confronted by my reflection in the mirror. "Well, do you have any better ideas? No? Shush up, then." I turned on my heel, picked up Susannah, pulled the long string to the bare bulb and snapped off the light.

On the ride back to church, I had a yet another stroke of luck. While digging for my hot-roller clip in the cushion of the borrowed car's back seat, I found seventy-eight cents and a pair of toenail clippers. Pretty good haul, I thought, and made a mental note to cushion-fish more often.

Nobody got saved that night, but it was a good start for the week. The crowd was great and JW and I sounded terrific together. Sometimes he fought the beat but that night he followed my lead and we came together perfectly. By the time we got to "He Touched Me," we had everyone *right there* with us and it felt like they were singing it in their hearts so loud that JW and I were only there to move our lips and hold the mic for them. It was incredible. When we sang, God moved on that room and everyone knew it.

The love offering looked exceptionally good for a first night, too, so all the Jaspers were in a cheerful mood when we finally made it back to the bus. Susannah was conked out and Old Rev and Merrilee were sitting at the table counting money. JW showered while I crawled onto my bunk and wriggled out of my church clothes and into jeans and a sweat shirt. I was still kinda worked up from the excitement of a great performance and I wasn't ready to sleep yet.

JW came out of the shower wrapped in a towel. Our bathroom was too small to towel off or dress in, which was a problem for most of us. Not JW, though. In one of his sillier moods, he once pointed out that he was the only person on the bus who could get away with walking around in his undershorts. It would have been awkward for Merrilee to be undressed in front of her grown son and horribly wrong for me or Old Rev to see each other bare-nekkid, but what was stopping JW? His dad was just another guy, his mom had changed his diapers and I was his wife, so he had nothing to hide from any of us.

From my bunk, I watched JW. Following the path of one water droplet as it slid down his Adam's apple and splashed onto his sternum, I was struck, once again, by his ridiculous beauty. Have Mercy, he was a pretty boy.

He shook his head like a dog and water flew everywhere, intentionally spraying me. I tried to look put out at him but got distracted wondering where he'd come up with enough sun to make that tan line just above his towel.

JW caught me looking. He turned his back on his folks, took the towel from his waist and dried his head, his neck, his shoulders. He dried his chest in slow, deliberate circles while he kept his eyes on mine, his smile shy and sly.

Which put me in a pickle. I mean, I was still mad at him about keeping my mail from me. I still thought he was being stupid and overbearing. I still thought he was letting Old Rev run all over our marriage. I hadn't changed my mind about any of that.

He winked at me.

Oh, what the heck. I could be mad at him tomorrow.

I cocked an eyebrow and rolled my eyes toward the bus door. He didn't bother drying off the rest, but dropped his towel, jumped into a pair of jeans, jammed on his sneakers and grabbed a t-shirt. Steering me down the bus aisle, he mumbled something to his folks about us going for a walk. We retrieved a sleeping bag from the cargo hold outside and took off, holding hands and running, through the churchyard and across the road. JW held the barbed wire up for me as I scooted through the fence, then he tossed me the sleeping bag and crawled through himself as I held the wire up for him. We quickly flattened a stand of blue gramma grass and spread the sleeping bag on top of it.

Oh, the stars, the stars, the stars. If you've never seen them on a summer-ending night on the prairie, stars so thick the sky is a shining silver backdrop and the blackness is nothing but scattered pin-prick dots, starlight so glorious and holy and tender; if you've never had the chance to see that, then I might have to wonder what it is you did that made God so mad at you. The best way to see prairie stars of course, is naked in a sleeping bag with a beautiful, worn-out boy stuffed in beside you, gently snoring, but I realize that might not be practical for everyone.

With my freest hand I wadded up our jeans and made a pillow. I inhaled the sweet, green smells of farm country. I traced JW's limp hand where it lay between my breasts. I recalled how good it felt to be on stage tonight, singing. I thought about my beautiful baby, sleeping peacefully in her bed. I thought about JW and our most recent and highly enthusiastic rendition of love. I thought about God. I told Him, *I'm glad I'm here. Thank you.*

JW wasn't quite asleep after all. "Ruby," he said, his voice sounding boyish, "Why did she say that? What did she mean?"

"Who?" I asked.

"Itty-Bitty Betty. Why did she say we are alike? I'm nothing like her. Nothing at all."

"I don't know JW. I can't believe you're still thinking about that. Do I need to worry about you after all?"

"No. You know who I belong to," JW answered and gave me a little squeeze.

I don't know why that answer unsettled me, but it did.

Later as my husband and I sneaked back across the fence and into the bus, careful not to wake his sleeping parents, I wondered. Who did JW belong to?

Chapter Five

Twice a year we dropped everything and made the trek to Mrs. Gibley's house in Iowa City. In late March we would swing by so Old Rev could sign tax forms, re-tag the bus, and renew driver's licenses for JW and himself. In late summer, we made sure to get back in time to pick up the Jasper's absentee ballots. Old Rev was big on doing your patriotic duty and exercising your voting rights. Well, for some of us. Somehow, we never got around to changing my voter registration from Salt Fork.

"When we get home today, you need to go ahead and put up Mrs. Gibley's storm windows for her," Old Rev said to JW as we hit the Iowa state line. "It's a little early, but the worst heat is over and, who knows? We may be in Canada by the time the weather turns completely."

Canada? No, no, no! Canada is the wrong direction. The wrongest possible direction, if you're homesick for Oklahoma. Merrilee's head jerked up, and for a second our eyes connected. She looked startled by that, too.

Old Rev went on. "You know, when Billy Sunday left us, it was quite a blow. But now I see how it all works. It's all a part of the Larger Plan. If it hadn't been for that wreck, we'd still just be the Traveling Jaspers, traipsing across the plains in an old school bus. But look at us. Now we have opportunities to expand across the whole continent, and even a new generation to raise up to continue our work. Such riches of blessing for a humble man." he shook his head in amazement.

At the mention of Billy Sunday, Merrilee had made the tiniest intake of breath, so faint she may not have realized she did it. Or maybe the little gasp of surprise came from me. Old Rev and Merrilee never talked about Billy Sunday other than when it suited Old Rev's purposes from the pulpit. But already, Merrilee was looking at her husband with her usual peaceful, unbothered gaze. Maybe I imagined that flicker of emotion. She must not count the cost when it comes to following the Reverend Lemuel T. Jasper, I thought. After all, Billy Sunday and the train wreck and every last thing that ever happened to Merrilee, aren't they small change to offer up in this life of Service to The Lord?

It all happened a few years before I came on board. Billy Sunday had been driving the bus on a foggy night in rural Idaho and did not see the train approaching. Yes, a train. The home-conversion 1964 Bluebird school bus that was the Jasper's former residence was totaled. The engineer and his crew would insist that they did indeed blow the whistle and slow the train as usual. The fact that the Jaspers survived at all more or less proved the crew's claim that the train was barely moving, but no lawyer in his right mind wanted to tangle with a Man of God in a courtroom in rural Idaho. Besides, there were no crossing arms on that deserted stretch of highway, so the Burlington Railway lawyers settled eagerly.

I once asked JW if he remembered anything at all about that night.

"We heard about that when it happened," I told him. "You-all were on our prayer list. It must have been really scary." I shivered in delicious fright at the thought. If we had been at a school bonfire right then and JW had been an average boy who had gone to a regular high school instead of a correspondence one with his mother for a teacher, he would have thrown his letter jacket around me right then, and I would have leaned against him. But instead, we were surrounded by parents and preachers and Sunday School teachers toasting their own marshmallows and safeguarding our souls. So JW only dug his fists deeper into his windbreaker pockets and averted his eyes from mine, looking into the bonfire instead.

"Accidents and things like that are hard to keep straight in your head," he told me. "But I remember how Billy Sunday was bound and determined to get to Texas ahead of schedule that weekend. Said the Lord was leading him to the sea, that we needed our souls refreshed by the waters. Told us all to go to sleep, he'd drive until he got tired. He almost never talked like that, and there's no arguing with a Word from The Lord, so we all went to bed. I don't know if I woke up before the crash, or when we hit. I heard Dad yell something, like, 'Praise God', and Billy Sunday was singing, really loud, *When the Roll is Called Up Yonder*, which was weird because he almost never sang. Anyway, all I remember after that was the lights of the sheriff's car, and wondering if we were in Texas yet."

JW was so serious, so fine-looking, as he gazed into the firelight, pondering the weighty unsaid things pressing on us. Big thoughts about fate and God's providence and the biggest one of all; please, please, *oh, please*, God, *we beseech Thee* to not Rapture us out of here yet because we will absolutely, positively *die* if we have to spend all eternity as virgins.

For an excuse to keep talking to him, I marveled at the drama of it all. I mean, surviving a train wreck, really. As conversation starters go, it's good in any circle, but in the church world? It's a guaranteed hit.

"Yes, it was God's hand, all right," he agreed. "And what's more, God used that accident as a means to provide us with a new bus. We'd been praying for one for years. That old school bus was worn out, and look at what God replaced it with!" He gestured with pride towards the sleek new motor coach parked on the far side of the churchyard.

"I saw Merle Haggard's tour bus on the highway to Tulsa, once," I said, "Yours looks exactly like it."

He laughed. "Don't be saying that! Mom will worry about it being too worldly, and she'll make us dent it up so it will look humbler."

"Maybe it needs some home-made gingham curtains. That would make it more modest."

"Sure, and we'll start traveling with a crate of chickens tied on top, too. Hey, maybe the Missionary Society would quilt us an awning, if we asked them."

My Grandma's friend, Doris, came by us right then, offering the sack of marshmallows and a pair of roasting sticks made out of wire coat hangers. She looked at me with a knowing smile that made me both embarrassed and brave at the same time. After she passed by, I said, "If they started on a quilt that big right now, they'd be done with it by the time you come back next year." I congratulated myself on bringing the conversation around to next year in such a crafty way.

"I'll have to ask Dad to hold this week open, then. We'd

hate to disappoint the Missionary Society." He pointed a lightly toasted marshmallow at me, a shy offering.

On the other side of the bonfire, Old Reverend also held court on the subject of the Great Jasper Train Wreck.

"God provides for his own, on that you can rely," he said. "Sometimes, He uses strange means, but that is not our business to question." Amidst the murmurs of agreement, I overheard my mother ask JW's mother about the wreck, and Merrilee replied something about her new hip healing nicely, and she barely noticed the pain any more.

Another net gain from that train wreck, aside from the new tour bus, was the expansion of the Jasper Family Ministries, Inc. While Merrilee recuperated in Idaho, Old Rev and JW continued their tour schedule and Billy Sunday stayed behind tending to Merrilee. Three months later, when Old Rev came back to pick them up in his fancy new bus, Billy Sunday was gone. He had slipped down to San Angelo, Texas, crossed the Mexican border and was halfway to Oaxaca. Said he'd felt the call to save the heathen in a more tropical locality. I never knew what the Reverend and Mrs. Jasper felt about that in private, but in public they were thrilled enough to operate under the more important-sounding new name of "Jasper Family Ministries, International." Suddenly Billy Sunday got his own mailing list, with his own prayer partners and pledges and everything, forwarded faithfully by the goodly Mrs. Gibley.

Funny how you run across the same people up and down the roads, but it happened to us all the time. Like Red Pinto Guy. He wore mirrored aviator sunglasses and drove with his window open year round, day and night. I saw him eleven times in two years. I know; I kept count. He was always alone. No idea where he went or why, but he waved at us every time he saw us. Reflector Man drove a pickup-truck with a cab-over camper and every square inch of it was covered in red and orange reflectors. We saw him three times. He was kinda hard to miss. A Kenworth driver with a life-sized stuffed gorilla riding shotgun was practically a rolling landmark. His CB handle was Amarilla G'rilla and we saw him at least once a month. Travelers tend to wear down a groove. Certain stretches of road can get to feeling like a home of sorts, and you always circle back to them. I guess that made the CB our town square.

"Bible Boy, is that you?" It was Itty-Bitty Betty on the CB again. JW picked up. "10-4, Betty. Surprised to hear you this far north, over."

"Looks like we're working the same territory. That's not good for business. Maybe we should divvy up. I'll take East of I-35 and you take west. What do you say?"

JW kept his temper better this time, but I could tell it still irked him to hear her to say that. "We are not in the same business, Betty," JW said, enunciating each word carefully. "I am here to save people."

Betty's voice was dry as she drawled. "So am I, Bible Boy. So am I." With that she was gone.

"Dadgummit all to Heck," JW said under his breath and I tried not to giggle. Leland used to call that "cusstituting." That's substituting cuss words. It's something of a gray area with Holiness people, so JW always tried to keep it contained around his folks.

Old Rev's ears perked up. "Did you say something, Son?"

"No, Dad," he answered quickly. He steered Old Rev

back to a topic that was sure to please him. "I've been thinking about Canada, too, Dad," JW said. "Sounds exciting. Got any leads?"

"Not yet," said Old Rev, "but we will, and soon."

Good Lord, Old Rev wasn't letting this Canada thing go.

"We do have a couple of standing engagements down south later this fall. And Rose of Sharon has asked us to come back for the last two years and we skipped them," JW reminded him. "Shouldn't we swing down that way first?" I held my breath. Yes, yes, yes we should go back home before we go trekking off into a foreign country.

"If the Lord calls us north, that's where we go. We have to go where the need is the greatest. I've known for some time now that God has a bigger work for us and ever since Billy Sunday left us, I've felt the Lord pulling me further north. He's calling me, Son. I hear Him." He looked high above our heads, envisioning that vast wilderness dotted with souls keening for salvation.

My pulse raced. They had both promised we would go back home to Rose of Sharon this fall. Both Old Rev and JW! They'd *promised*! I clenched my teeth against a torrent of words threatening to burst.

I had to do something. Susannah and I could not go to Canada for heaven only knew how long, following Old Rev as he wandered in the wilderness like Moses in a leisure suit.

Right then Merrilee asked Old Rev if he would like to see our performance outfits for the week and she led him to the back of the bus. The closet back there was her little kingdom. Designed by Merrilee and stuffed with beautifully coordinated clothes, shoes, scarves and jewelry all perfectly organized with ingenious, space-saving racks, hooks, and shelves, it rivaled any big-name star's touring bus. Those twelve square feet were the only spot on earth where Old Rev deferred to Merrilee. We all pretended not to notice it.

As soon as they were out of earshot, I scrambled up beside JW.

"I don't want to go to Canada, JW," I said, not whispering, exactly, but definitely not in a loud voice. "I want to go home. You promised we would go home. It's been two years. Mom and Dad haven't even seen Susannah."

He kept his eyes on the road. He said nothing.

"JW."

"I know, Ruby, I know. I did promise," he said, his own voice high and soft. It struck me as a bit childlike, the tone in his voice. "But, Dad, see, he thinks, well, he says—" JW swallowed. He tried again. "If God calls, you know, we have to, I mean, God! Ruby, what am I supposed to do?"

"You're supposed to keep your promises to your wife," I hissed and scrambled back to the love seat as Old Rev and Merrilee closed the closet and came back to the couch. I picked up a magazine and hid my fuming face.

I'm not going to Canada, I decided. I'm going home. I don't care what the Jaspers say, I don't care what JW wants to do about it. I'm going home. I'll just have to think of a way and that is all there is to it.

By the time we got to Iowa City, I had an idea. If Old Rev, Merrilee, and Mrs. Gibley would go outside for a bit to talk to JW while he worked putting up storm windows, I could have a moment alone at Mrs. Gibley's desk. A second was all I needed. Just long enough to whip an addressed letter out of my back pocket, slide it in the postage meter and pull the handle. The last time we were at Mrs. Gibley's, I'd just tossed my letters home into the outgoing mail box with all the rest of the mail, but apparently Mom never got them. So this time, my plan was to get the postage on it, then maybe slide it into a mailbox somewhere else down the road. I couldn't believe that I had to sneak around to mail a letter. I only wanted to write to my folks, to let them know I was ok. Well, that, as well as tell them how our new schedule would put us less than half a day's drive from home next week. I had to get that letter in the mail right away. Please, God, let me pull this off, I prayed.

The tiny bungalow was crowded and hot with all of us inside, so after a quick hug from Mrs. Gibley, JW headed outside and Old Rev and Merrilee got down to the copier business. I would have liked to take Susannah out in the yard, but instead I loitered inside.

Old Rev and Merrilee and Mrs. Gibley fussed over the copier, Susannah looked for things she could grab, and I edged toward the table where the postage meter and mailing baskets sat. Even if everybody was preoccupied across the room, I couldn't use the meter right then; it made a loud *ker-chunk* sound that would have given me away.

Mrs. Gibley voiced her exasperation at the new copy machine. Merrilee clucked sympathetically, then turned around to face me and asked if I'd ever used one of these "new contraptions." Dang you, Merrilee. It's almost like you know what I'm up to.

"Oh, no. I've never used one. I wouldn't be any help there. What else could I do, though? Mrs. Gibley, is there anything over here you need done?" I was close enough to see the table top now, and I could barely contain my excitement; there were three loose stamps! Just lying there! Not on a roll, or anything. My fingers twitched. I wished I had Merrilee's swift hands.

A sound like a gunshot suddenly rattled through the walls of the little house, followed by JW yelling something that sounded an awful lot like a real cuss word. Startled, everyone dropped their copy papers and rushed toward the back door. Praise the Lord, here's my chance. I snatched up a stamp, grabbed Susannah and followed the others outside, giddy with success.

JW looked sheepish. "It's alright. Just wasps. Sorry to scare everyone," he said.

Old Rev looked at him with suspicion, like maybe he'd almost heard the same dirty word I'd almost heard, too, but he said nothing. Merrilee wanted to inspect JW for wasp bites, but he waved her off. Mrs. Gibley muttered something about how maybe JW's wife could have been helping him and told JW about the wasp spray in the storage shed. Once everyone was convinced that JW would survive, Mrs. Gibley and the Jaspers trooped back into the house to tame the copier.

Susannah and I stayed outside, clumping around in the small fenced-in grass patch. JW wolf-whistled as he passed by, and I flashed him a smile to show him that I was flattered. Satisfied, he trotted happily around to the front of the house with his arms full of aluminum-framed window panes.

I was aching to get my letter into a mailbox, but even alone in the backyard, Susannah and I were as trapped as ever. Mrs. Gibley's yard didn't have alley access. All the houses on her block backed up to a common chain link fence that ran the length of it and were separated from their neighbors on each side by more chain link.

Everybody could see everybody's back yard business from there — the battered trash cans on one side, the car on blocks on the other, the swing set in the yard across the back fence. I felt sorry for kids growing up in those yards. I knew professional bird dogs who had bigger runs. Even a toddler like Susannah quickly ran up on her boundaries there. She wrapped her baby fingers around the wires of the back fence and howled as she rattled the bars of her prison.

The back door opposite Mrs. Gibley's banged open and a little girl in a faded Wonder Woman cape and leotard struck a super-hero pose in the doorway. "I am WONDERFUL WOMAN!" she bellowed, her small fists held over her head. "I WILL SAVE YOU ALL! I WILL SAVE THE WORLD! I WILL SAVE! THAT! BABY!" She punched the air in our direction, gave herself a drumroll and leapt from the top of the porch steps, leaving the storm door flapping open behind her. Charging across the yard with her cape fluttering and chunks of hair loosed from a dishwater blond ponytail flailing, she zoomed and looped and flapped until she skidded to a stop in front of Susannah.

"Hi," she bent down, hands on knees, and said to Susannah, "I'm Abby."

"Hi!" Susannah answered.

I gasped. "Oh! You taught her a new word!"

"Hi?" Abby wrinkled her nose. "She didn't know 'hi'?" Abby was less than impressed.

"Well, no. She is a baby."

"Oh." Abby said. She flicked her tongue toward the corner over her lip where the remnants of a PBJ remained out of reach. "Can she do anything at all? Can she play?"

For an answer, Susannah pulled at the fence and pushed

her little face right into it, the diamond-shaped wire space squishing her slobbery little nose and mouth into a fat blob. "Hi hi hi hi hi hi hi," she prattled, making Abby laugh.

"Come over here to my side," Abby said. "We'll play Justice League. You guys can be bad guys. You hate America, but I'm saving it."

"We can't come over there," I said. "There's no gate." But my mind was racing. We would be leaving as soon as JW finished swapping out the three windows in the front. Our visits "home" rarely took an hour. Had it come to that, trusting a jelly-stained four-year-old to rescue me?

"But we are still playing," I rushed to explain. "We are prisoners in a foreign country. They caught us spying. For America," I added, before she could ask.

She nodded wisely. "They kill spies in that other country. Want me to kill that guard with the windows?"

"No, no; we can't do that." Yikes, Abby. You play hard. "Don't kill anybody. We have to stay in here and spy some more. We have important messages to pass to the president. Can you help us?" I pulled the folded envelope from my jeans pocket. Her eyes flashed. "I can read that," She said.

"Can you?" I was surprised. She looked too young to read.

"Yes. For real." Pause. "No; for pretend."

I wasn't sure how to decipher that, but I didn't break character. "Understood." I unfolded the envelope as dramatically as possible and showed her the addressed front. "As you can plainly see for yourself, this letter simply must reach The President of the United States. The future of our nation depends upon it. Do you have a mailbox at your house, or do you take your mail to the corner mailbox?" I licked my precious stamp and stuck it to the corner.

"Is that a real stamp?" she asked. "Or a play-sticker?"

I looked at her the way I thought a steely-eyed spy would. "Yes, of course it's real. It has to get all the way to Washington, D.C. I repeat, do you have a mailbox at your house?"

She nodded vigorously, shaking loose the rest of what had to be the worst haircut I've ever seen, most certainly self-inflicted. "I can reach it all by myself, if I stand on the big flower pot."

"Excellent." I rolled the envelope into a c-shape and pushed it through the fence to her. She took it out and held it in front of her eyes, puzzling over the writing.

"Is that a 'M'? Or a 'N'? Your humpies all run together."

"It's code." Come on, Abby. "Now you have your mission. It's urgent. You must do it immediately. It's Top-Secret. Super-Duper-Secret-Squirrel Top Secret."

This whole time, Susannah had been rattling the fence and yelling her new word. But suddenly, I realized she was no longer greeting Abby, she was winding around my leg and hollering "Hi! Hi! Hi!" behind me. Inside my head, an alarm bell clanged.

"Looky at you! You learned a new word!" JW appeared by my side. He swung Susannah up into his arms, tickling her. While all his attention was on our daughter, I motioned Go! Go! to Abby, but she was planted firmly in front of us, flapping my letter at me. JW leaned in for a kiss on my lips to celebrate Susannah's new word.

"Hey! Lady! Are we still playing, or not? Is he the mean prison guard, or not?" Abby demanded. JW turned to look at her and I held my breath. If Abby shifted the letter a half-inch, JW would see the address. But JW gave her a look of mock outrage and played along. "No! I'm the good guy! I've come to rescue these beauties."

Abby cocked her head, considering. Our eyes locked. "For play, or for real?" she asked.

I swallowed. "Real."

Her body still, her face deadpan, she kept her eyes on mine as she held up my letter with the addressed side toward her and ripped the envelope, with my precious stamp, right down the middle. She quartered those pieces, wadded them into a ball and stuffed them in her mouth.

"Mfffrg grmmfph frerrf" she said as she turned and flew away.

I kicked myself all the way back to the bus. How stupid, Ruby. Trusting a girl not much bigger than Susannah with your letter and your only stamp. Sick with disappointment, I trudged up the steps with Susannah in my arms and flopped down on the love seat. I handed Susannah a board book. I didn't even want to look at it with her. The plot of Pat the Bunny was a little too emotional for me at the moment.

JW trotted up the stairs carrying a stack of LP albums he had retrieved from storage in Mrs. Gibley's basement. The bus's stereo system was top-of-the line and JW often listened on his headphones while he drove. I watched JW choose some records, slide them out of their covers and stack them on the spindle. While he unrolled the wire on his headphones and plugged in the jack, I flipped through the album covers. The Florida Boys, The Dixie Echoes. The Cathedrals, The Happy Goodmans. Really?

I raised my eyebrows. "Practicing for your next nursing home gig?" I asked. Sarcasm wasn't generally well-tolerated in this family, but I wasn't in the mood to censor myself. Besides, at the right moment, JW would have found that funny, because we were always privately making fun of Merrilee and Old Rev's favorite music.

But he didn't laugh. He snatched the albums from me and pointed to the handwriting scrawled across the picture of a quaint country church. *Property of Billy Sunday Jasper*, it said in black felt-tip ink. *Do not discard*. JW leaned over his driver seat and tucked the album covers beside his cassette collection. He clamped on the earphones and cranked over the bus engine. OK, fine then. We'll both be in bad moods, I thought. Me, I deserved mine, but what was his problem?

Over at the dinette, Merrilee was sorting mail and I pretended not to watch her. I wasn't sitting close enough to read over her shoulder, but from my spot on the love seat I covertly monitored her movements. Like I was about to be tricked in a shell game, I trained my eyes on her hands as she picked and flipped, stacking letters and cards in various piles. I watched hard, but for the life of me, I couldn't see any mail that should have been mine. Old Rev or JW had probably already told Mrs. Gibley to take care of that herself. I'm sure she was glad to do it, too, the old bat.

Mrs. Gibley opened all the envelopes as soon as they arrived so that she could deposit any checks for us, but Merrilee always handled the more personal correspondences, looking for prayer requests and so on. Most of our prayer partners were content with our monthly newsletter, but Merrilee was always alert for a big donor with gall stones or wayward daughters or such who needed extra prayer and a special line or two added in Merrilee's meticulous handwriting. Her tattered devotional Bible was open and at hand so that she could include precisely the right verses for each ailment and anxiety.

I was surprised when Merrilee picked up an envelope with our own Jasper Ministries, International logo in the return corner. I watched closely, intrigued. Why would we be mailing something from ourselves?

Susannah climbed up on my lap and started fussing and tugging at my t-shirt. She wanted me to lie down with her and feed her a little before her nap, so I was gathering the two of us up off the love seat to head for my bunk when I saw it happen. So fast, so well-timed, so slick, so secretive, I almost doubted what I saw, but it did happen. Right under our noses, Merrilee slipped something out of the envelope and buried it in the leaves of her Bible.

I couldn't believe it. But I saw it. I did. Unbelievable.

Whoever would have thought that Merrilee had a sneaky streak?

I lay on my bunk feeding Susannah and listened to Merrilee's humming grow lighter and change into soft singing. She really was in a good mood. Nothing was cheerier to Merrilee than a good sin song. She started with "What can wash away my sin?" then after all five verses, segued into "Come, ye sinners, poor and needy." Off the top of my head, I could think of about fourteen hymns with "sin" in the first line, and as chipper as she was, she would hit every one of them before we got to Kansas.

Wow. I was still stunned at the whole idea of Merrilee having a secret sin. That is, if hiding things from your husband was a sin. I wasn't sure. I kinda hoped it was. I liked the idea of Merrilee having a secret sin of her own.

"How about McDonald's?" JW called back to us. "Does

everyone want that for supper? There's one twenty-four miles ahead." He sounded like he was asking our opinions, Merrilee's and mine, but he wasn't. He was really asking Old Rev could he please, pretty please, stop at his favorite restaurant. After all, he's been a good boy, driving all day without whining.

"That would be fine, Son," granted Old Rev. "Affordable and efficient. What more could you ask from a meal?" So we soon pulled in alongside the eighteen-wheelers on the industrial side of the lot. JW unfolded his body from the driver's seat slowly, like an old man. He stumbled down the steps and sprinted to Ronald McDonald's door. JW hadn't taken a restroom break since leaving Mrs. Gibley's that morning. Sometimes, I don't think JW gets enough credit for how hard he works.

Susannah and I dawdled until we were the last ones on the bus. I watched the Jaspers walk toward the Golden Arches before I picked up Merrilee's Bible and gave it a ruffle, watching the soft parchment pages fan out to reveal her flattened treasures. Mostly devotionals and prayers clipped from magazines or cards from prayer partners, but there were a few more interesting items, like a frayed ribbon bookmark braided long ago by childish hands and a brittle sprig of lavender hand-pressed in wax paper. I was surprised to find a library card from the Hot Springs, South Dakota Public Library, issued to Merrilee Doe in 1947. I'd never heard Merrilee's maiden name, I realized with a shock. And I didn't know that Doe was a real last name, anyway. I thought it was only used for made-up things like Jane Doe. I flipped through more pages and found a strip of S&H Green Stamps, a post card picture of the small-town motel in Idaho where Merrilee had stayed with Billy Sunday after the train wreck, and a hasty sketch of a neat little bungalow, drawn on the back of a Dairy Queen napkin.

Then I found it.

Buried in the leaves of Merrilee's personal Bible was a snapshot of a beautiful, golden-brown toddler boy with hair and eyes as shiny-black as a new pair of boots. He smiled up at me with Billy Sunday's unmistakable crooked eyebrow and toothy grin. I turned the photo over. Printed in neat block letters was a one-word question: *PLEASE?*

Hands shaking, I shoved the photo back where I had found it, in the book of Isaiah, Chapter 49, verse 15. I knew the verse: *Can a mother forget the baby at her breast, and have no compassion for the child of her womb?*

I gathered up my own baby at my breast, the child of my own womb, and hurried to catch up with the others. I wasn't going to tell JW, and most certainly not Old Rev, what I'd found, even though I was dying of curiosity. I knew what Grandma Daisy would say about something like this; *let's just leave that in the nest and see what hatches.*

Chapter Six

Merrilee murmured something about fasting, but she did order a Dr. Pepper. You can't get that everywhere, so it was the first one she'd had in ages. I had JW get hamburgers, fries and the essential strawberry shake for Susannah and me to-go so that she and I could spend more time walking. This little break wouldn't be nearly enough exercise for her, but it was at least something. Susannah's lack of fresh air and exercise really worried me. It couldn't be good for her. Besides, if Susannah didn't get enough exercise, she couldn't sleep well at nights, and, well, that wasn't good for any of us.

Another young mother had the same idea about traveling breaks with her two preschoolers. She watched her little boys fly off the benches at the picnic table while I held on to Susannah's hand and helped her march importantly up the sidewalk on some urgent baby errand she had assigned herself. The mother and I caught each other's eyes and smiled knowingly.

"Has it been a long driving day for you, too?" I asked as Susannah and I toddled past.

"Oh my God, yes!" she groaned, not noticing me flinch at her casual use of the name "God." I hadn't talked to anyone "outside" for such a long time, I'd forgotten what it was like. "Your daughter is beautiful!" she said, and I immediately wished I could be her best friend.

"Oh, thank you! I was thinking how precious your boys are. They must be fun."

"Not on a six-hour road trip. You know, they should build playgrounds next to these roadside restaurants," she said. "Wouldn't that be a good idea?"

"We were in a McDonald's in Omaha a few weeks ago, and they actually had one. It was so handy, I hope they build more," I answered. The littlest boy, a wiry, tow-headed thing with ketchup on his shirt, flew off the bench and landed in front of Susannah in a crouch. She laughed, so he did it again, this time with a silly face. His mother and I laughed, too, so his older brother copied him. Susannah plopped her diapered backside down on the sidewalk, squealed, and clapped her hands at the boys. The little one leapt to her again, this time chanting, "Hi, Baby! Watch your bumper! Wanna see a mutton-thumper?" Susannah laughed a hard, baby-gut laugh. Rewarded, the boy climbed back onto the bench as his older brother, also a tow-head, but minus the ketchup, flung himself at Susannah, too. He asked her the same Suess-like question. Susannah was elated with this big-boy attention, and these boys decided that nothing in the world could ever be more important than keeping this tiny girl laughing. They repeated it again and again, tirelessly.

"What a couple of show-offs I've got!" their mother said. "That's little men for you, isn't it? The rest of their lives, now, they'll be breaking their necks to impress a girl."

Watching Susannah play with these little boys made me

think of how she should be back home, playing with all her cousins.

But did all of her cousins live in Oklahoma? What about that baby picture stuffed in Merrilee's Bible? That tiny crooked eyebrow, Merrilee's secrecy, and the silence from Mexico all pointed me to the same conclusion; Billy Sunday had a baby down there, and the Jaspers weren't talking about him. Did JW know he had a little nephew? Did Old Rev know he had a grandson?

In Mexico. Which is pretty dadgummed far from Canada.

Now, there was a new thought. Maybe Merrilee didn't want to go to Canada, either.

"Ruby Fae?" JW popped out the door, "Let's go. Mom took your dinner to the bus."

I grabbed Susannah up, interrupting her game and provoking her baby temper. She wailed, frightening the little boys back to their mother's side. "You boys better learn early how scary an angry woman can be," she joked as we left.

Susannah squalled even harder as I lugged her to the bus. "You really need to correct that behavior, Ruby." JW said to me over his shoulder. "In a couple more weeks, she won't be a baby anymore. We can't let her keep throwing fits like that, or she'll never learn self-control."

Self-control? She hadn't even had her first birthday and we were talking about self-control? Geeze. Throwing a fit is a normal part of toddlerhood, the way I saw it, but JW was totally unnerved if she cried. He was certain I was doing something wrong or we wouldn't all have to suffer so. It infuriated me when he said that. How would he like it if absolutely no one ever listened to what he wanted, what he thought, what he had to say? He'd pitch a ring-tailed fit, too, if he couldn't even tell you what he wanted for supper.

Fortunately, it was a long walk across the parking lot, and Susannah forgot she was mad by the time we got to the bus, so she soon settled happily at the table with her French fries. I put the shake in the freezer for later.

Up front, the CB was squawking with chatter, but one voice caught JW's attention. "Break one-nine for that rolling church-mobile I'm spyin' here in the Big Mac parking lot. Is that what you drive, Bible Boy? How's business? I saved four souls today. How about you?"

"Ruby, c'mere, quick," JW motioned me up to the front of the bus. "You try. Maybe you can get somewhere with her." He handed me the microphone. "What do I do?" I asked.

"Hold the button down when you talk, let up when you're done."

"What do I say to her?" I asked JW. "I don't know how to talk to a hooker."

"You're a woman. Say something." JW urged. "God keeps putting her in our path. We're supposed to save her. I just know it."

I cleared my throat and clicked the button. "Hello, Itty-Bitty Betty. This is…" You weren't supposed to use your real name. I knew that much. I searched for inspiration, and my eyes fell on the scruffy toy in my hands. "Bunny-wunny here. I'm, uhm, also Mrs. Bible Boy. It's nice to meet you." I let the button up as I made a self-conscious snort. "That was so dorky," I said to JW.

"Bible Boy's got him an old lady? Go figure," said Betty.

"Yes, ah, 10-4," I answered. I looked to JW for help, but he rolled his hand in a "keep it going" gesture. "We—we're singers. We sing together. Do you like music?" I asked. I made a horrified face at JW and slapped my forehead. What kind of a question was that to ask a hooker?

JW waved my embarrassment aside. "Just bring it back around to Jesus," he said.

"Yeah. I love music," Betty answered. "I'm thinking about getting myself a guitar and learning some of the old Country and Western stuff." Betty's voice had a wistfulness about it that made her sound much younger than her fake, breathy-girly voice did. "Like Patsy Cline and Wanda Jackson."

"Oh, I love Wanda Jackson. She's from Oklahoma, you know." I answered, a little surprised. Betty must have had some good roots, if she knew the Queen of Rockabilly. "What's your favorite song?" I asked, then I remembered to add "Over," like you're supposed to.

"*Silver Threads and Golden Needles*," Betty sang the title into her mic in a thin, reedy voice. "Over," She tacked on the end.

Ignoring JW, who was waving his hand and hissing "You're not supposed to sing! That's against FCC regulations," I clicked the mic and sang along with Betty. But I stopped myself before I got too far, because in that song, Wanda sings about how her love can't be bought with money, which didn't seem like a very polite thing for me to sing to a prostitute I barely knew.

"Breaker one-nine, Mountain Man here; any chance I could talk one of you pretty singing ladies into singing a private concert for me?" came a third voice.

I gasped. JW grabbed the mic from me and slammed it down. But even before he switched the radio off, Betty's girly voice had already promised Mountain Man she'd wait for him on channel zero-five.

After our burger and fries, I got Susannah into her jammies and started her bedtime routine, even though she was not the least bit sleepy. She put up a little fight, and I saw Old Rev stiffen. JW glanced in the rearview mirror uneasily, and Merrilee hummed louder, *There is a Place of Quiet Rest.*

That's how I knew it was time. Time for my terrible, secret sin. A bad one. Worse, oh so much worse, than neglecting to tell your husband about his grandbaby.

I slid out of my seat to get the strawberry shake from the freezer, pausing for a second by my bunk on the way. Leaning in behind the curtain, I fished around under the far corner of my mattress for a small silver card and punched out a pink capsule.

Benadryl. Adult strength.

I would have felt much better about this if it had been a child's dose, but I didn't know what else to do. *Forgive me for stealing*, I prayed. *And forgive me for...whatever sin this is.*

"Here's Bunny-wunny!" I said, straightening up in the aisle of the bus again. "He was in my bed. Silly Rabbit." I handed him to Susannah, then got the shake from the freezer. I took the lid off and stirred it. "This is almost too solid, now. Needs stirring." I was talking to no one in particular. "Oops! Spilled a little!" I said, still to no one, as an excuse to move out of view by the sink. I set the shake on the counter and quickly added the contents of the pink powdered capsule. I ran a little water as though I were washing up, then continued stirring as I came back to the dinette and sat down beside Susannah. Merrilee said something about such a big shake for such a little girl, and I said brightly, "Oh, but Mommy shares it, too!" and took a big, long suck from the straw. Susannah would drink it all if I'd let her. She loves ice cream and can put away an astonishing amount, but I was trying to estimate how much I could safely let her have. I didn't mind drinking the extra. Benadryl always knocked me out as well as it did Susannah, and sometimes I don't sleep so well, either.

Chapter Seven

You're not supposed to admit this, but youth gatherings are pretty romantic. I know lots of married couples who met at camps or retreats. That's off the record, of course, but everyone knows it's true. Where do you think little Holiness babies come from?

Even JW and I fell in love at district youth camp. We'd known each other forever, but we'd never admitted to anything between us until that summer camp right before I left home for college. The Jaspers were never the main singers or speakers at youth camp; that was usually somebody who specialized in teenagers, somebody who wasn't afraid to wear a skinny knit tie and was good at Pac-Man. But the whole Jasper family always came as staff or sponsors or something, and that year, Old Rev was the Camp Choir director. Camp Choir was made up of kids who spent one of the break-out sessions getting a song ready to perform for the big nightly service in the tabernacle. Merrilee accompanied on the piano, of course.

The song we were working on for the Thursday service, "Rise Again," was a favorite. Everybody wanted to do the solo on the first verse, which is why Old Rev announced that we'd have a quick try-out session for everyone who was interested. JW was picking up the sheet music after practice when he came to my row.

"You're going to try out, aren't you, Ruby? You're a really good singer," he said. The girl next to me applied a fresh coat of strawberry Lip-Smacker and openly eavesdropped. JW was on every girl's list of possibles for a couples-only song at the roller skating party on Saturday night. "No, it's not a good range for me. I'm an alto," I answered. JW knew music. He wouldn't have said that if he hadn't meant it. A warm feeling crept into my belly, a warmth that began somewhere inside me in a place I'd never noticed before. "You are the one who should do it," I told him. "It's right in your sweet spot."

"Nah that would be too weird. Having my daddy pick me, and all," he answered, emphasizing "daddy" so I'd know he was too old for special favors from a "daddy." I caught that.

"Yeah, I see what you mean. That would look silly," I said. "But, still, it would sound best with you. Your voice sounds exactly like the record." The choir loft was emptying out. Lip gloss girl sighed, surrendered any unspoken dibs on JW and left. The solo hopefuls crowded around Merrilee and Old Rev at the piano, so JW and I were sort of alone.

"We should sing a duet sometime," JW blurted out. "You and me. You're really good." He reshuffled the sheet music and I watched his hands do it. They were wide, square-nailed, man-shaped hands.

"When did you hear—"

"With your show choir, remember?"

"Oh, yeah, right."

"I get to hear you every year," I said as we slowly stepped down from the choir loft. "And you're really good, too.

If you'd gone to high school in Salt Fork, you'd definitely have made show choir."

"That would have been great," he answered, his voice betraying more longing than he knew.

We came down the stairs together, landing on the same stair at the same time. They were barely wide enough for two people, but we stayed in step anyway, careful not to touch.

Which was a good excuse to watch my feet instead of his face as I said, "I would have tried to be your partner."

His bare forearm brushed mine and he jerked it away.

"Oh, no-no-no. Nothing good could have come from that," he said. He was being goofy now, making fun of our church elders. "It's not the dancing itself that's a sin," he began, wagging his finger. Every kid in our denomination could quote this saying, and so I finished it with him, like a rousing battle cry, "It's what it could lead to!"

At the bottom of the stairs in the main sanctuary, we looked around to make sure no grownups had overheard that spirited bit of rebellion. Grinning, we faced each other.

"Hey, you should bring your guitar to afters tonight," he said. "Sit by me and we'll do a song together."

"OK," I said. This time I got up the nerve to look him in the face. "I'd love to sing with you." His eyes, I noticed, were the same inky dark blue as his father's.

That's only one silly little love story that began at a church youth rally, and it happens to be ours. Somebody else's love story could begin here, today at this one, I thought, as I watched through the window of the church while a couple hundred kids poured out of church vans like clowns from a clown car. In the parking lot, kids were mingling and greeting, bashfully forming and reforming tight little knots as each group's boundaries loosened and blurred, gradually annexing somebody's cousin or last year's camp bunkmate, then someone else that somebody else knew. The scene was all so familiar, it hurt. One skinny boy with a leather and wooden cross hanging around his neck clutched a big black New Testament awkwardly in front of him as he bravely crossed the crowd to reach a group of boys he knew. A flock of girls in Chic Jeans and sparkly eye shadow tossed their hair at him and made sure he noticed they were ignoring him as he passed.

Once inside, the kids mobbed the donut and juice tables then arranged themselves, cross-legged, on the floor of the combo fellowship hall/gymnasium. JW and I waited beside the portable stage while the host church's youth director got things rolling. He quieted everybody down, made announcements, prayed, and told some inside jokes that were greeted with whoops and cheers. Finally, he introduced us. *Show time!*

JW hopped on stage and let out a long blast on his trumpet. "Rapture Drill!" he shouted. "Everybody in the air!" They leapt to their feet and I was already at my keyboard, banging out the intro to a souped-up version of "I'll Fly Away." I leaned into my mic, "This is only a drill," I intoned, "in the event of an actual Rapture, these shoes will be unoccupied." They hooted and hollered at the corny joke. Knowing they'd never have gotten away with making fun of The Rapture if the grownups had been around was what made it so funny. I started them singing the familiar words while JW led a serious of wild, arm-flailing leaps as he yelled, "Rapture Jacks." The crowd went wild and I loved it. I'll admit it, still. If it's a pride-sin or not, I can't say, but I could live on stage

I picked all contemporary songs that the kids could sing along with, like Keith Green, Evie, and even one Rez Band song. I taught them a brand new one that they'd never heard, from a young singer named Amy Grant. They loved that, too.

But even though I knew what the kids liked, I also knew I wasn't one of them anymore. I was in a whole different class now. I was married and had a baby of my own. I hadn't seen my mom and dad for two years and had traveled all over the country. I could have sex and it wasn't even wrong. You would think all that made me a grown-up. But part of me thought I should still be sitting cross-legged on the floor, gawking up at the professional musicians who were practically recording stars. Which we were, in a way; we had real albums for sale, on both cassette and LP. Hard to believe, but we were a big deal at those things.

After about an hour, we took a break while the youth had a snack and played party-mixer games. Merrilee, who had been watching Susannah in the nursery, brought her to me. My baby reached for me eagerly and my heart, like it always did after I'd been away from her, exploded with that ferocious, white-hot love. We clutched at each other while she covered my cheek with sloppy baby-smooches and I sang to her "Oh, Susannah! Oh, don't you cry for me!" I was so smitten with her, I hadn't noticed JW calling my name.

"Ruby Fae, c'mere." There was excitement in his voice, but he tried to hide it. "Come on, I need to talk to you." He took my arm and rushed me through the sanctuary doors where we ducked into a small room off to the side. It was the bride's room, a windowless little room at the back of the sanctuary where brides would wait before the ceremony. A little larger than a walk-in closet, it had giant floor-to-ceiling mirrors covering three walls, which made Susannah squeal with delight at the extra mommas and daddies and babies. I put her on the plush rose-colored carpet and she tottered over to make friends with one of her doubles.

"Whoa," JW said, "This is cool! Look at you! You're infinite." We turned this way and that. "Looky there," he said, giving me a playful slap on the rump. "I told you that you have a cute butt. Now do you believe me? Look at that!" I looked, and he was right; I did have a cute butt, but that was not what I was noticing. What I saw was our little family, JW and I laughing, Susannah squealing and playing. I loved my little family in moments like that.

JW turned me around and we posed, prom-picture-style, with his arms wrapped around my waist. He pushed up close behind me and began swaying, which was probably the closest he's ever come to dancing.

His lips started down the side of my neck so I gave him a gentle nudge. "Hey, Mister! There's a kid in here!" I said to his reflection. "Besides, what did you have to tell me?"

"You're such a killjoy," he said. "But listen, you're gonna like this. I got a letter from Reverend Dixon." JW held up a letter and waved it at Mirror Ruby.

I pushed away so I could face him, the real him. "Reverend Dixon? He wrote you? When? What did he say?" Reverend Dixon had been my pastor at Rose of Sharon since I was in second grade. You would think he'd have written to me, but still, it was a letter from home and I was excited. "Was it addressed to just you? Did he even ask about me? What did he write you for?"

"It came straight here, not through the home office, and it was to me, but he did ask about you and sends his prayers. He wrote to me because he's inviting me–" Was I imagining it, or did JW suddenly look a little taller, a little older? "—he's inviting me to be the interim pastor while he's on leave!"

"What? No way!" JW is good at preaching already, everybody says so. And he should be; he was in the pulpit before his voice had even changed. But pastoring a church is different. He was way too young.

"Only while he's on leave," JW corrected. "His mother-in-law has terminal cancer, so he and his wife want to take off a few months to spend more time with her. They live over in Osage County, too far to drive back and forth a lot."

OK, that made more sense. Reverend Dixon would still be available in case of real need, like a death or something, but JW could handle the regular preaching, easy.

"Where would we live? If they're only taking a leave, they won't move out of the parsonage, will they?"

JW held the letter out to me. "Right here, it says that the Randalls almost have their house built, so they offered to let us live in their trailer until they sell it. We can pull it up behind the church. And get this," he said, jabbing his finger at the letter. "He says the board voted to keep paying Reverend Dixon while he's on leave, so they can't pay me a salary. But that's OK, because they decided it would be a good time to work on the parsonage, so instead, they will pay me out of the building fund to re-finish the floors and cabinets!"

I think that was the happiest I had ever seen JW with his pants on.

But then again, I was excited, too.

"Let me see that." He didn't even notice how bossy that sounded, he was in such a good mood.

I skimmed over the letter, and it confirmed everything JW told me. And more:

One more thing you should consider, JW, as you and Ruby pray over this decision: the church at Rose of Sharon has a reputation for encouraging its young pastors. I'll tell you the same thing Reverend Caldwell told me when I took over for him; I was a raw, green, by-the-book know-it-all when I got here, but these people put up with me, going about their business being good folks, setting an example. Eventually, I learned to shut up and do more, to point and holler less. That must be the farmer coming out in them.

"We're going to do this, right?" I said. "I mean, we practically have to." Wait, Ruby; use the right words. "JW," I made sure my voice was filled with awe, "you've been called!"

Old Rev burst in before he had a chance to answer .

"Praise the Lord!" he enthused. "This is fantastic!" The shock on our faces reflected back at us. Had Old Rev been eavesdropping? But as he continued, we realized he was excited about something else, entirely. "JW, look at this room! It's perfect for us! Exactly what we need to put the finishing touches on our duet before we get to Colorado. Look at these mirrors! We can get thirty minutes' work in while the kids are at lunch. And if we get over here early in the morning before people start showing up for Sunday School, we could get another practice in before we hit the road. I tell you, God takes care of all the details, right?" This all was something to do with the new sermon deal that Old Rev and JW had been cooking up, some whole new twist they were all excited about. They were convinced it would be revolutionary, a true innovation in preaching. The greatest thing to hit the pulpit since pre-cut communion wafers.

JW's face changed to reflect the expression on his father's. "Yes, Sir! This is exactly what we've needed! This is going to be terrific!" I stepped back from JW. The center of gravity in his universe had shifted away from me, and I didn't want to be sucked into the void with him as he surrendered to the pull. I reached down to pry Susannah away from the mirror where she was covering her own reflection with slobbery kisses. I looked up and caught the expression of disapproval on Old Rev's face. "Come on, Susannah," I told her as I swooped her up into my arms. "Let's go find some Windex. I'll teach you how to clean a smudgy mirror."

It was a little hard to get back into the performance after JW's news. Onstage, I kept thinking about leaving. I couldn't wait. Maybe JW and I could even launch our own part-time youth ministry, doing stuff like this. The two of us together, like a real team and not just Old Rev's kids. We could call ourselves Ruby and John. Maybe we could cut a record, even, just JW and me. My head was suddenly filled with ideas for what we'd sing and what we'd wear and where we'd go. I could see it all so clearly. A gush of excitement and a new love for JW came crashing over me as I finished up the singing and sat down to watch him bring the message.

JW talked to the kids about Satan, how he is a roaring lion, seeking whom he may devour, all that. He talked about all kinds of things he'd been told teen-agers face. You know, drugs, sex, rock music, etc. Drugs, he had to address from hearsay. But that's ok, because most of those kids, the kind who would wake up early on a Saturday morning to spend the day at church, didn't know any more about drugs than JW or I did. Sex, that was easy. Anybody could preach that one: Save it, or else.

Rock music, though, now, that was where JW truly did shine. It was the one sin that JW could repent of with authority, I happened to know.

He prowled the stage, his preaching mic pinned to his shirt pocket, his Living Bible clutched in his right hand.

"Hey guys, clearly, there is a choice laid out for you, a fork in the road. 'Narrow is the way that leads to Salvation.' That's one path. The other?" With his left hand, he held up an album cover, and the audience, as one, shrunk back. *Highway to Hell.* He froze, silent for a beat, holding it above his head. "It's OK, guys, it's empty. Just the cover, see? The album was shattered into a million pieces on an altar in Texas one night. And the boy who did it gave the cover to me and said, 'I want you to take this, JW, and tell kids everywhere, how an ordinary preacher's kid in a little town west of Ft. Worth once believed Satan's lies, and was speeding down this very highway in a life full of drugs, crime, prison, and death, and it all started when I began filling my mind with Satan's music."

That was a true story. There was such a boy, and he believed that his own sins and his parents' broken hearts could be blamed on the Satanic music beamed at him from an FM album-rock station in Dallas. He came forward after one of JW's messages and gave him that album cover. JW had been really moved by that, because he himself had once been in danger of falling to the very same sins.

At the same youth camp where JW and I had fallen in love, after hearing a speaker preach against rock music, JW had brought all of his albums to the bonfire and tossed them in. He challenged the rest of us to do the same. None of us had our vinyl sins with us; you don't bring them to camp. The only reason he had his was because Merrilee and Old Rev were there, too, with their bus. They had been shocked that their boy had been carrying this filth with them, right under their noses, but they were more proud of his public confession. Some of us, mainly girls, promised JW that as soon as we got back home, we'd burn our records, too.

I guess there was probably something to all that, the music from the devil business. Look at that other famous preacher's kid, Alice Cooper. Everybody knows about him, biting heads off live chickens and stuff.

But as for the rest of his line? I wasn't entirely convinced.

"It's bigger than you think, guys. Satan's hold on the music industry goes deep. Back to the British Invasion. That's right. The Beatles, The Rolling Stones, all of them, puppets of Satan. Follow their strings, and you'll find ties to Satanic Cults, British Military Intelligence, and the International Drug Trade." He launched into an explanation of an intricate web, explaining how these minions of Satan were stealthily laying the groundwork in the minds of Young America for a bloodless takeover of our country. What exactly the British wanted us for wasn't clear, but the coup would be complete soon unless we got a handle on it.

"It's buried in the very music itself; even Christian rock and contemporary gospel music have their roots in darkness," JW told his young listeners, his pretty face full of concern for their spiritual condition. The girls' eyes went all wide and glassy. JW could have been telling them to burn the feathered hair right off their sun-bleached heads and they would scramble over each other to get in line as long as he was holding the matches.

After a tiring but successful day (forty-three saved,

eighteen re-dedications, and four calls to full-time ministry) I was glad when Susannah went down for bed easy. She got so much attention from the kids at youth meetings that she always played hard and went right to sleep afterwards. Finally, I had my chance to get JW alone.

"Would you like to go for a short walk?" I asked. We were both tired, too, but I knew he wouldn't turn me down.

He leapt off his bunk and shoved his feet into his sneakers. With his hand on my forearm he steered me out of the bus. His hand worked its way down the small of back and into my rear pocket. As we crossed the parking lot, he pulled me close and my heart soared. If we had a chance to be on our own, then I could speak up now and then, get my own way once in a while. If I didn't have to worry about his touchy pride all the time, if he weren't always posturing, trying to impress Old Rev, we could be great together. I knew we could.

JW walked me around to the back door of the church, which had been left open for us in case we needed to use the phone or the kitchen or something. The building was dark and empty, but JW led me purposefully. He already had a place in mind. Should I talk to him first, or afterwards? He walked faster, relying on the dim red glow from the exit lights to illuminate our way. Definitely after, I decided. When we bypassed the fellowship hall and the foyer, I knew where he was taking me. He opened a door. We stumbled into the pitch dark room and he shut the door behind us.

Well.

That was a new one.

"Take off your clothes," JW said in his most honest voice, "but don't open your eyes."

I did what he said, but for once, instead of making me feel weak and silly, I felt confident. Strong. Like a woman who *decides* things, you know? Because I was *choosing* to mind him. Maybe when we were back home, I might mind him now and then, like that, for fun, but only if I felt like it. I heard the click of the light switch and the blackness behind my eyelids changed to a lighter darkness once the fluorescent overhead fixtures began to buzz. I imagined all my naked selves looking back at me from the three walls of the bride's room. I giggled, but kept my eyes shut tight.

Mostly.

A little later, we were lying still on our backs and naked as Eden, one leg each in a lazy tangle, the rest of our bodies not touching, separated only by enough space for the heat left between us.

When I noticed the carpet scratching my back and the hint of a yawn in my throat, I decided it was time.

"I'm so proud of you," I said. "Your first preaching assignment already." Lightly I ran one fingernail up the length of his thigh as far as I could reach without moving. He shifted, burrowing further down into the floor.

"Your Dad must be proud, too," I said, and skimmed my fingernail back down toward his knee again.

He shifted again and mumbled, "Uh, I haven't told him yet."

Careful, Ruby,

"I'm sure you know the right time. You're right. It could be a bit of a shock to him, but he'd never stand in your way of obeying God." I reached slightly higher on his leg this time and moved my finger a bit faster.

"No, no he wouldn't do that," JW said, and I switched to

a two-finger caress. "Maybe after we're done in Colorado, I'll ask him to swing down and drop us off," he said.

I lifted my hand away from his skin. "Yes...that would work...but two weeks is a long time. It sounds like Mrs. Dixon's mother is pretty sick. What if the board doesn't feel like they can wait that long?"

He flung his forearm over his eyes.

"You're right," he said, and I put my whole hand on his leg now, pulling it closer to me before I resumed stroking it. "I'll call Monday," he said, and my fingers wandered farther.

"You know," I mused, "we could buy bus tickets from anywhere. That wouldn't cause your folks any extra mileage going out of the way," His skin quivered and inside, I was also quivering, but with hope, not lust. "Every little town you go to has a bus stop." *Come, on, JW, work with me here.* "I don't think bus tickets are very expensive."

Suddenly, he rolled up on his side, on one elbow, blocking the glare of fluorescent lights. "I can afford bus tickets for my family. I work hard and I have money of my own. So if I want to take my family on a bus trip, why can't I? What's he going to do? Ground me, a grown man?"

In answer, I reared up, toppled him over and climbed on. Just to, you know, agree with him.

I woke up happier than I had been in a long, long time. We were going home! Just the three of us! We'd be on our own, we'd make our own rules for our marriage, and we would raise Susannah however we thought best. I wouldn't have to worry about acting submissive anymore and I would even have my own spending money!

We had laid on the floor of the brides' room all night,

talking, planning, agreeing. In fact, I agreed with him two more times, without even having to say a word.

I looked over at JW's bunk and saw that it was already empty. I stretched and listened to Susannah stirring in her crib bunk above me, babbling at Bunny-Wunny and realized that we were alone. Where'd everybody go? I crawled out of bed, stood in the aisle and peeked at Susannah. She stuck her fat little hand through the bars of her crib bunk. "Ma-ma, Ma-ma, Ma-ma," she sang. She could already make little melodies, but her lyrics were rather limited. I unlatched her bed rails and pulled her toward me. "Oh, lucky girl," I swung her around twice while I crooned an on-the-spot new song for her. "You are such a lucky, lucky, lucky girrrrrrrrl."

While Susannah and I got ready for the day, I told her all about her new life.

"You can help Grammy Mac gather the eggs, and Grampa Mac will take you for rides on the tractor, and you'll play with all your cousins, and Daddy will put a swing up for you in the barn." And Old Rev could drag Merrilee to California or Canada or the Australian Outback, for all I cared. Merrilee would have to fight that one on her own.

I rummaged through the kitchenette for some breakfast, found two slices of bread and popped them into the toaster. It was still early, not yet seven. I wondered again where everyone was. We needed to get going because the regular church crowd would be showing up soon. Since we were only booked for the youth yesterday and not the Sunday morning worship service, we'd planned to travel that day. It would look rude to be pulling down camp and leaving right as the rest of the good Christians were arriving for worship. Oh, well, that was Old Rev and JW's problem, not mine. Seated at the table with Susannah and our peanut butter toast, I let my mind drift back to last night.

Even alone with Susannah, my cheeks flushed when I remembered the mirrors in the brides' room. Which suddenly reminded me; I did know where JW and Old Rev were, after all. I snickered, thinking of JW practicing sermons with his dad, looking into the very same mirrors he'd looked into the night before and trying now not to think about the view.

"Let's go find Daddy," I told Susannah. We took our time. I let her poke around, pulling on my finger, detouring across the parking lot to kick at a rock and stomp on a stray leaf.

Once inside, I heard preaching coming from the brides' room. The door was open and Merrilee had pulled a folding chair inside to watch the rehearsal.

For a moment, I thought it was some weird acoustical trick of the little room that amplified JW's — no, Old Rev's — no; I couldn't tell whose — voice. Were we this loud last night? I wondered, my cheeks reddening yet again. But when I got close enough to look through the doorway, I stopped so abruptly that Susannah was thrown off-balance and bumped into my legs, dangling from my finger. I couldn't take my eyes off the scene in front of me.

The Reverends Jasper were dressed in identical suits. JW's hair, usually feathered back from the center and falling into soft, golden waves framing his face instead now gleamed with Bryl-Cream slicked back from a razor-straight part on the left side. Exactly like his father's, except Old Rev always parted his on the right. Their identical ties were also single-Windsor-knotted in opposite directions, as though they'd each tied the other's.

JW's was clipped with a bar from the right side. Old Rev's, with the same tie-bar, from the left. JW's silk pocket square was in the left pocket. Old Rev's, the right. They stood and moved in absolute symmetry. If you'd folded them in half, they would have matched perfectly.

Each had his outside hand raised, his face upturned toward it, looking at heaven.

"And God, the RIGHTEOUS, the BLAMELESS, the great and JUST..."

Voices thundering, they brought their outside feet forward one step, slammed their upraised hands down into a mighty, synchronized clap and I felt the thunder in my own chest.

"...shall SMITE THEE, O, Sinner!"

They clapped again.

"SMITE THEE, I say!"

Dropping one knee to the floor, his hands clutched together, JW turned to his father. Carefully keeping his face to the mirror so the audience could see his look of penitence and fear, JW raised his clasped hands to his father, saying, "Oh, Father, tell me; is it too late for the sinner to come home? Must we all, each one, partake of this chastisement? Are you not a merciful father?"

Old Rev changed characters and dropped his gaze to the imaginary congregation in the mirror and like an old-time melodrama actor, narrated from aside, "...says the filthy sinner!"

Shifting to face both JW and the audience at the same time, his inside hand hovering above JW's head in blessing, Old Rev said, "God, the Father Almighty does indeed, have Mercy in the right hand..." he stepped away again and slammed his hands together to repeat the thunder-clap. JW matched the clap and backed Old Rev's voice up with his own, repeating the stereo effect "...and JUDGMENT in the left!"

JW hopped up, stepped forward one step and two steps to the right as Old Rev melted away behind him. Together, they raised their hands above their heads and in one voice roared, "Observe the PUNISHMENT of the wicked, behold the PENALTY of the immoral!"

I couldn't tell who was talking. I couldn't remember which one I was seeing. Their two selves dissolved and blended into one. Where was my husband? I couldn't see him. All I could see was Old Rev and more Old Rev, reflecting back at me in an eternally damning, diminishing chorus line.

I couldn't move. I wasn't sure I was breathing. My eyes bored into the mirror in front of me, willing JW to meet my gaze, to look, to sense me, to turn around, to grab my hand and run with me far, far away.

But he never took his eyes off his father's reflection.

I was relieved when we were back on the road. JW's slicked back hair bothered me, but I kept quiet. The day after tomorrow we'd be headed home and he could wear his dad's own pajamas all the way to Oklahoma if he felt like it and I wouldn't care one bit.

I rode up front beside JW most of the morning. JW played with Susannah while he drove. I rubbed his neck and shoulders when he got squirmy and tired. We talked about all kinds of stuff. We even kicked around a few hypothetical baby boy names for possible future use.

And we talked to Itty-Bitty Betty again. Or rather, I did. JW just encouraged me along. "It's our last chance to reach her," JW said when we heard her little voice come on the air. "Just, you know, try to get her to talk to you again."

"Hey there, Betty, it's me again. I mean, Bunny-Wunny." I made a face at JW. I always felt kinda stupid on this thing. But JW said I needed to get used to it because everyone would be using them all the time, instead of phones even, before long.

"Hello, Mrs. Bible Boy. You keeping it between the ditches?"

I looked at JW, stumped. He said, "It's like asking if you're doing ok. Say, 'Yes, ma'am, how 'boutchyer own numbers? They all good?' Come on."

"Uhm, I think so. Yes," I said. "Thanks. And how are you doing?" JW rolled his eyes, but I ignored him.

"Not too bad," Betty answered. "I think I'm about to get me a guitar, like I said last time. Is it hard to learn? Over."

"If you can find someone to teach you it's easier," I answered. "But just fiddle around with it and you'll get it, eventually."

A man's voice broke in. "Breaker one-nine for Lil' Bitty Betty. How 'bout you fiddle around with the Alabammer Jackhammer here? C'mon back."

Itty-Bitty Betty was always on duty. "You got it, Trucker," she purred. "Meet me on the Dime Channel." And she was gone.

JW sighed. "I guess all we can do is pray for her now," he said as he switched the CB unit to "off."

I laid down with Susannah at nap time, but I was so excited about going home that it took me a while to drift off. It was late afternoon by the time I woke up; the summer sun lingered uncertain in the sky. The restless time, Mom always called it. You know, when it's too early for bed but too late to start anything new. I decided to put some music on the stereo to try and shake off my funky, fidgety mood. I lifted the lid on the turn-table and reached for the records he'd left there, when suddenly JW looked up in the mirror and said, "Hey, wait; I was getting ready to play this new Reba Rambo song." Before I could say anything he popped a cassette in and switched on the cabin speakers.

That was fine. I hadn't set my heart on any particular music. But since I was so antsy and had nothing better to do, I reached for the album covers JW had scattered. Might as well match them to the records and put them away. They were the ones he'd picked up from Mrs. Gibley's, Billy Sunday's old gospel records. Odd, that JW had chosen those to listen to. But maybe he was feeling a little nostalgic at the thought of leaving the bus. After all, it was his childhood home.

"Hey, Ruby, sit up here with me," JW said quickly, his eyes on me from the rear-view mirror.

"Uhm, OK," I said as I glanced down at the turntable. That's when I almost laughed out loud.

Billy Sunday's records weren't good old wholesome, four-part-harmony hymns at all. The records that slid out of those serene cloud-and-cross-covered album jackets were really Blue Oyster Cult, Judas Priest, and Black Sabbath. And JW had been listening to them on his headphones.

Well, how about that. Looked like JW could keep secrets as well as any of us.

Chapter Eight

Merrilee and I were proofreading Old Rev's collected works. His plan was to publish them so we could sell his most popular sermons on our merchandise table along with the records and cassettes. It was grueling work. English was never my favorite subject, but I knew the basic rules. That was more than I could say for Old Rev. I didn't know much about his schooling, but I think he went to a little Bible College in Kansas where punctuation must not have been a requirement.

Looking for misspelled words was even worse than usual. It was hard to concentrate, because all I could think was *we're going home!* Really. JW promised that he would buy our bus tickets as soon as we got to the next town, and in the morning, like ol' Huck Finn, we'd light out for the territory. We'd be on our way home.

Home. The longing for it squeezed my chest until I was nearly dizzy. I closed my eyes and could almost feel the hard, hot winds blowing my last two lonely years away.

Merrilee cleared her throat and my eyes popped open. I muttered an excuse about not sleeping well last night and tried to focus on the papers in my hand.

A stack of sermons on Hellfire lay on my lap, demanding

my attention. But lucky for me, I knew all about Hell, so I had a good head start.

The first sermon I remember hearing about Hell, I really could smell the smoke. The whole church reeked of it. Two days of grass fires had turned the countryside into a black-crusted skillet, scorched and smoking in the evening air. Everyone in the community had been hit. The Kinney family and Old Mr. Hatley had both lost new barns. Grandma Reenie lost a chicken coop and fifty good laying hens. Dad's water truck had overheated and blown a head gasket, and where we'd get the money for a new water truck now was a good question for The Lord to answer. My cousin Wit lost a sweet old hound named Barley, and that grieved me quite a bit, but even a five-year-old like me knew that was nothing compared to the families who had lost cattle. And everyone had lost good grassland. Hundreds and hundreds of acres of pasture were nothing but blowing ash now, leaving worries of overdue bank notes and outstanding feed bills hanging as thick as the smoke in the evening sky.

Our backs stuck to the wooden pews and the small sanctuary smelled like a used matchstick. All of us, even the little kids, were weary and dazed. But no matter. The fires were out, no homes were lost, and the lone bodily injury was Earnest Brine's arm, broken tripping over a garden hose. All the more reason to start revival week services right on schedule. There were prayers to be said and thanks to be given and, after all, the evangelists had come all the way from Iowa to be here, so the least we could do was go and hear them.

I usually sang loud and hard along with the all hymns whether I knew the words or not, often sitting on Grandma Daisy's lap with an open hymnal, Grandma helping me trace the notes as they slithered up and down the staff. But that night was too hot to sit on any lap and I was too tired to sing. Beside me, Leland was worn-out, too, and kept slumping over onto Chuck, who shoved and poked at him to keep him away. Dad and Mom, seated together on the other end of our pew, didn't even bother to thump him quiet.

The singing droned on, verse after verse with no one really giving a full-throat effort. Before long, I toppled over sideways and stretched out on the pew. My eyes closed and scenes of the day's nightmares blended into the words and the melody blurred into a sleepy background hum. In my dream I heard again the roar of the fire and the frantic screeches and squawks of Grandma's chickens as I tried to herd them away from the coop. But they wouldn't follow me out of the pen; instead, they panicked, scattering and ricocheting off the chicken-wire fence. Mrs. Bonny Wobbles, a particularly nasty-tempered old layer, had even turned on me, pecking me on my bare shins until she drew blood and I screamed. That was when Mom had appeared, grabbing me up and running me to safety. But in my dreams now, Satan was sitting on the burning roof of the flaming chicken coop, laughing and eating smoking hot chicken drumsticks while a legless Mrs. Bonny Wobbles shrieked and demon chickens jabbed tiny burning pitchforks into my legs.

"Cast into a lake of fire, I say," roared the voice from the pulpit. I jerked awake. My Mary Janes whacking against the wooden pew sounded like a shotgun, but beside me, Leland only snorted in his sleep. "A lake of unquenchable, eternal fire. Eternal. Ever burning, burning, burning at the flesh, but never consuming, never ending. This is the wages of sin, my friends." I snapped to attention, sitting back upright. If God was talking about fire, I needed to hear it. "This is the natural consequences, the unavoidable end for the liar. The thief. The killer. The whoremonger. The sinner. And who is the sinner? Each and every one of us." The preacher paused, mopped his sweating brow with a handkerchief. My heart seized. Did the preacher mean even us kids? He'd said everyone. I held my breath. The last thing I wanted was more fire headed my way.

The preacher continued "But Reverend, you ask, What if I'm not a killer? Will I still go to Hell?"

My chest eased slightly. I'm definitely not a killer.

The preacher went on. "Or a whoremonger? If I'm not a whoremonger, will I still go to Hell?"

I had no idea what a whoremonger was. Could I accidentally be one? *Please, Dear God, don't let me be a whoremonger*, I prayed.

"Oh, my dear friends," the preacher's voice was warm and pleading now, "I think of you as friends, no, as family, I've known you all my life and I think of you as my family and loved ones; I speak the truth to you when I say that every sin, no matter how small, even the most harmless lie, the stolen penny toy, the unkindly thought toward your brother—is a sin in God's eyes as surely as the vilest deed."

I gulped.

If that was the scorecard, I was three out of three since suppertime. I'd lied to mom when I told her I was wearing a slip under my dress. Under my bed at home, right now, was a growing pile of little green plastic army men that I was stealing, one by one, from Chuck's and Leland's armies. I'd managed to pilfer another while they were dressing for church tonight. And right before the service started, I'd called Chuck a hog-face. My stomach roiled up in me, remembering.

I was eternally damned for sure.

A tear slipped down my face. I'd always thought God liked me, but suddenly I wasn't so confident. I didn't want Him to hate me and I for sure didn't want to go to Hell and burn and burn and burn until always and forever, which was what eternal meant. More tears came, but the piano had started up and people rustled to their feet, fumbling through hymnals. No one noticed my sobs growing louder.

Over the music, the preacher's voice flowed, deep and loving, "Ooooh, won't you come to Jesus tonight? Meet him here at the altar, confess your sins, and enter his eternal favor. Won't you come forward now?"

I couldn't get out of my seat fast enough. I rushed past Leland, now sprawled on the pew and snoring with gusto. Chuck blocked my way to the aisle. "Where are you going? Get back in your seat," he ordered.

"Stop bossing me around! I'm going to go get saved." I shoved at him.

"Don't be stupid. He doesn't mean you. You're too little to know what it means even," he said. The gentle commotion that goes with altar calls had begun, people singing louder, praying in audible whispers, shuffling aside to let people into the aisle. I was already overwrought with the magnitude of my sins and now Chuck's know-it-all big-brother attitude incensed me so thoroughly that I forgot to keep my voice down.

"I NEED to be SAVED!" I wailed, "I NEED TO GO MEET JESUS! I need to get saved NOW!"

Mom leaned down, reached around Chuck and pulled me to her. "Honey," she whispered, "Maybe we can talk about this on the way home."

"Hallelujah! Even the youngest can hear and know the

Word of the Lord!" the preacher shouted happily. "Jesus said to suffer the little children! Come forward, Little One! Don't be shy! Come on! Come forward."

I was sobbing hard. Snot came out of my nose and black flecks of soot came with it. Mom wiped at my face with her handkerchief, which, like everything else in our half of the county, now smelled like the Devil's own laundry. "Please, Mom, I need to be saved! Now!" I was trembling. What if something terrible happened right this instant like lightning or an earthquake? I couldn't die with God still mad at me.

Mom looked at Dad. He shrugged and reached to pick me up as though to carry me to the altar on his arm, but I broke away and ran down the aisle to the front of the church.

The preacher went down on one knee to meet me, and I remember still, how very blue his eyes were that night. Dark, inky blue. And so, so earnest. He understood. I needed to make God like me again, and this man would help me get back on God's good side.

"What's your name, if I may ask?" He spoke softly, and I appreciated that we were having this conversation privately. It made it more official.

"Ruby Fae McKeever," I choked out.

"Ruby Fae McKeever, why do you need to be saved?" he asked.

"Because I lied to my mom about wearing a slip and because I stole army men from my brothers and because I called Chuck a hog face." I admitted. I couldn't unload my sins fast enough.

"Ruby Fae McKeever, do you know how to pray?"

I nodded.

"Can you pray out loud, right here, and ask God if he will forgive you for those sins?"

I nodded again. "Will that save me?" I asked.

"Almost," he answered. "Then you ask Jesus to live in your heart and help you not to sin anymore."

"Wait—" I asked, "—do I say 'Dear God' or 'Dear Jesus'?"

He considered the question carefully. "You could say either, and know that the other one is listening. Or you could say both. Either way would be fine, I think."

"Okay," I took a deep breath and bowed my head. Was the wind picking up outside? What if a tornado came right now? "Hurry, I need saved fast."

The preacher bowed his head and I screwed my eyes shut tight. In one big rush of words I prayed, "Dear God and Dear Jesus both I am sorry I stole the army men and lied about wearing a slip and called Chuck a hog face please Jesus live in my heart and don't let me sin again, ever. Amen."

All I can compare that feeling to, the feeling that I had when I lifted my head from that prayer, that instant where all the internal pressure of my soul was relieved in one mighty, rushing swoosh like that — the only thing that has ever come close to that was the feeling I had the day Susannah burst out of me and into the world. Not her being born, that's not what I mean. I mean the split second before you comprehend that it was an actual baby, that lightning bolt of jubilation and shock, when your body rejoices because whatever unbearable mass that was once inside you is now safely outside and it did not kill you on its way out. That feeling. That's what it feels like to be saved.

It must have shown on my face, that feeling, because

I remember the preacher nodded and said, "Yes. You are now saved."

That's my first memory of Old Rev. Him, looking me square in the eyes, pronouncing me saved and promising me that I would never have to worry about Hell ever again.

I finished proofing my first set of pages and asked Merrilee to hand me more. Along with the typed pages, Old Rev often included random clippings from magazines or Sunday School materials that he wanted to quote, and it was part of my job to follow the lines and arrows drawn from page to page to follow his thinking and figure out what quote went where. So I thought nothing of it when Merrilee set a little pamphlet on top of the next stack of papers she gave me. I scanned it, looking for clues as to what Old Rev wanted from it.

"Little Pearls for Jesus," by Mrs. Pearl Welby, was the title of the booklet. I was doubtful of Mrs. Pearl Welby's credentials. Her picture showed a thin-smiling, peasant-blouse-wearing woman with a graying ponytail surrounded by chubby, cloth-diapered toddlers. The pamphlet looked like some home-grown publication for barefoot parenting from a 1960's Jesus Freak commune. I browsed through the paragraphs of Mrs. Pearl Welby's "wisdom".

```
If Baby is allowed to become attached
to a beloved chewy toy,
Oh, Dear Mama, you are starting her
on the road to all manner of future
bad habits. Have you seen the
gum-smacking teen? pity the poor
child, as she no doubt learned the
seeds of grossness long ago, as a babe
```

```
with a pacifier. The young woman prone
to all manner of oral sins, such as
gluttony and smoking and,oh, dear, even
the wanton kissing of boys in cars,
could have avoided
such heartache, had only her
loving mama been diligent
enough totake away her favorite
teething toy in time!
```

This was a joke. Surely. But no; there was more:

```
If caught early enough, though, these
deviant babies
can start learning about the Fruits
of the Spirit, like self-control.
Of course Baby will fuss, but oh,
Mother, out of love
for her eternal soul, you must
persevere! Who knows? Maybe giving
up the rubber dolly could be the very
means by which Baby learns the meaning
of sin and
repentance! This could even lead Babby
to Eternal Salvation, if Mother doesn't
miss her opportunity! And,tarry not,
Little Mama. After the first birthday,
you may be too late. Oh, for the love
of Sweet Babby's
everlasting soul, Dear Mother, do not
delay. Deal with this today!
```

Let me get this straight, I thought, as I skimmed back over the pages. If I don't take Bunny-Wunny away from Susannah sometime in the next two weeks, she's going to wind up in Hell.

I was speechless.

Merrilee looked at me in that bland way of hers and murmured something about finding this author helpful when she was raising her boys.

All the while, Susannah happily shook Bunny-wunny from her mouth by one soggy ear, like a puppy who won at tug-o-war. I tried, but no matter how hard I looked at it, I couldn't find the sin in that. Thank the Lord we'd be home before her first birthday, and Mrs. Pearl Welby and Merrilee could just keep their helpful pamphlets to themselves.

"Heeeeeey, good-lookin' whaaaaaaat you got cookin?"

JW sang at me, hovering beside my reflection in the mirror as I frantically worked clips and hot rollers out of my hair. We were getting ready for evening service. Merrilee and Old Rev were already in the building, so we finally had a minute alone on the bus.

I threw my arms around his neck and jumped up and down. "Did you get the tickets? Did you get them? Did you?" I squeezed the words out between my squeals and kisses on his cheeks and jaw. He laughed and put his arms around my waist, pulling me closer.

"I've been wondering, Ruby Fae, why did your momma name you 'Ruby Fae'? She should have named you 'Grace," he said, his mouth close to my ear.

"Why?"

"Cause you're so amazing."

I groaned. "But did you *get* them?" We'd been parked a couple of hours, and first thing, he took a long walk by himself around town. He'd had the perfect chance to go find the bus station.

"Stop teasing me! Did you buy the bus tickets yet?"

He squeezed my waist a little too tightly, and I squirmed.
"Did you?"

"No."

I went very still in his arms. "Oh," I said. "Why not?"

Every moment of our shared life could have been packed into the pause he hung in the air between us.

"Because the bus agent is only there from eight to ten. There's only one bus out of town. We'll get our tickets in the morning, when we leave."

Relief surged out of me as JW released me and I turned back to my makeup and hair tools. Grabbing a wide-toothed comb and yanking it through my hair, I made a mental promise to thank JW properly in the sleeping bag later. Heck, I would have thanked him then and there, but we were already running late for service. Meanwhile, Susannah had been winding around my legs, pulling my pantyhose cock-eyed, yet I barely noticed her as I worked. I set my comb down and JW immediately picked it up and began singing into it like a microphone. "Ruuuuuuby.....don't take your love to town..." Ignoring him, I popped open a tube of blue Great Lash while Susannah reached for the lace on the hem of my half-slip and started tugging it down. I ignored that, too, as I glanced at my watch.

JW leaned in. "Hey, Ruby," he said, low and close to my ear. "Whaddaya say, after church tonight, you and me, we play like I'm Moses and you're Aaron."

"Huh?"

"I'll let you hold my staff."

OK, that one got me. I snorted. Out loud.

His face lit up with a victory grin.

"JW, that is the stupidest line yet." But I had to laugh anyway, dang it.

He bent over and scooped up Susannah, "You're all ready for church, aren't you, Punkin? Why don't I drop you off at the nursery? We'll let Mommy get ready for church in peace."

I stared after him, open-mouthed, as he and Susannah bopped down the bus steps and across the parking lot. He'd never done that before. I know it doesn't sound like much, but fifteen minutes to myself was a huge luxury. Apparently JW had been doing some thinking about our new start as well. I hummed as I finished getting ready for the service. One last time.

Because we'd get the bus tickets in the morning. JW said so.

Maybe it was because that would be my last service and I was feeling a little sentimental — I really would miss the performing — but the congregational singing was especially dear that night. The voices were so rich and true that I invited everybody to sing along on the choruses at every chance. There's nothing west of heaven as beautiful as a hundred different voices folded into a single prayer of a song. And when you are up front, with everyone facing you, you get the best acoustics, the music wraps all the way around you, and you can see it on peoples' faces, when they feel it, too. I will always love that. It makes me feel, oh, I don't know how to say it. Maybe the word would be *open*. Like my edges are gone, and I'm a flooded river and all this music from all of these people flows from them right through me and straight up to God Himself. That's what it feels like.

I finally sat down, feeling all soft and mellow and mushy and full, as I settled in with my Bible open on my lap. When JW and Old Rev started up, that meant I had at least a twenty-minute break, so I let my mind wander off and stretch its legs. I was so excited about tomorrow, I could barely sit still. To calm my nerves and distract my thoughts, I fluttered through my Bible, pausing over the papers and what-nots stashed in the pages. A faded Sunday School award for memory work, a senior picture of a cousin, an old love note from JW. *Know why Solomon had 700 wives? Cause he never met you.* All kinds of paper knick-knacks were tucked in there. A bulletin from a church in Joplin, a picture of Chuck and Leslie and the baby — my little nephew I would finally get to meet. And an offering envelope with Grandma Reenie's lime pickle recipe scribbled out on the back, which I'd intended to give to Mrs. Olson. That stopped me. I would be home in time for the Lime Pickles at Christmas!

For a long time, I'd thought Santa left jars of homemade pickles under everyone's Christmas tree. I didn't realize it was only a Schuller Family tradition until I heard the story of how Christmas Pickles got started. Mom told me once, while we were bent over the sink, our hands raw from rinsing the lime off the cucumbers. You soak the cucumbers in builder's lime — yes, the real stuff that you buy at the hardware store — and you have to be very careful to get every bit of lime off or it will eat right through the cucumber skin and turn the flesh to mush. Since Mom and I took over the Christmas pickle-making from Grandma Reenie a few years ago, that would leave all of her brothers with no lime pickles under the tree at Christmas. They would never let Mom live that one down. No lime pickles? You might as well cancel Christmas.

"Your Uncle Charlie was fourteen years older than me," Mom told me one pickle day as we sliced our way through a small mountain of spears. "So when I was a little girl and he went off to war, I thought he was a full-grown man. I didn't think about how he was really just a high school boy, until I saw your brother Chuck in his FFA jacket the other day. He looked so much like Charlie, I don't know how Momma—" She shook her head quickly, dodging the thought the same way you do a persistent mosquito when your hands are full. "Anyway, we all rode in to town to the depot to tell him good-bye. The other boys were all excited. They thought it would be a great idea to have a war hero in the family, but I pouted. Charlie was always my favorite, and I thought he was leaving me on purpose. Your Grandpa Pake didn't say a word, which wasn't like him at all, if you can remember." Mom's sure fingers flew on the cutting board. I worked slower and more carefully with my knife. Partly because I wanted to hear the story, but also because I wanted to keep my fingers. I'll never be as kitchen-handy as Mom.

"Buster, he was about eight then, looked in the sack lunch that Momma had packed for Charlie and hollered, 'Hey! You gave him two pickles! No fair!' The train was getting ready to leave, so Charlie grabbed his lunch bag, gave both his pickles to Buster, kissed Momma on the cheek and told her, 'Buster can have 'em. Make me a jar of my own for Christmas. The war will be over and I'll be home by then, for sure.' Your Grandma Reenie pointed her chin at him and said, 'Alright, I will, but if you don't get home to eat them, don't blame me if they're all gone. We'll eat 'em without you.' I still remember how he laughed at that; he was so young and strong and rarin' to go." Mom cleared her throat. "Start some more lime water, please, Ruby Fae." She did not look up at me.

I took a measuring cup to the pantry where I scooped two cups of builder's lime out of a twenty-pound sack. A dusting of it landed on my skin and I blew it off as quickly as I could, but the burning and itching had already begun. I rubbed my hand on my jeans and then, more carefully this time, I poured the lime into one of the empty gallon glass jugs set out beside it. I carried it to the sink and began filling it with cold water.

"He wasn't home that Christmas, though, was he?" I asked Mom. I had a general idea of Uncle Charlie's story, of course, but had never heard this part.

"That summer, Mama put up an extra quart of pickles, just for him, tied a Christmas ribbon around it and put it on the shelf in the cellar with the others. Come Christmas, that jar was under the tree. So she opened up his pickles, passed them around and said, 'If he wants some bad enough, he can get himself home to eat them.'"

"And next Christmas?" I asked.

"Was even worse," she answered. "Wiley and Will had turned eighteen, so they had to go, too. And even though brothers weren't supposed to be sent to the same front, they asked for special permission to go together. They somehow convinced somebody that keeping twins together would be more efficient. We all tried to be cheerful anyway, but that was a tough one. Guthrie was always good at drawing, so he made all three of the boys Christmas cards with a picture of Santa Claus feeding pickles to Rudolph and saying, 'You weren't here to eat your pickles, so we ate 'em all.' They didn't get those cards until almost August, because the censors thought it was some sort of code. The boys had to tell their story over and over again until somebody finally believed them, but all their mail was held up after that for the rest of the war. Our German last name probably didn't help."

Mom stopped talking then, but I knew the rest, anyway. The twins eventually did come back, but Uncle Charlie never did get to eat his pickles. My mom's favorite brother, Charles Lindbergh Schuller, the laughing Future Farmer of America, the full-grown boy who was always kind to his littlest siblings, did not return from the war. He lies forever still under an American flag, in a quiet garden overlooking a beach off the coast of France.

Now, I wonder what Grandma did with his pickles that first year. I know that we never eat pickles in honor of people who died, only for people who are somewhere else and can't get home for Christmas. There's no jar under the tree for Grandpa Pake or my Cousin Missy's three-day-old baby, either. Grandma Reenie considers them all home now.

Last year, everyone ate a jar for me and even a little half-pint for Susannah, and Mom mailed me Polaroids of everyone eating them. We Jaspers spent Susannah's first Christmas at a KOA in the Big Thicket of Texas. There was no room for a tree in the bus, but it wouldn't have mattered, anyway, because Jaspers don't believe in Santa.

After the service, we all changed out of our church clothes. Merrilee and I hung ours carefully away, but the men tossed their suits on JW's bunk. Almost before their pants hit the bed, Merrilee was there, hanging up their slacks and un-knotting their ties for them. It's always best to look helpful, so I slipped JW's suit coat onto the heavy wooden hanger and reached for the other jacket.

This is the very last time I clean up after JW, I decided. When we get home, he can learn to use a hanger and a hamper like a grownup.

I picked up Old Rev's jacket and heard a paper crinkle in the breast pocket.

I froze.

I had to look at it, the paper in his pocket. I didn't want to. But I had to. I watched my hand as it reached slowly. I pulled the paper out and my insides deflated and slopped out on the floor.

Of course.

In Old Rev's pocket was the wadded-up letter from Reverend Dixon.

Just when I was starting to think maybe, maybe, JW might grow up, leave Old Rev, and take me back home like he'd promised. But I should have known. JW had already given the letter to his father. Heartsick, I stuffed it back in the pocket, dropped the jacket on the floor and staggered back to my bunk. We weren't going to the bus station tomorrow morning. We weren't going home. The only bus I would be on was this bus, right here.

Of all the things JW ever did to me, that one hurt the worst.

Chapter Nine

Susannah and I spent the next day on my bunk. I spoke to the Jaspers only when I absolutely had to and I gave JW flat, vacant smiles when he tried to flirt with me. I fantasized about being invisible. Once, in passing, Old Rev misspoke and called me by Merrilee's name. That's how quiet I was. If I couldn't really leave, I'd disappear right in front of them. That was the only weapon I had.

I was so determined to hide that I took a deep breath, gritted my teeth and closed the curtain around my bunk. As long as I faced the window and kept the outside blinds open, I had a good view. Even my claustrophobia was too depressed to put up much of a fuss.

At a busy Shell service station somewhere on I-90, we pulled in for a quick break. I took Susannah out to stretch her legs and that's when I saw a cheerful splash of Oklahoma State University Orange on a bumper sticker in the self-service lane. My heart leaped. Oklahoma Cowboys! I was so excited. Five young people in t-shirts and cut-offs piled out of the little Nova and the driver, a bearded guy about my age, was wearing a Pistol Pete t-shirt. I caught his eye and pointed to it, mouthing "Go 'Pokes!" His face lit up like I knew it would. All Pokes are family, and if you run into one outside of Stillwater, greeting each other is only the polite thing to do.

"Hey! We're heading back for the semester. You, too?" He asked as he reached for the gas pump.

"No," I shook my head and pointed down at Susannah hanging onto my hand. She had discovered the short curb that edged the cement island around the gas pumps and was working her little legs, tackling the new skill of stepping up and down. "No, I left in'77," I told the college boy, "I have this little Cowgirl to raise, now."

"Cute baby." One of the girls from his car came up behind him. "Did you say you were Class of '77?" she asked.

"No, I didn't finish," My face flushed when I said that. I don't like to think of myself as a dropout. But she didn't seem to notice. "You left in '77? You missed it, then! Cause, oh, man! I mean, Streaker Night in '77 was wild, I'll give you that, but last year was out of control!" They both started laughing. "The news said there were ten thousand people on The Strip that night, if you included everybody on the roofs."

"Wow! Were they all streaking?" I asked.

"Aw, nah!" He said. "Mostly gawkers. But there were a bunch that did it. I bet I saw a hundred before midnight."

The girl shoved at him. "How could you count them? You were too drunk."

He threw an arm around her. "I remember you, though. You were with all those girls on roller skates, wearing nothing but knee pads and gloves, and you grabbed my cowboy hat as you streaked by."

"That was not me! That girl was blond!" she protested, but still laughing.

"Was she?" he teased back. "I didn't notice."

"You didn't even know me yet, before Streaker Night," she said, then gave me a look that meant *men, right?*

Streaker Night in Stillwater was exactly what the name said. On the night before spring break, starting at dark, if you were outside on campus, sooner or later somebody would come flying past you wearing nothing but their God-given skin and a pair of good tennis shoes. Chuck would never admit to it, but Leland told me he'd seen him the year Chuck was a junior and Leland a freshman. Leland said he was watching from the roof of his dorm with a bunch of other freshman, but he would know that long-legged, lop-sided gait of Chuck's a mile away. Leland also told me that he already had a plan for his next Streaker Night because he knew a place where he could get a Batman mask and cape.

Me? I missed streaker night altogether. Before my first spring break, I was already Mrs. Reverend JW Jasper and instead of streaking around a college campus in my birthday suit that night, I was covered to my neck in polyester, onstage in a church somewhere, singing hymns.

"Remember the Sirloin Stockade? Down on Washington Street?" The college boy asked.

"Yeah, my roommate waited tables there." I wondered what had happened to Amy. If she was still waiting tables, if she ever passed algebra. We got along ok, but weren't quite friends. She'd been an assigned roommate. No other girls from Salt Fork High had come to OSU with me that year, so I went potluck. Even though I hadn't thought of Amy in a long time, I would have given anything to see her right then. My Susannah tugging at me was the only thing anchoring me, the only thing keeping from deteriorating into a puddle of self-pity and regret.

"You know the giant bull statue in front of the Sirloin?"

the college boy continued. "Some of my buddies loaded it onto a flat-bed trailer and we pushed it down the street, all the way to Theta pond with Nature-Boy, here," he jerked his thumb over his shoulder, pointing toward his friend coming out of the gas station restroom, "and a couple other guys, drunk-nekkid, war-whooping and singing, 'I'm an Indian Outlaw' all the way, riding it like they're King of the Rodeo. We shoved it into the pond, then everybody started jumping in, clothes or not. There were news helicopters circling, businesses throwing t-shirts to the crowds, one campus cop even stripped down to his gun belt. It was a crazy night." The memory of it cracked these two up, and I started to laugh, too, but I saw JW coming toward us so I cut it short.

I introduced my husband and the girl gave me a *well done* look. "These guys are going back to Stillwater, to school," I told JW. "We were all talking about OSU stuff, making me feel nostalgic."

"Oh, nice!" JW said, his wholesome smile nearly blinding us. "We both have good memories of Stillwater. Remember how much fun we had at that Student Bible Association party, when I came to visit you? We must have played ping-pong 'til almost midnight."

They went silent.

I could actually see them shift the gears of their brains. I could tell they were wondering, first, whether or not Preacher-Boy and I really did belong together, and if so, were we a couple of weirdos or just regular-religious, and finally, had they said something to offend me? Because, after all, nobody meant any harm; we were all family here.

I wanted to reassure them that I didn't think they were Pagan Hippie-Folk, not anymore, anyway. I wanted to say, hey, let me grab my suitcase and squeeze in. OSU will take me back; I'm almost a sophomore. But instead, I grabbed Susannah and swung her up onto JW's shoulders. I had already learned a dirty little secret of motherhood, that babies can be useful for smoothing over awkward social situations. She squealed with delight and I made our excuses to leave. JW assured our new friends that we would pray for their safe travels. He offered to do it right there, on the spot, but they declined. Politely.

After another round of "Go Pokes!" and "Pistol's firin'" we broke apart. The students headed into the gas station for Cokes and I decided to call off my silent treatment and ask JW if he'd watch Susannah long enough for me to go to the ladies' room by myself. Since she was already on him, hanging onto his forehead and bucking for a ride, I figured he couldn't exactly refuse. Taking her into a public restroom with me was such a pain. There was nowhere clean to put her down. Besides, I never passed up the chance to go to a real restroom instead of that footlocker of a bathroom on the bus. As mad as I was at JW, my claustrophobia overruled.

"Please?" I added, in an attempt to sound sweet.

"Okay," JW said slowly. He had a strange, thoughtful look on his face that I couldn't read. "But why do you need to go here? Why can't you use the bus?"

What was his problem? He knew why I hardly ever used the bathroom on the bus.

"JW! You know why!" I didn't want to say "claustrophobia" out loud, because when Old Rev had first heard about my claustrophobia, he told JW to lay his hands on me and cast that demonic spirit of fear *down* in Jesus' name. Saying that word again would only start a new round of demon-slaying, and I really, really just wanted to go all by myself in a real ladies' room with a real sink and enough room to turn around. That's all I wanted. "It's perfectly safe here! It's broad daylight, and there's all kinds of families."

At that moment, one of the OSU girls came out of the gas station and rounded the corner towards the ladies' room. "Look!" I pointed, "She's going in there, too. She's very nice. I won't be alone."

From her perch on JW's shoulders, Susannah shrieked and squirmed, trying to get her horsey of a daddy to giddy-up. JW's face smoothed into a placid, picture-perfect smile and his blue eyes were suddenly wide and clear. "All right," he said. "I'll be glad to watch our little angel." He jiggled her once, then, making clop-clop noises with the roof of his mouth, turned to trot around the side of the bus. Susannah's delighted giggles followed me across the parking lot.

OSU girl and I ended up washing hands at the same time. She smiled at me in the mirror, but it was a careful smile. Guarded. Once she realized I belonged to the bus with the giant cross on the side, she had marked me down for party-free, weekday-only conversations.

"I forgot to tell you that one of my brothers is a senior at OSU. Do you know him? Leland McKeever?" I asked her.

"You're kidding!" she squealed. "You're Leland's sister?"

"No way! You know him? Really?" See? I told you we're all like family.

"Oh, everybody does! He's the funniest guy on campus. Out at the Cimarron Ballroom, he's half the party all by himself. He cracks us up with his dancing. One night, he got real drunk and started lassoing everybody in sight. The bouncers came after him, but he lassoed one of them, too. My Kappa little sister tried to go out with him, but she said all he wanted to do was drink and dance. I mean, she said that was *all* he wanted to do, you know? He would never..." her voice trailed off.

"Listen," I told her. "I need you to do something for me. Please." I dried my hands and put one of them on her arm. "Tell Leland you met me." My eyes welled up.

"Hey, are you all right?" She asked, genuinely concerned. I nodded. "I just, really, really miss him. Please tell him that. And tell him I tried to write home, but I'm not getting any mail back. They're keeping it from me." The tears were getting harder and harder to blink away. "Please, tell him to tell Mom, tell everybody, that they're keeping my mail."

"What do you mean? I don't get it. Who's keeping it? The people on that bus?"

I grabbed some paper towels and wiped my face. "Yeah, they are, they're hiding my mail from me, because, oh, it's complicated. But listen, I gotta go, I only have a second." I'd already been in there too long. Good Lord, I thought, JW will come barging in here if I take much longer. OSU Girl, though, wasn't finished with me.

"Your husband can't do that to you! He doesn't have the right to keep you from writing your family! You should, you know, you should, do something about that. It's not right!" Her hands were on her hips, her eyes flashing.

"What? What do I do?" I asked.

"Well, for starters, you tell them to give you your mail!"

"And then what?" My hands were now on my hips, too, and I felt my own face getting hot. For a moment, I imagined storming out there and telling those Jaspers to keep their dang hands off my dang mail. Yeah. *I could tell them that! I could!* I could feel it. I could almost see it. Almost. "But what if they won't?" I asked.

"Well, if they won't, you call the police. It's a crime to steal mail, you know."

Call the police on my husband and his family.

Sounded easy enough, right? But I had my suspicions that fire-bombing your life was a little more complicated than that.

I shook my head. "I can't do that. He's, you know, my husband. But, please, I need you to tell Leland you saw me, and that I want to come home, but I can't."

Her eyes narrowed, her brow furrowed. "What do you mean, you can't go home? Will he not let you leave or anything?"

"No," I said, a little confused. "It's not like that, I mean, I could go home, I guess, it's just that I'm married, and he says I can't, so, you know, I can't. I mean, I love him, I don't want to leave him..." my words limped away from me.

"Oh my God. You sound like that Patty Hearst. They said she fell in love with her kidnappers, too, and acted like she was married and all. Is that guy really even your husband? Oh my God, what if you're, like, kidnapped?" she gasped.

"What? No! I'm not kidnapped. I'm really married!" I held up my wedding ring, like it would clear everything up. "And we're Christians, so, the Bible says, you know, I have to—" Suddenly I realized I'd been in the bathroom far too long.

"I've got to go. Please, just, please, tell Leland what I said." I was probably already in trouble and I needed to get back to Susannah. I turned to go, hitting the door at a run, but it wasn't fast enough.

The bus was gone.

They were all gone. The bus, the Jaspers, JW and Susannah.

Susannah.

I ran around the building to the side where the trucks fuel up. Two semis were parked at the far edge of the lot, but no bus. I looped the building again and once more. It wasn't there. I ran out to the road and looked east and west and all around, but they weren't there, either. I ran thirty or forty yards along the shoulder. Still no bus.

How could they have forgotten me? JW knew where I was! I *told* him where I was going! Did he think I'd gotten back on the bus? Did he think I'd gone in our bus bathroom after all? I stomped my feet in frustration. Now what? They had to come back for me any minute. It couldn't take that long to figure out they've left me.

Except.

I'd been hiding out on my bunk all morning, with the curtains closed. They were probably still half-closed.

Maybe they thought I was back in my bunk, sulking. It could take them hours to miss me.

I turned back, walking slowly. My shoulders slumped. My feet dragged. Tears ran down my cheeks.

I ached for Susannah and burned with fury at the rest of them. How could they have left me? How did JW not take a second to look around and say, *gee, I don't see my wife here, anywhere?* And Susannah! She had to be looking for me. Didn't Merrilee think it was strange that I just dumped Susannah on her? I never did that without asking. Did she think I abandoned her? Oh, God, don't let Susannah think that. Not that. I couldn't bear Susannah thinking I abandoned her. A sob bubbled up in my chest.

I trudged back toward the station, wringing with sweat. My fair, freckly nose and cheekbones were already crackling with sunburn. My throat was parched, and I didn't even have quarters to buy a Coke while I waited. I had never been so utterly miserable.

But when I reached the awning of the service station, I saw that oh, it was worse, so much worse, than I thought.

My suitcase was sitting on the sidewalk.

Chapter Ten

"Call the police! Call the state troopers! They took my baby! They took my baby!" I was hysterical. Someone pulled me into a little office and someone else got on the phone. The first someone tried to get me to sit down on a rickety office chair. He tried to talk to me, to get me to describe the bus, tell him our names. Maybe he got intelligible answers from me, I couldn't say. Someone else brought me my suitcase, thinking that it would somehow reassure me, but I knew it would be empty. I didn't keep it packed and JW wouldn't have bothered. He wasn't leaving my things; he was leaving a message. *You've been left behind.*

Somebody patted my hand and told me that the sheriff was a few minutes away, and someone else handed me a tissue. Hour-long minutes passed as I sat, hugging myself, rocking back and forth. Eventually, I stood and mumbled something about waiting for the sheriff outside. The man who had taken charge commandeered a helpful and concerned woman from among the customers to go stand with me, to try and comfort me. Someone prayed out loud and everyone but me said "Amen." Someone else muttered something about kids on milk cartons. I paced the sidewalk, staring at the parking lot and willing the bus to appear, but all I could see was a handful of cars and pickups fueling up and the two semis still parked at the far side. The OSU carload had already left, and I know it's awful to admit that it mattered, but I was glad they weren't still there to see this. This was all so made-for-tv-movie-drama trashy.

We heard a siren in the distance and it was a relief to everyone. Surely The Law could fix this. Or at the very least, take this crazy, weepy woman off their hands.

The drivers of the two semis must have suddenly decided they wanted to be somewhere less cop-filled, because both trucks roared to life and began to ease their way off the lot and back onto the highway. One eastbound, the other the westbound, they split like stage curtains parting and rolled away to reveal the main attraction hidden behind them.

Our bus.

There was a beat of stunned silence while everyone took it in.

Suddenly everyone had something to say, all along the lines of, "Say, what's going on here? What are you people pulling?"

I broke away and ran as hard as I could toward the bus, leaving my empty suitcase behind.

When I reached the bus, the door opened, and I hurtled up the steps past JW in the driver's seat. I didn't bother with him; all I could think of was Susannah.

She was on Merrilee's lap, fussing and squirming. I stomped over and snatched her up without a word. We buried ourselves in each other's necks and swayed together, comforting and calming one another. When I caught my breath, I looked up at the rearview mirror and shot rays of pure hatred toward the back of JW's head until he looked up at my reflection. He still had that perfect, smooth, look on his face.

"Next time you decide to flirt with a bunch of college boys, Susannah and I won't come back for you," he said calmly. He checked the highway traffic and hummed a little Gospel tune as he pulled out of the lot.

I wanted to tear the bus apart and set it on fire. I wanted to slam JW's perfect smile into the pavement. I wanted to knee him in the groin.

I didn't, though. Instead, I straightened my blouse and tied up my hair and said nothing.

But inside, I seethed. I did not deserve that. Even more, *Susannah* did not deserve that. I mean, she's OK, she's too little to know what had happened, but would that have stopped JW if she wasn't OK? If she'd been old enough to bang on the windows and cry for her mama as the Jaspers drove off without me, would that have made any difference?

I studied the Jaspers as we rolled down the highway together. Everyone was quietly occupied. Old Rev was scribbling out a sermon longhand. JW was driving, of course, but reading a newspaper at the same time. Susannah was dumping plastic blocks all over her bed. Merrilee was sewing.

Merrilee.

I pretended to read a magazine, but really, I was watching Merrilee. Had Merrilee approved of her son's little bus-hiding stunt? I couldn't imagine that she would, she never liked commotion of any kind. She would not have voiced any disagreement, though. Even though she birthed JW, raised him, trained him and taught him all twelve grades of school, she saw him as a full-grown man, a preacher in his own right, and therefore, in authority he was a full rank above her.

In fact, in the Jasper Hierarchy of a Godly Family, the organizational chart would have looked like this:

GOD/JESUS

The Holy Ghost

Old Rev

JW

Any Other Pastor In The World (providing he was representative of one of the pre-approved denominations of the Jasper's choosing)

Merrilee

Me and Susannah

Bunny-Wunny

So even if Merrilee had objected to "leaving" me, she wouldn't have spoken up. She believed a woman should not offer an unsolicited opinion. She felt that would not be in keeping with a quietness of spirit. I turned another page of my magazine and watched Merrilee at the same time. Her fingers wove the needle and thread up and down on a row of sequined roses with the same even and steady beat they have on a piano's keys.

Funny. If you were to ask me what Merrilee looked like, I'd probably start by describing her perfectly shaped pianist fingers and her soft, girlish hands. She did have beautiful hands. But then again, she never had to cook or do dishes because we always ate at restaurants or church members' houses. It wasn't like she spent much of her life on housework, either, because it took about five minutes to clean her entire "house." And she never did any gardening or farm work, so it made sense that her hands looked like a magazine ad for Jergen's Lotion.

But they were gifted hands. On an instrument, at the sewing machine, with a make-up brush or even with barber scissors, her hands were confident, creative and inspired. Merrilee's figure was slim, but not striking. Her features, agreeable, but not remarkable. Her facial expressions and mannerisms, well, they were pleasant, but not engaging. Overall, there was nothing unattractive about her looks, it's just that they were sort of general-purpose. It was like her face and body could have belonged to anybody, and only her hands were truly hers.

From our record collection, I pulled out three Jasper Family LPs and considered the photos on the album covers. The first two were from before my time. Billy Sunday and JW looked like they were about eight or ten in one, fifteen or sixteen or so, in the other. Old Rev was smiling broadly, the Proud Papa in the younger photo, but he was the somber family patriarch of a Kelly-Green-Tuxedo Tribe in the second. The third album was the one we recorded last. I had replaced Billy Sunday and JW was grown, but with his boyish beauty intact. He looked like Donny Osmond, if Donny Osmond were blond, clutching a large red new testament in one hand and me in the other. And me? I looked wildly happy. That picture was taken at our wedding. And Merrilee looked exactly the same. The expression on her face in all three pictures was identical. Precisely, pleasantly, forgettable.

I put my hand up to my face, feeling my cheeks, my lips. Lightly, I skimmed my fingers up my nose and across my brow. I recognized the expression from the inside-out. It was the same as Merrilee's.

That evening's service was going to be different. Old Rev had wrangled our way onstage at the evening worship

service of a three-state district conference for some off-
shoot independent Baptist denomination meeting in
Decatur. The crowd would be nothing but pastors and
deacons and board members and their wives. It wouldn't
be a hard night, because we weren't the whole show, for
once. Old Rev and JW wouldn't be giving the sermon,
they'd only say a few words. We would do three, maybe
four songs, tops. But the audience would be packed with
the leaders of a hundred different churches, and if it went
well, our schedule could be booked solid for the next three
or four years. Merrilee and JW were a little keyed up about
it, but Old Rev was unperturbed. "The Lord is our
booking agent," was all he'd say.

Merrilee was fretting about everybody's clothes,
especially the dresses. She and I each had ten matching
dresses in various solid colors, all of them made from a
soft, draping polyester blend, and Merrilee had made them
all. She carried a sewing table and machine with us, packed
away with the music equipment under the bus in the cargo
hold. My mom was good enough at sewing, but Merrilee
was amazing. She didn't need patterns, only pictures and
measurements. Her skills came in very handy during my
pregnancy; dressing me was no problem. Well, no more
problem than usual. It turned out that Dressing Ruby was
a regular item on the Jasper's business agenda. There was
always the modesty issue, for instance. Since we traveled
so widely, we ran into a lot of different opinions on how
a good woman should be covered. What would be
considered appropriate in one church was shocking in
another. Decently covered in a rural church out west
might be laughable and dowdy in a metropolitan one up
north. So Merilee had shrewdly devised an adjustable hem
system for each of my dresses, where my hemline could be

raised or lowered to fit each church's preference. That was only my dress, mind you. Since she was always at the piano and never on stage, she could pick her one length and stick with it.

And then there was the decoration problem. Everyone likes to think that they aren't judging on appearance, but that's not true. Churches think they like the idea of everyone being plain and simple and unworldly, but when they find themselves having to stare at someone for fifteen or twenty hours in a row during revival week, they secretly want to see something a little more interesting than a bunch of ordinary people dressed in homespun and feedsacking. But Merrilee had also solved that challenge. Our dresses had all sorts of hidden snaps and buttons and hooks-and-eyes where we attached or detached ribbons or rhinestones or seasonal decorations or even bands of sequins that matched a church's new sanctuary carpet, if needed. Whatever you wanted to look at, we tried to show it. Have sequins, will travel, that was us. You want plain? Book an Amish family. Us Jaspers, we sparkled.

But the Pastors' Retreat was a serious dilemma. Merrilee didn't know how sparkly that particular pocket of Little Baptists liked their singers. Little Baptists are different than Big Baptists, who are almost as shiny as non-denominationals. When we sang for Big Baptists or Non-denoms, we got to pile on all the glitter we had, and they loved it. JW disapproved of that aspect of their beliefs, but me, well, I thought it meant they might be a little more fun than the no-shines. I never found out for sure, though; it was just my hunch.

I confess, I always did like sparkly things more than a good Christian should. Mom says I must have caught my magpie disease from her, because she loves sparkle, too. Hers is understandable, though, because when she was a kid, Pilgrim's Holiness women were still plain. No make-up, jewelry, anything like that. And don't even ask about pierced ears! My Grandma Reenie never even had a wedding ring, because it was considered an unseemly ornamentation in her day. Eventually, though, what was once a firm rule became more like a guideline, then only a soft consideration. There was no grand pronouncement from the pulpit or anything; the thinking just sort of *shifted* a little. Maybe first a good old farm wife would show up at church with a watch somewhat fancier than its job strictly called for, hiding it under her quilted Bible cover until someone asked Shorty if his wheat had done any good this year, and he pointed to her wrist with a sheepish grin saying, "Oh, not too terrible bad. Ask Mama there, what she did with her share of the crop." Then maybe one of the preacher's high school boys, the one everyone was so proud of for always getting on the honor roll, spent some of his hog show winnings on a class ring and everyone understood, because youngsters are supposed to get foolish now and then, and, besides, don't you imagine that calculus business must be a terrible hard day's work? Even Grandma Reenie finally began sporting a colored-glass-studded tree-shaped brooch at the little kids' Christmas pageant. After all, Christmas only comes once a year, isn't that right? So by the time I came along, jewelry itself was no longer a sin, but your attitude about it could be. You know, just don't be show-offy or go spending as much as a year's feed bill on something flashy to try and impress people.

I listened as Merrilee dithered about a formula for calculating the precise amount of glitz this denomination would accept as righteous. She had a stack of newsletters from other ministries, a couple of Sunday School quarterlies, and five issues of a Christian Women's magazine spread across the table alongside three bolts of ribbon and spangle trims. I'd seen her get worked up about our costumes before, but she was dead serious about this show. Merrilee had both of her Bibles opened, her NIV *and* King James translations, searching for the last word on women's wear and jewelry and doo-dads and earbobs.

I could have helped her out. One of my cousins married someone from a Freewill church not fifty miles from Decatur, and I was at the wedding. I could have told Merrilee exactly how short the dresses should be and how much jewelry everybody wore to church around there. But since Merrilee felt a woman shouldn't offer an unsolicited opinion, I decided I'd best keep my mouth shut. Don't anybody mind me, nosiree. I'll just sit over here keeping my spirit quiet like you taught me, Merrilee. Besides, sparkly clothes and spotlight fever are what got me into this fix in the first place.

Chapter Eleven

It was at the Farmer's Co-op Annual Shareholder's Meeting and Barbecue Dinner that I first saw the Salt Fork High School Swing-Singers on stage, the girls in their shimmering dresses, the boys in their sequined vests. On a Saturday afternoon in the spring of my eighth-grade year, I beheld those upperclassmen rock stars dancing grapevines and step-ball-changes, singing "I Can See Clearly Now, the Rain is Gone," and my breath caught, my skin tingled. *Here, now,* I thought. *This is a miracle they never told me about.* When that feather-haired senior, Curtis LeRoy Crabb stepped up to the mic and sang "Precious and Few," I even wept a little. Partly because I knew, I *knew,* he was secretly singing it only to me, but also, because I felt betrayed. Why had no one ever told me? How could they have kept this from me? Why hadn't I known about this until now?

After the final number, a rowdy swing-dance version of "Rockin' Robin," the Co-op members and their families meandered over to the cafeteria for their Styrofoam plates piled high with pulled pork, corn on the cob and wacky cake. But I lingered in the empty auditorium, brooding on this new kind of Sign and Wonder. What did it mean?

What had happened here? How could such a magnificent thing have come to pass in humble Salt Fork, Oklahoma? Those ordinary kids, classmates of my brothers, regular old high school students, had latched on to something big and holy and brilliant and turned it on the audience until we all gloried in it, every last one of us, together. I had felt something akin to that before, but never outside of church. There could be only one explanation; God had been here. Yes. That had to be it. He'd been here. I had heard Him. I had seen Him.

And I meant to get in on that, next time.

All summer long I practiced for the auditions. I stayed out in the yard after dark, a transistor radio pointed toward Dodge City, singing along and holding my curling iron for a mic, copying the dances I'd seen on American Bandstand. I memorized each motion, each step; but something was still wrong. I was too stiff. Too anchored. Too earthbound. I didn't know what was off, but I knew I'd never make the cut.

It was Leland who finally saved me.

"You know they'll teach you, right? You don't have to know it already," he said.

"What?" I whirled around to face him. He had sneaked up on me. I'd thought he and Chuck were still in town, doing whatever it was that driving-aged boys, decently raised, did on Saturday nights in Salt Fork.

"At the auditions. They don't expect you to already know it all, they only want to see if you can catch on. They line you all up and someone does a few steps and you copy it. They teach you right there, at the try-outs."

"You mean, like a game of Simon Says?" Relief flooded through me. I could follow directions as well as anybody, when I wanted to.

"Yep." said Leland. He sat down on the porch steps, pulled off his cowboy boots and tube socks, rolled up the sleeves of his plaid pearl-snap shirt, and joined me in the yard. "Like this."

He walked five paces ahead of me and stopped. "Just watch first. One, two, three, go." Whistling "The Hustle," Leland, all long, lean limbs and cocky cowboy glee, expertly strutted off a few easy measures of disco. "Ok, I'll repeat it once, calling out the steps, then you join in," he said over his shoulder. "Right foot back, two, three; tap-lean-clap; turn! Right foot back, two, three; tap-lean-clap; turn!"

Maybe it was Leland's encouragement. Or the relief of knowing that I wasn't that far behind, after all. Or maybe it was the bumper crop of stars overhead, which have been known to make people way crazier than that on an Oklahoma June night. Most likely, though, it was the dawning knowledge that Leland had definitely done this before and seemed to be, as far as I could tell, unsinged by hellfire. Whatever it was that caused me to be Filled with The Spirit that Saturday night in front of the hen house, it sanctified my joints and unstuck my soul.

Leland and I danced all night. He taught me The Hustle, The Bus Stop, The Box Step, and a little something he claimed copyright to called "The Possum Stomp," which he assured me was a big hit at parties. We worked on swing-dancing and line dances and disco steps until finally we went just plain nuts to whatever the DJ in Dodge City gave us. When we got hot and thirsty, we danced over to the hydrant, gulped and splashed, then danced on out past the hay barn. We danced on top of the picnic table and under the clothesline and in the driveway. We danced clear through the darkest part of the night, until right before sunrise, when the radio battery died and the stars all came onstage for their final curtain call and we flopped down in the soft, sparse buffalo grass of the front lawn.

"How come you knew all those dances?" I asked him.

"I know stuff."

"Yeah, like pigs and steers and football, not show choir."

"Show choir's for pansies."

I flung an arm over and gave him a half-hearted punch on the bicep. "Is not."

Leland didn't reply, and I didn't expect him to. We both watched the sky lighten one, then two shades as the stars melted into it. I yawned. So did Leland. An early rooster warmed up his throat with a few abbreviated crows.

"I hope you make it," he said to me. "But if you don't, try again next year. You will then, probably."

The first breeze of the day stirred, and over by the corral, the windmill blade woke up with a feeble squeak. I yawned once more. "We're gonna fall asleep in church today."

"God will get over it," Leland answered, then rolled himself over onto his belly, smashing his nose and right cheek into the grass. Flinging his arms out wide, he closed his eyes and let out a snore.

I didn't make show choir right off, because I was a freshman and there's a certain justice in this world tending toward upperclassmen. But eight weeks into the semester, when Wendy Jo Kelly's sequins could no longer stretch around her quickly-rounding belly far enough to deflect the gossip, I got my big break. I tried to be sorry for Wendy Jo, who would be timing her contractions before our spring concert, but I was mostly concerned with catching up on those early weeks of practice I'd missed. I didn't have time to think of anything else, not then, and not for the next four years. I lived for show choir.

JW saw me once on stage with the Swing-Singers, in the fall of my senior year. The Jaspers were parked out at Rose of Sharon church for our annual week-long revival, but I had missed every evening's service that year because I was so busy in town with show choir. The Swing-Singers were getting ready for a contest in Dallas — a very big deal, complete with an overnight trip and a visit to Six Flags. We were all excited. We had extra practices every night. Mom hadn't exactly been happy about that, me missing so much revival, but she didn't make me go. After all, a show choir is like a team, Dad had said, and I'd made a commitment to my teammates.

On Saturday afternoon, we had a fund-raiser on the square in Salt Fork. The Jaycees sold hamburgers and chips for us, the booster club had a bake sale, and the youth group from the Big Baptist church even sold snow cones and gave us half. The radio station was there, giving out balloons and talking to the mayor about the volunteers who'd painted the bandshell. It was that sort of a thing. The junior high show choir and the girls' ensemble and the jazz band also played while people milled around, visiting with each other, trying not to spill their plates and waiting for whichever thing their own kid was in to take the stage.

We Swing-Singers stood behind the Crape Myrtle bushes trying to stay hidden off-stage until our big entrance, but it was hard to behave like professionals when everyone could clearly see us. We waved at friends and generally fooled around while the junior high kids sang. I was motioning to my friend Pam that I wanted her to take a picture of me during my solo on "Rainy Days and Mondays" when behind her, I saw JW and his parents standing with Reverend Dixon and his wife. Of course the Dixons would be there, their youngest boy was in the Junior High Jazz band, but I hadn't thought about them bringing the Jaspers. Honestly, I hadn't even given JW much thought at all, lately. But now here he was, and I could see that JW was a year older and a year taller than the last time I'd seen him. And a year cuter.

We were almost ready to go on, but the alto section had suddenly fallen out of formation. They had noticed JW, too. A cute new boy in a small town is never inconspicuous, and the girls were busy making up wild, hopeful theories about who he was and how he'd landed in Salt Fork that day.

JW saw me, flashed his movie-star smile, and waved. I waved back, and the choir went berserk. OK, I hate to admit it, but I sort of had a reputation back then. No, not that kind of reputation, the other kind.

"Ohmigosh! Look! He's waving at Ruby!" Mitzi Wampler said, "And look! She's waving, I mean, *waving*, waving, at him! Like she actually notices him! Can you believe it?" Mitzi gave an exaggerated stagger and threw her hand over her heart in a dramatic it's-the-big-one-Ethel fake heart attack.

"Good luck, Goober," Jimmy Radford, Salt Fork's third-string quarterback and my usual dance partner cheerfully saluted JW. "Unless you're a monk or a legally-blind, asexual mute with really good manners, she's got no time for you." JW couldn't hear him from across the lawn, but he could tell Jimmy was addressing him, so he nodded agreeably.

"Uh, guys?" I said, "I'm standing right here. I can hear you making fun of me."

"We're just calling 'em like we see 'em," Mitzi said. "Or are we wrong? Are we missing something? No! Wait! Is it true? Look at Ruby's face, Jimmy! She *does* have something going on with Tiger Beat Cover Boy over there! Ruby, you little fox! Telling all the guys, 'Oh, no! I can only date boys who share my beliefs,' and all the while you got Cover Boy in your pocket! Whoa, I underestimated you!" She elbowed me.

My face burned with embarrassment. She had pegged me. I had let all the boys in Salt Fork think I couldn't date boys outside my church. I told myself it was my high standards that kept me from going out, that was all. I almost believed me, too, when I insisted it had nothing to do with being nervous or shy about dating. But here was JW, sweet, familiar JW, whom I'd known all my life, my other life of home and family out at Rose of Sharon. Here he was in my town life, my worldly, sparkly, show-choir life. For the first time, I saw JW through the eyes of the Salt Fork girls.

Huh. It did make me think.

Jimmy Radford was still grousing. "Watch out, Ruby. He's an out-of-towner. He may wish to *engage in ungentlemanly conduct*."

"For your information, Jimmy, he actually is a preacher." That shut Jimmy up. He pouted as we took our places.

When I got onstage though, I felt an extra jolt of energy that leapt from me to my partner, to the next couple, and right on down the line until, as Mr. Cole told us later, we'd given the performance of a lifetime. "I wish we could have been at contest today," he'd said. "Can you guys do that again in Dallas?"

Red-faced and panting, Jimmy said, "Ruby was on fire

today! I was half asleep, but she pulled me along and I had to keep up."

"Well, do that again next week, OK, Ruby?" Mr. Cole said.

I promised I would. But even in my innocence, I suspected that I wouldn't be able to without the dazzled and slack-mouthed JW in the audience. I knew he had never before in his church-filled life seen such a show, and he'd certainly never seen me lit up like that, singing and dancing in my shiny, slinky, show choir get-up. He couldn't take his eyes off me. I hadn't looked at him once from the stage, but I still knew he was watching me. I could feel it. And I'll admit it, still; I liked it.

A year later, JW would tell me that he'd gone straight back to his bunk on the bus that day and prayed for me and my soul and any future children that God might see fit to bless us with. Prayed fervently, I imagine.

It was no use going back and asking if things would have turned out differently had this or that thing happened or not. If I had been on the back row that day, or if JW hadn't come to town, or if I'd had a head cold, even. There was no use asking it. I was married to JW, we had Susannah, I lived on a bus, and I could get as mad as I wanted, but it didn't change a thing. As Grandpa Pake would say, sometimes you gotta dance with the one who brung ya.

Chapter Twelve

For the preachers' conference, we had planned a special treat. A guaranteed hit, a ringer. Yep, that's right, a solo from Old Rev.

Old Rev only sang for special occasions. Which was for the best.

Oh, his voice was good enough. With a booming, resonating, old-fashioned, Gospel-Singing-Jubilee-style baritone that the older folks pined for, he could rattle the rafters when he wanted to. And he dearly loved the dramatic use of dynamic markings. The liberal sprinkling of a *sotto voce* whispering mid-melody, the startling blast of a *sforzando*, a long, drawn-out *crescendo* so measured, the gradual build-up so agonizingly slow, you'd think you'd be the one to die of breathlessness before he reached the end of his note. And, if a person could be objective, Old Rev's appearance never hurt his overall performance. You could take one look at Old Rev and see that JW's fine bones and good hair came from his father, so when Old Rev sang, you saw why he was once himself the Golden Boy of the Gospel Circuit. I've heard claims that once, in his younger days, Old Rev sang at an event where Gloria Gaither herself heard him and offered him a job singing back-up on tour, but he turned her down because he didn't think those Gaithers were ever going to amount to anything. If that was true or not, I never knew, but whether he was preaching or singing or praying over a pie social made no difference. Old Rev could hold a stage, make no mistake.

But Merrilee was the only one who could ever accompany him. She was the only one who could anticipate his improvisations, his changes in tempos and sudden injections of related hymns that transformed the piece into some medley hybrid that no one else could see coming yet made perfect sense when you heard it. The whole concept of harmony baffled him. The idea of two voices singing two completely different notes that melt into a single liquid beat of intertwining music as unsplittable as an atom flummoxed him to the point of exasperation. He was not an ensemble man. He was strictly a soloist.

That night he sang *The King is Coming,* and, oh, it was majestic. Royal robes unfurling. Trumpets resounding. Holy hosts singing Amazing Grace. Our world deserted, nothing left but empty haunted marketplaces and the over-ripe wheat harvest still standing in the field. All we've ever known abandoned for the bright, shining halls of heaven.

From my seat on wife's row — and it was crowded tonight, there were lots of wives smiling up at their husbands at this church full of preachers all vying for pulpit time — I gazed at Old Rev, and I couldn't help it. I was mesmerized. He wasn't just singing, he was prophesying, sharing a divine vision in song, and suddenly I could see it as clearly as if the heavens had opened and scrolled the scene before me. Tears ran down my cheeks as

I imagined The Second Coming. My shoulders shook with the effort of keeping my sobs quiet and inconspicuous. What if Jesus did come back, right now? Tonight? I'd never see Oklahoma again.

After the service, the nursery was crowded with pastor's wives and their littlest ones reuniting after a long and tiring evening. Most everyone but me seemed to know each other, so the gathering-up process had a girls' club feel. Heels were kicked aside, purses and Bibles dumped on top of a toy kitchen set. One bubbly wife ducked behind the cubbies and shimmied out of a girdle with a delicious sigh and everyone laughed. Since this was the first night in the conference, everyone was staying somewhere in town overnight and for most of these women, this would be the best vacation they'd get all year. The host church had laid out an after-service dessert and coffee table in the fellowship hall, so none of us were in a big hurry. For once, the men could wait. Jammies and bottles and breasts and blankies came out as rocking chairs were claimed and these preachers' babies, who had all learned early on that they had to be good sports about things like bedtime routines, settled in.

Everyone was very friendly, first complimenting our music and clothes and then trying to include me in their conversation. But I was too wrung out to put much effort into small talk, so I gracefully faded out, just rocking and feeding and appreciating the warmth.

Eventually, a girl of about five or six popped in and said, "Daddy wants to know how much longer you're going to be." It was unclear to me which Mommy she was addressing, because three mommies got up and took their leave. A few more women drifted off until I was left with the last two women in the room. One sat cross-legged on the floor holding a pajama-clad toddler who had been asleep for quite a while, the other was in the rocker beside me, burping a tiny, nearly-newborn across her knees. She turned to me with the kindest face. I wasn't positive, but she may have been the wife seated next to me during the service.

"Ruby, I'm glad we are getting a chance to talk. I feel led to speak with you. Please forgive me if I am offending you, but can I ask you something?" She laid a gentle hand on my arm.

Oh, great, here it comes. She saw how emotional I'd been during Old Rev's song, and now she's going to ask me about my eternal destiny. I couldn't fault her; it's our thing, it's what we do. But I'd started the day with being abandoned by my husband and having my baby kidnapped, then I'd traveled seven hours to get here, performed in front of five hundred people and breastfed a toddler. I was kinda tired. But I smiled and said, "Of course I don't mind. I appreciate your concern. Go ahead."

She glanced at the cross-legged mother and I suddenly knew they'd already discussed me. Oh, well. That didn't offend me, either. I'd probably have done the same with my friends. I braced for the "If you died tonight, do you know where you'd spend eternity?" question.

"Ruby, are you safe?"

What?

I blinked and jerked my arm back. I didn't know what to say. Am I? Safe? I made an awkward noise of surprise, some blending of "Huh?" and "What?" I looked from one woman to the other, saw a spark in their eyes. "Safe? Of course I'm safe. JW doesn't really intend to, you know, the only bad time was an accident — he just gets so — I mean, sure, sometimes he scares me, but he wouldn't ever really hurt, not really— "

Now they were the startled ones. Their eyes nearly popped out of their heads, and it hit me.

Duh.

They hadn't said "safe." They'd said "saved." They had asked if I was *saved*.

Oh, crap. What have I done?

The three of us stared at each other, wide-eyed. First no one spoke, then we all did at once.

"Oh! I thought you said–" I tried to laugh it off.

"What were you going to say?"

"He doesn't intend to do *what?*"

"Never mind, how silly of me, forget I said anything."

"You can talk to us."

Silence.

I buried my face in Susannah's hair.

"Ruby?" This came so softly. It was tempting. It was. To tell.

But it was so much harder than I realized, saying these things out loud. Especially to these sweet women, who all had that well-loved-wife look about them. I didn't want to admit anything sordid and embarrassing to them. I wanted to pretend I was like them. But something in me took over my mouth and I did it. I spilled it. I told them about JW leaving me at the truck stop, about his threat to run away with Susannah. I told them everything. Even though I was disgusted and shamed hearing my own words, my story, once it started, wouldn't be stopped. It sickened me to think what my thoughts would have been if our places were switched. What I would say to a woman whose husband refused her money or contact with her family and thought nothing of pinching her arm or shoving her down. What advice I would have for a woman who was scared of her own husband. Nevertheless, the words and the tears kept on coming.

By the time I was done, they had scooted in close to me and managed to hug me without waking or dropping our babies in the process. They produced tissues, murmured sympathy. Stroked my hair.

The mother with the toddler prayed over me. The other one prayed for JW. I was touched by their concern. I believed they truly cared, and there was a comfort in that.

We kept at it until Toddler-mamma's husband, who stood at a discreet distance from the door, made a coughing noise to let us know he was in the hall. We all had one last squeeze-y hug and broke up our huddle.

The older wives were bustling about the fellowship hall, washing out the coffeemakers, snatching third helpings from kids, drying silverware. Unexpectedly starving, I found a scrap of coconut cream pie still on the kitchen counter, but no fork. An aproned, silver-haired lady picked a fork off the dish drainer, dried it on a tea towel and handed it to me.

"I can tell by the mascara running down your face that The Lord moved you in the service tonight, too," she said. "It's such a joy to know that even though this is your daily job, your heart is still tender. You keep that tender heart, Dear. Guard it carefully, just like the scripture says."

For the first time, I questioned that common saying. A tender heart? Tender, like sensitive and caring? Or tender like "it's sore, don't touch it?" And how, exactly, was I supposed to guard it? Suddenly I was exhausted and I didn't know how to answer this nice lady. I nodded dumbly and shifting Susannah's sleepy dead weight against my shoulder, I wolfed down my pie one-handed.

I found JW in a crowd of jacketless, loosened-necktie preachers, talking to them so seriously and looking so mature. He excused himself for a moment to take me aside. "Mom has already gone to bed," he said. "You look tired, too. You go on to bed if you want. Dad and I'll be along later." He lowered his voice. "A few of the senior pastors have invited us over to the parsonage to visit some more." He sounded self-important, and I knew what he was thinking. The parsonage! The senior pastors! *We're in!*

Back on the bus, I rolled Susannah into her bunk and got ready for bed. My own bed was a welcome comfort, but I was still uneasy. Because, for all their kind concern, it seemed that still, none of those sweet ladies knew exactly what it was that I should *do*.

I was sleeping hard, on my stomach, when I felt a heavy weight suddenly crushing my lower back.

My yelp of surprise went only as far my mattress because a steely hand was crushing my head, face down, into my bed. I panicked and tried to buck up, but JW was straddled on top of me, pinning my arms and forcing my nose and mouth into the sheets. He leaned down and whispered in my ear. "How does it feel? How do you like being smothered? Huh? You like it? Well, that's what you're doing to me. To us. To our ministry. You're cutting *my* air off. Crybaby-ing about how I treat you. Making them think I don't have my own house in order. They talked to *my father* about it. My *father!*" His fist twisted my hair and jerked. My head came up long enough for me to gasp for air, then he slammed it back down again. I made a muffled grunting sound. He leaned down and whispered again. "Why can't you just be good? Why, Ruby? Why? Why do you humiliate me in front of my father like that?" He ground his weight hard on my hips, his weight crushing me. I moaned. I was suffocating. I concentrated on blowing out very slowly through the small crease in the sheets where I could still get air. He shifted his weight and I could tell he was hard, but I also knew he would never, ever do anything about it, here, with his mother on the bus. Instead, he leaned in and whispered, "I could do it for real, you know. Leave you. Drop you off somewhere and run off with Susannah. Let us Jaspers raise her right. She'd forget she ever had a mother. And you would never find us."

He gave my head one last crushing push, then climbed off. I rolled over and moved as far away as I could. I made my body as small as possible and ran my shaking hands up and down, all over my body, touching, petting, reassuring me that it's all mine, it's all here, it's still solid, and everything works.

The bus door swished open, gravel crunched underneath my window, and I realized Old Rev had been outside, waiting for JW.

"Did you handle it?" he asked.

"Yeah," JW answered. "She's sorry."

Pause.

"I'm disappointed in you, Son. I thought you were more of a man than that."

A quick scuffle, a gasp and the bus shuddered as something slammed into the side of it.

"I'll do better, Dad," said my husband in a tight, pained voice.

A second thud, and the bus rocked again.

"You are forgiven," Old Rev said as something slid down the side of the bus. A long, long quiet passed where no one moved or spoke until Old Rev broke the silence, "It was the Lord's Will. If next year is already booked up, we won't be open to The Lord leading us in a new direction."

JW sounded flat. "Are you talking about going north? Is that what you want to do now?"

Old Rev paused before he answers with a voice full of emotion, "It's not about what I want, Son. It's The Call. That's all that matters. That's all that's ever mattered."

I heard a single Jasper sob. I couldn't say whose.

One set of footsteps faded away.

I laid awake the rest of the night. Listening. Thinking. Planning. Even praying. By morning, I was exhausted, but clear-headed. Calm. I hummed as I went about my morning routine. I smiled and chatted with the Jaspers. And I wasn't faking, either. And no, it was not strange that I felt better after JW's bullying than I did after those sweet ladies' loving prayers and concern.

Because now, finally, I knew what I had to do.

Chapter Thirteen

Early the next evening, we pulled in at a truck-stop diner about an hour out of De Moines. I looked out the window, saw what I was hoping to see, and turned to Susannah. *Hang on to your Pampers, kid. This might be a wild ride.*

I lagged behind everyone else as they got off, fiddling with Susannah, her diaper bag, and so on. I watched through the bus window until all three of the Jaspers were inside. Then quickly, I grabbed my guitar case and opened it. Pulling up the red velvet lining, I snatched the envelope with Mom's letter and the cash, stuffed the bills down my bra, grabbed Susannah and the diaper bag and jumped off the bus.

Once inside, I watched JW, Old Rev and Merrilee go through the door to the café section. Merrilee turned and saw me in the entry, so I motioned toward the ladies' room. But I watched through the plate glass door and as soon as they were seated in a booth out of sight, I turned the opposite direction and made a beeline through the entrance area into the gas station and up to the counter. Yep, there it was. A sign. *Thank you, Jesus!* No, I mean, a real, actual sign, one that said "BUS STOP — Greyhound/Trailways — Tickets Sold Here" was tacked to a bulletin board behind the cash register.

"Does Greyhound still have that one-way-anywhere-for-fifty-nine dollars deal for the summer?" I asked the man behind the counter, "Mike," according to the embroidered patch over his pocket.

"Yes, we do." Mike said, "Good anywhere to anywhere, but only 'til Labor day, so you gotta hurry. And are you eighteen? I can't sell one to anybody under eighteen, without their parents. That your parents you came in with, there?"

"I'm eighteen! I mean, I'm over eighteen." Oh, why hadn't I worn make-up? I looked about thirteen without it. "Look! See, I have a baby of my own. I'm old enough, and I need a ticket!"

"Ok, ok! Hold your horses! Is she two yet?" he asked, pointing at Susannah. "If she's two, you need two, see?" He held up two fingers. Yes. I see.

"No, not even close. One ticket, please."

Mike reached under the counter and pulled out a big blue binder. "Oops, that's Trailways." He put it back, fished around some, pulled out a gray one, thumped it down and opened it. He flipped through the pages of carboned copies of used tickets to the last one. "Huh. Looks like somebody sold the last one outta this book. You're supposed to re-fill it when you do that." He turned and hollered back to the service area. "Hey, who sold the last Greyhound ticket? You didn't refill the book!"

He muttered as he bent down behind the counter.

"The last one? But, you have more, right? I can still get on the bus? I have to get on the bus!" My voice shrilled upwards as I leaned into the counter, clutching a squirmy Susannah.

He banged open cabinets and drawers down below while he answered, "Oh, yeah, sure, I think so. We should have some more here, somewheres."

I kept looking over my shoulder, expecting a Jasper to appear. Susannah grabbed at a Dipsy-Doodle Bird perched by the register, dunking slowly into a water glass. I caught her hand in time to keep her from knocking it over and spilling the water. She wailed in frustration and bucked against me. *Hurry up, Mike.*

"Ah, here we go." He plunked a big cardboard carton in front of me, pulled out a pocket knife and slit the packaging tape. I balanced my squalling daughter on one hip while I dug my money out of my bra. Mike pulled a shrink-wrapped packet of forms out of the box and then a packing slip, which he pored over. "Gotta inventory these, log their numbers. You know, people could Xerox them, these days. Gotta account for all of them."

I wanted to scream at him to hurry up. Pretty soon, JW would start wondering what's taking me so long and send Merrilee to the bathroom to look for me. Susannah's fit grew noisier, gaining power. She pounded at my shoulder with her chubby little fist and wailed.

Come on, Mike.

After an eternity, he was satisfied with the organization of his binder.

"All right now, Ma'am, that's one Anywhere-Fare at fifty-nine dollars, so with tax, that comes to $61.95. Cash, money order or credit card. No personal checks."

Tax! "What? I didn't think there'd be tax! I don't have any more money! I only have sixty dollars!" I waved my wadded-up twenties at him.

"Well, I'm sorry, but that's the cost. You gotta pay the tax."

"Please, I gotta have a ticket." My voice rose higher, Susannah keened louder. "I have to get a ticket! I have to get us to Oklahoma! I have to get my baby home!"

"You don't have two more dollars," Mike said, "then you can't get a ticket."

Susannah, still grabbing for the Dipsy Bird, kicked out in frustration, and things started falling off the counter. By reflex, I caught the first item as it fell, a cardboard March of Dimes display, nearly full of donated dimes stuck in little slots. I slammed it down on the counter, face down. A few dimes bounced out.

"There! I have enough money. Please, I need a ticket!"

Mike looked alarmed, and I couldn't blame him. Stealing from crippled children is the mark of a desperate person, no matter how you look at it. What else might I be capable of?

"Ok, Ok! Easy, now!" He held up two hands like it was a stick-up. "Look, it's gonna be alright, lady. I'll loan you the two dollars, myself, Ok? It's gonna be all right."

He ripped my ticket out of the book, did his necessary accounting, and rang up the sale. When I finally had the ticket in hand, he said to me, "I don't know why you're in such a hurry. There's not gonna be another bus through here until midnight."

But I was already on my way out the door.

I stopped in the bathroom, so if Merrilee came looking for me, I'd at least be where I said I'd be. I could make some excuse about not feeling well, or Susannah making a mess, or something. But what next? Midnight. I had to wait six hours. I propped Susannah up in front of me in the dry sink and we watched in the mirror as I re-did my pony-tail.

We both searched my face for reassurance that everything was going to be fine. Yes. Fine.

I decided to go in and eat with the Jaspers, like nothing was wrong. That would be a good idea, anyway, because I didn't have any money left to feed Susannah and me during the long bus ride home. I would get as much food as I could at dinner and figure out the next step, well, *next*.

Sure enough, Merrilee came in to ask if I was alright. I told her something or other, and Susannah and I followed her to our place in the café.

I ordered a huge hamburger steak dinner, but no gravy, and an extra steak finger and side of green beans for Susannah. Mom would have approved of my protein-filled plate. She believed that most people could benefit from more beef in the diet, but JW looked surprised at my sudden increase in appetite. I carefully ate every last bit of my salad and swept a handful of packaged club crackers into the diaper bag. Susannah dug into her green beans, but mostly played with her steak finger.

My plan was to put most of my meal in a takeout and stash it in the diaper bag and drink lots of water so I could breastfeed Susannah more than usual. That should be enough food to get us back to Oklahoma. But what would we do until midnight? JW was planning on driving a few more hours before we stopped for the night. He'd want to leave right after supper. What would I do until then? I fantasized about casually saying, "Hey, guys, Susannah and I are going home. I have a bus ticket, I don't need anything, so you can go on and leave us here." Yeah, right.

The sign in the window said both the diner and the gas station closed at ten. After-hours bus customers had to wait on a bench in the lighted entryway. I would be waiting all alone. Mike and the waitresses and cooks, all gone. No customers. No phone.

"Susannah Grace Jasper," At the sound of her full name, Susannah looked up at Old Rev; her green-bean smeared face wore a curious, cautious expression. Old Rev rarely talked to her. She was intrigued by his sudden attention, but wary of his tone. He pointed to the floor under her high chair where she had flung the steak finger and said, "This is an unacceptable waste of food." Her eyes followed his finger to the meat on the floor. She remembered how it got there, and threw two green beans down to join it. Quite sure that she had followed her grandfather's instructions to the T, she chortled and kicked her feet noisily at the underside of the high chair tray. I sucked in a breath and looked around. Plenty of people. We were safe. We'd be on our way home soon. But I couldn't stop the chill crawling across my skin.

With an effort, Old Rev turned his gaze back toward his own plate. Quietly, evenly, he said, "A babe in arms, of course, wouldn't be expected to appreciate the blessings of God's daily provision for us. But a child, even the smallest child, can be made to understand. I trust that you will see to that when you begin her character training after her birthday."

Old Rev, actively interested in training my sweet baby's character. That terrified me. I willed my body to sit very still. My teeth clamped tight to keep them from chattering.

Only a few more hours. *Hold it together, Ruby Fae.* Think. *You have to* think.

I took a big gulp of ice water. I wished I were more mechanically-minded. I'd find some way to sabotage the bus, so we'd have to park it here tonight. Over at the corner booth, the waitress smiled and talked with a family she knew. She seemed nice. What if, I wondered, what if I just walked over to her and told her my story? Would she help me? Would she think I was crazy? Would she call the police for me? What would I even tell them, anyway? I mean, it's not like I'm kidnapped. Nobody made me marry JW. In fact, they tried to talk me out of it. So could I tell the police that I once thought I wanted to be married to this guy, but now I have changed my mind? That didn't seem like their jurisdiction.

It occurred to me for the first time, if JW would really hurt me that might be of interest to the police. But pinching? Pushing? Is that against the law? I did a quick mental inventory and could only think of one smallish bruise at the moment. Not too incriminating. "Officer, he pulled my hair," isn't reporting a crime, it's tattling.

"Will there be anything else?" The waitress was back at our table now. "How about some ice cream for this little sweetie?" she asked. "No, thanks," I said, "She'll only make a bigger mess."

Suddenly, the café door swung open and Mike came into the dining area. I ducked my head, suddenly finding urgent business in the diaper bag. *Please, please don't talk to me.*

"Oh! There you are!" he made straight for our table. I didn't look up, but he came to our booth and tapped me on the shoulder.

"Ma'am, sorry, I know this is an inconvenience, but I got a call from Bismarck. They are running late, maybe an hour, even, behind schedule, by the time they get here. They authorized me," here he paused and stood straighter and taller in his Texaco Star shirt, his posture now befitting a sworn officer of the Bus Counter, "to offer you this voucher for your troubles. It's good for a free extra ticket next time you ride." He solemnly produced an envelope with the Greyhound logo across the front and held it out to me. I tried to look confused rather than terrified, but it fooled only Mike and the waitress.

"I'm sorry, you must be mistaken," I sputtered, "I don't know what you mean, what ticket are you talking about?"

"*Ruby! No!*" JW sounded shocked, hurt, even.

"Your bus ticket, the one you just bought?" Mike said.

Old Rev said nothing, but everyone else talked at once.

"Oh, honey, a freebie!" said the waitress, delighted at my good fortune. "Good for you! Now, you won't have to pay for a return ticket to, to, well, wherever, you know, your family is. That's lucky! I mean, if you're not in a hurry."

"Ruby! No! The baby! Think of her!" JW said, his voice rising.

"But I don't have a bus ticket," I insisted.

"You mean you lost it already? Ah, shoot, I saw you put it in your baby-bag, there," says the ever-helpful Mike.

"Ruby!" JW repeated my name, his voice breaking. "Ruby!"

"It's not me." I protested doggedly. "I'm not the one. I didn't buy anything, I can't buy anything, I don't have any money!" I held up my empty hands.

Desperate, JW lunged across the table and grabbed my hands, knocking his drink into Old Rev's lap. "Please. Don't leave me. I'll change. I will. Just don't go." He continued begging as Old Rev yelped at the ice water hitting his crotch and shoved at JW to get him out of the booth so he could stand up. I leapt up from my seat, pulled my hands away from JW and yanked on Susannah, untangling her feet out of her high chair safety strap. She began crying. The waitress, sensing she had been overly-cheerful about our little family dining experience, decided to concentrate on the ice water and helping Old Rev. He waved her off and tumbled out of the booth. Mike, voucher still in hand, backed up two steps and stood with his mouth open, watching the show.

With Susannah finally freed, I decided to make for the ladies' room and lock us inside. If I refused to come out, maybe somebody would call the police. I didn't know what else to do. I grabbed for the diaper bag.

It wasn't there.

Neither was Merrilee.

Through the diner window, I saw her disappear onto the bus, diaper bag in hand.

My ticket was still inside it.

Susannah and I ran after her as JW ran after us. He caught me right outside the café door, his hand gripped my arm. His voice now changed, no longer breaking.

"You're not going anywhere, Ruby."

He was right.

Some things you learn from your parents and you remember the very day they taught you. Like when Dad showed me how to back a stock trailer without jackknifing it. Or when Mom showed me the right way to walk in the 4-H Style Show. And some things they never set out to teach you; you caught it by example. Like knowing how to put on your panty hose or how to properly shake hands and say "Nice to meet you."

I wonder how it was with JW and Old Rev. Did he set out to teach him these things? Did Old Rev set JW down and say, "Listen, Son; stay away from the face and neck, because that will cause questions. A little on the arms is

OK, but never the fingers because we can't do without a piano. Arms, legs and upper body, now, they're fair game."

Or did JW just learn it all, bright boy that he is, by watching?

Chapter Fourteen

The next day, I couldn't hide it.

I moved slowly. I didn't pick Susannah up, or let her sit on my lap.

I looked at my watch a lot.

I sneaked a peek at my Benadryl stash and considered breaking my bedtime-only rule, but decided against it.

I felt humiliated whenever someone talked to me. I vaguely wondered why I should feel ashamed, but then again, I was not inclined to think about it very long.

That day lasted forever.

Even worse, it was a layover day. We were just killing time in a little South Dakota town, saving gas before zigzagging up to Minnesota again. If it had been a travel day, I could at least have hunkered down in a corner, stared at a magazine and ignored everyone. But since JW wasn't driving, he could spend the day hovering over me, "nice-ing" me to death. Not apologizing, mind you, because husbands can't be wrong, but exhausting us both with sweet, desperate gestures that meant *I need you to like me, even though I had to hit you. You understand, right?*

It went on all day and it was unnerving. He ended every sentence with a compliment. He told me to order whatever I wanted from the Montgomery Ward catalog. He brought me a new Reader's Digest, a vanilla (his favorite) shake and whittled JWJ + RFJ on a little wooden heart. I wanted to do nothing but hide in my bunk, but I could only lie on my left side and only for a few minutes at a time, so I couldn't get a break from all his husbanding.

The weirdest part was when Merrilee said I didn't need to help her with the laundry, then asked JW to help her carry it to the laundromat for her. Even crazier, Old Rev jumped to help them. He did swipe the keys out of the ignition, I noticed, before he said in a gentle voice, "The baby seems a bit under the weather, Ruby. Perhaps you should stay here with her." Then I was alone on the bus.

That was better than having all the Jaspers watching me, but I was far from comfortable. I paced, concentrating on my breathing the way I had when I was in labor. Susannah toddled after me, giggling, thinking it was a slow-motion chase game. I don't know how long we did that, but we kept it up until we wore the game out. Then I decided to try sitting in the most comfortable chair on the bus, JW's driver's seat. I pulled out a few "emergency toys" I'd been hiding for Susannah, a few new things that might keep her occupied a while, and barricaded her safely in the stairwell. Then I gingerly lowered myself into the seat. I was fooling with the various seat adjustments and the selection of back pillows and supports JW kept on hand, when my eyes fell on a blinking green light below the dash. The CB. The volume knob was turned to zero, so I turned it up.

The channel was empty. I took a deep breath and clicked the button. "Breaker one-nine," I said, then looked down at the channel knob. I wasn't on channel nineteen, I was on channel ten. "I mean, one-oh. Breaker one-oh. This is Bunny-Wunny. I need some help. Please, can somebody help me? I need the police." My heart pounded. I took a deep breath. "My husband beat me up. I need help."

"Breaker, breaker," a man's gruff voice answered. "Listen up, Bunny-Wunny. We've worked hard to get this stretch of highway cleaned up. So you can just tell your pimp or your perv or your so-called husband to haul your business on down the road. Maybe set up shop in Nebraska or Kansas. They're not so fussy down there. Out."

Before I had time to process that, another voice, a familiar one, cut in. "Breaker one-oh for Mrs. Bible Boy, skip down two. Out." It was Itty-Bitty Betty.

I switched to channel eight. "Break for Itty-Bitty Betty. This is Mrs. Bible Boy," I started to say, but she interrupted me. "Go to twelve." I followed. "Meet me on two," she instructed, and so on, until finally on channel eighteen, she was ready to talk.

"Sorry, Bunny-Wunny," she said. "But they come down hard around here. Now listen up. One: never do that again. They'll only find you and arrest you or molest you or both," she said.

"But I'm not—"

"Two; an accident, got it? Next time, say it's an *accident*. Everybody will try and help if they think you've had an accident. But only if you've never been heard working that area before. If you've worked there before, forget it. And only use the 'accident' line once. It only works once, you copy that?"

"But I really need help. I'm scared. I'm not safe. I'm parked in—"

She came back swiftly, her voice hard. "Never," she hissed, "never tell where you are. Make him tell you, first, then you find him. And Bunny-Wunny, Honey, you wanna be safe, you get off the road. Over and out." And she was gone.

I couldn't even cry. It hurt too bad.

When he got back from the laundromat, JW tried even harder. He told me I was pretty, changed two diapers, gave me his pillow and asked if I'd like anything from the Ben Franklin store.

There was, in fact, one thing I did want, and this was a good chance to get it. I knew he wouldn't give it to me without a hitch of some sort, but after last night, he owed me. If he wanted me to play happy-wifey, I should get something out of it and we both knew it.

"Alright," he agreed too happily, too quickly. Anything to put last night behind us and get back on my good side. "Let's call home."

While Old Rev and Merrilee puttered around in a Safeway store with Susannah in the shopping cart, JW and I stood outside at a pay phone. He pulled a handful of change from the pocket of his jeans, picked out the pennies, put those back in his pocket, then weighed the rest in his hand. "This oughta do it. Ready?" I forced a thin-lipped smile in his direction and nodded. What? He couldn't hand me the money himself? I couldn't be trusted with a few quarters now? We both knew the answer to that one.

He deposited some coins while I hung on to the receiver wishing I could crawl through it. As I dialed, I could picture the black wall phone on the daisy-covered wallpaper by the refrigerator. I could almost see Mom wiping dishwater, or maybe flour, or potting soil, from her hands with a corner of her apron and lifting the receiver. "Good afternoon, you've reached McKeever and Sons Livestock and Seed Wheat," she'd say, in case it's somebody about farm business, and then she'd sound so happy when she realized it was me.

Which is exactly how it happened, exactly what she said.

"Hi, Mom. It's me."

"Oh, Ruby Fae!" she said, sounding truly delighted. "How are you sweetheart? Where are you?"

"We're in South Dakota."

"Oh! South Dakota? I thought your newsletter said you would be in Missouri this month."

"Yes, but we've made some changes. I wrote you about that, in my last letter." Dangit! I'd already said too much. Why did I say "letter"? JW won't want me to tell her I'm not getting my mail. I chanced a look at him, but he didn't meet my eye.

"Honey, I haven't gotten a letter from you in ages. Are you all getting your mail?"

Can I pull this off? Right under JW's nose like this? Am I slick enough?

"No." I tried to say it lightly enough not to alert JW, hoping that Mom would pursue it. "Not me. Not at all." I tried to sound pleased as punch.

Mom was silent for a beat. "Not you? What do you mean, not you?"

Mom! I can't spell it out for you! Help me out here!

I chuckled, too heartily. "Oh, you know how it goes," I said.

Mom missed another beat.

"Ruby Fae, are you alright?" she finally demanded.

"No. Not really." I said, still sounding picnic-pleasant. But my pulse was racing. Come on, Mom.

JW chose this moment. "Tell your mom 'Hi' from me," he said.

"JW says 'Hi,'" I told her.

"Is he there? Put him on the phone." I tried to predict the outcome of such a conversation, and I didn't think it would be a good one for my immediate future. I ignored her demand and thankfully, JW couldn't hear it.

"Oh, she is so sweet these days, Mom. She's walking like a champ. I wish you could see her. You wouldn't believe how much ground a little girl not even a year old can cover."

"You're not even making sense now! Is something wrong with the phone? Can you not hear me?" Oh, I heard, all right. I heard the worry in her voice. Good. Maybe she was catching on now.

"What's dad up to? How does he like the new round baler? I bet he and Chuck can haul hay in no time, now that you don't have to hook each bale up by hand."

"Put JW on the phone! Now!" Mom yelled too loudly. I looked up at JW and winced. He'd heard her volume, if not her words.

"What's wrong?" he asked, aghast. He'd grown up with Merrilee, so the very idea of a woman yelling troubled his soul.

I put my hand over the receiver, made a silly face at him and said, "The cat. He gets on the table."

Which was a bald-faced lie. My mother would eat a cat whole before she'd have one in her house, let alone on the table.

"The church we are going to next sounds really nice." I

blathered on. "It's in Minnesota, but it's somewhere out in the country, like ten miles or more from town."

"What town, Ruby Fae? Where in Minnesota?" She demands. "Where are you now?"

Suddenly I drew a blank. Where in the world were we? What was the name of this town? And where were we going? I wracked my brain, but it escaped me. I looked at JW. Surely this was an approved subject of conversation. Where in the world I was? "I can't remember. Hold on a sec, let me ask JW."

I looked up at him, inches from my face. Hovering. Politely.

"What's the name of the next town again? I forgot." I asked.

To my horror, he grabbed the phone. "Hi, Mom Mac! It's JW! How are you all? Is it hot enough for you yet, there?" Mom answered loudly enough that I could hear it, too.

"John Wesley Jasper, what is wrong with my daughter, and why isn't she answering my letters?" she demanded.

JW's face darkened and I remained very still. I could salvage this. As long as his parents weren't around for him to lose face, I could work with him. *It's going to be OK. It's going to be OK.*

He pulled out his sweetest-boy charm. "Oh, Mom Mac, we've had some trouble getting our mail forwarded to the right places lately. You know how the post office is. And then we changed our route which made it even worse. And, I hate to say it, but between you and me, Dear Old Mrs. Gibley isn't quite as sharp as she once was. Why last week, she sent us some of Billy Sunday's mail." Pause. "I bet Ruby's letters are piled up somewhere between here and Mexico."

I couldn't hear Mom's response. She was talking at a

normal volume again. Not yelling. I couldn't believe it. He'd calmed her down. My stomach fell to my shoes. Even Mom is suckered by his charm? On the phone, without even seeing his dazzling smile and adorable dimples? From a thousand miles away? Mom, please, please. I silently beg. Come and get me.

"It's a little town called Lake Falls." Pause. "Oh, you've heard of it?" Pause. "No, a long ways west of Bemidji." He laughed easily at something she said. "Yes, this one makes Salt Fork look like a big city. Yes, she probably does feel at home. Plenty of cows everywhere." He looked at me, his eyes unreadable. He nodded as though Mom could see him. "I worry about her, too. Taking care of the baby must be tiring. You're right," Pause "Oh, of course. I understand. That's a good idea. Does that all come in one pill? The vitamins and the iron?" Pause. "Uh-huh. Yes, we do. We pray and read the Bible together every morning. Uh-huh." Long pause. "Will do, then. Sure. Bye, Mom Mac. You, too."

Mom. Your granddaughter and I are strapped into a bus with a cruel man and his crazier parents. We are not anemic. We don't need more iron. Or Vitamin C. And we certainly don't need even more Bible study with the Reverend JW Jasper. We need you to come get us.

Oh, if only I could talk to you alone!

JW handed the receiver back to me, watching. I put it up to my ear.

"Mom?" Couldn't she hear the misery in my voice?

"Ruby, you're going to be alright." Her voice was gentle, but firm. I couldn't believe it; JW had persuaded her that I was alright. But I wasn't. Not at all. I felt hope leave me, gradually swirling down inside my skin and draining out through the soles of my feet. I was afraid if I answered, I would burst into tears, and that would not go over well with JW.

She continued. "Listen to me, honey. Remember what your daddy and I taught you about being a good wife, about minding JW, and God will take care of you. Do you hear me?"

I answered slowly. "Yes," I finally said. I never, not ever in a million years, would have thought Mom would be in the mind-your-husband camp.

"We love you very much, and we will see you soon. I'll hug and spoil and feed you and Susannah both, and we'll make her a big chocolate seven-layer birthday cake together, OK? You go on now, get some rest and take your iron pills. Your blood is probably still poor."

"Mom. I already told you. We changed our schedule. We're not—"

"Ruby, hug Baby for me. I will see you soon. Now go be a good, submissive wife. Remember everything we taught you. Go on now. Scoot."

"OK." I swallowed. "Bye, Mom. Love you."

Pause.

"I love you, too."

Chapter Fifteen

A good, submissive wife. Like Mom and Dad taught me.

What was she talking about? I didn't remember them telling me any such thing. In fact, all the teaching about being a good wife that I could remember came from Old Rev's sermons on submission. And I'll give you one guess as to who was supposed to do all the submitting.

But I never heard any talk like that from Mom and Dad. Well, except this one story, that Dad told me once about the dry years, back when they were newlyweds.

Mom and Dad were married during the Little Dust Bowl. No, not the big one, the little one. Everybody knows about the Big Dust Bowl, the Dirty Thirties, about Okies and all that, thanks to Hollywood and Mr. Steinbeck. What people forget, though, is that for everyone west of the ninety-eighth meridian, the fifties were even drier. In fact, they were driest decade on record.

"People were desperate for rain." Dad said. "So every fly-by-night shyster and his crooked-legged cow-dog came through here promising to end the drought and bring a downpour — for a reasonable fee, of course. Every third day, you'd see a poster for a rain doctor of some kind; scientists and cloud-seeders, hot-air-ballooners, voo-doo makers, water-witchers, and duded-up Cherokees, pretending to be old-timey medicine men, everything you could think of. One feller blew in, pretending to be Moses, another one came through, claimed he was Zeus."

"Did people really pay them?" I asked. "Even though they were all fakers?" I may have still believed in Santa and the Tooth Fairy, but I had already been schooled well in the hard truths of rain and drought. The only supernatural forces at work there were in God's hands, and He ran things as He saw fit.

"Somebody must have, because they kept on coming. And then you got the roaming preachers! They flocked in here like Canadian Geese. They'd set up tents and start preaching out sin and praying down rain. I bet there was some tent revival or other in Salt Fork every single week for six months straight."

"Did you go to all that church?" I asked in disbelief. Dad firmly held that twice every Sunday and Wednesday evenings at seven was church enough for anyone. He said that even Jesus Himself only showed up at the semi-annual revival weeks at Rose of Sharon out of a sense of duty.

"I didn't feel any obligation to those off-brand preachers. They had nobody overseeing them, nobody to report to. Who's to know if they were really who they claimed to be? What's to keep them from preaching salvation in this town and selling bootleg whiskey in the next? I was not sure about those free-lancers, not at all. Anyway, we didn't pay them much mind, but then one day, somebody kinda halfway-famous came through town, somebody we'd heard on the radio here and there."

"Was it Billy Graham?" I asked in awe. "Or Oral Roberts?"

"No, no; no big preaching star like that. Just somebody

known back then." Dad said. He shook his head. "You gotta remember, your momma and I'd barely been married a few months. I was young and real, real nervous. We didn't know your brother Chuck was on the way yet, but I suspected one or the other of you would be along shortly. I was worried sick about the farm, if I'd be able to hang on to it, how I'd be able to feed you all, whether or not I could keep your Momma happy, things a young married man worries about. Then your momma hears on the radio that this half-known preacher is at Salt Fork, holding a tent revival out at the fairgrounds, and so we thought it might not hurt to go, give him a listen."

So Dad decked himself out in his pressed-best Levis and white straw Resistol, Mom in her heels, hose, and hat. It would have been a real date, but on a Monday night. With preaching. But everyone else must have thought so, too, because it looked like everybody in the county was there. Cars were parked all the way to the American Legion Ball Field.

"Did everybody get a seat?"

"Oh, sure! That tent was so big, I kept looking for elephants to come in,"

The singing started a good hour before the actual service, but Mom didn't want to miss any of that, it would have been the best part. The heat would have been miserable, but big metal water cans sat on tables at the back of the tent, so ladies dug in their purses for the little collapsible tin drinking cups that the Salt Fork State Bank always gave away at their fair booth and filled them from the drippy spigot. And of course, Hasting's Family Funeral Home (Serving You Since '32) had donated hundreds of cardboard fans with Jesus Knocking on the back, which would have helped somewhat.

The sun had set by the time the singing was done, so then the ushers could roll up the canvas on the west side of the tent, too, and let the wind blow all the way through. The lights snapped on, which meant the generator was cranked up. That meant the preacher had to use a microphone and speakers to be heard over the kerosene engine that ran the generator that ran the microphones and speakers. "It was a real show. And he was a good preacher. Told good stories, read lots of verses. His message was that God would send rain once we all repented. And people were desperate for rain, remember."

"Lots of people came forward, then?"

Dad nodded. "The altar was filled with people on their knees the very first night. People weren't even waiting for the end of the week."

"That was good." I put in.

"Oh, sure. Repentance is good for everybody."

"Then what happened?"

On Monday night, the preacher had stuck to the general sins, nothing specific, mainly catch-all things, like falling away, forsaking God, riotous living and so forth. That first night, he was casting a wide net. That was all well and good; Dad had no quarrel with that type of preaching. The second night, the preacher narrowed the sins down to the Ten Commandments. Nobody could take issue with those either, and the altar was full once again. Wednesday night, the preacher started in on more modern sins, like drinking, gambling, and immodest evils of a various nature. There was some squirming going on in the seats that night. But by Thursday night, the sins were getting more specific. Movies, dancing, and pants on women were keeping God from pouring out his showers of blessings, people were told. The front of the tabernacle was filled with kneeling repenters, and more fell to their knees in the aisles.

On Friday, the thermometer soared into the hundred-and-teens for the tenth record-breaking day in a row. The town's oldest department store announced it was giving it up and going out of business. The weatherman apologized to everyone and the air conditioner at the movie theater broke down. The sun broiled, the red clay soil cracked open, dust devils whipped through the county, and bankers mailed out thick stacks of frightening letters.

"Was it as dry as this?" I asked.

Dad flicked his hand and made a dismissive "pffft" sound with his teeth and lips. "This? This is nothing. Barely a dry spell. You were born in a wet year. Your whole life has been green. You don't know about drouth." He used the old word for "drought", saying it like it rhymes with "south". He went on with his story.

The souls suffering in the hellish heat of the revival tent that night were already parched and thirsting for hope, but that traveling preacher had everybody riled up until they were downright ravenous for a bite of God. *Showers of blessings, showers of blessing we need! Mercy drops 'round us are falling, but for the showers we plead,* they sang, with fear in their stomachs and dust in their throats. Whatever that preacher was selling that night didn't matter; they'd come to buy it.

That final service, his message was how the country was going to Hell, and the solution was to fix the proper order of things, starting at the very beginning, in your own home. He preached from the third chapter of Peter, from whence he proclaimed the glorious virtues of the submissive wife.

It was actually Mom who hit her knees first that night. The altar up front and the aisles were already full, so she turned and dropped over her folding wooden chair. Dad was the next one to kneel, and together, they pledged to do better. They would follow this teaching and order their little home, all two-hundred-square-feet of it, in this, the correct, way. Dad would be The Head and Mom would Submit. If God truly was withholding Oklahoma's rain because of sin, it wouldn't be on their heads. They would be the very model of an obedient wife and her husband of authority.

"How long did you do that?" I asked.

"About a week." Dad answered.

"Why'd you stop?"

Dad's thumbs made a gesture like a small shrug. "It wasn't any fun," he said.

He would ask Mom what she thought about selling off their last yearlings, and she'd answer, *I think that whatever you think is best.* He'd ask her if she wanted to ride with him in to Salt Fork to the John Deere House after a tractor part, and she'd say, *if you'd like for me to go, I'll go.* Did she want the clothesline in the back yard, or the side? *Wherever you'd like to put it, Sweetheart.* Got that new stock tank set in the northeast quarter. It should be filled by sundown. What-say, after supper we go splash around in it some? Cool off? *If that's what you want to do, I want to, as well.*

No, Dad said, it just wasn't any fun at all.

"But, Dad, if it was in the Bible, you had to do it, didn't you?"

"Well, your Momma asked me if I liked her always minding me like that. And I told her no, Ma'am, I did not. She thought a minute, and she said, 'Harvell, you could order me to stop minding you.' So, I told her, 'Stop minding me. And that's an order." He turned to look at me as he cranked the old truck to life. "Ruby Fae, some day, when you get to be a grown-up lady, you got to be careful. Some folks can get some pretty funny ideas."

"What do you mean? What kind of funny ideas?"

"Oh, you, know, about, ah, married stuff, and the like."

"You mean like a husband? A husband might tell me I have to mind him?"

Dad snorted, "The kind who say you have to mind are the kind you better not mind."

"But what if he tries to make me?"

Dad looked at me straight. "Then you hightail it back home. I don't care how. Just get home. Either outrun 'em or outsmart 'em. Whichever one you think you can get away with. God never said you had to lose all your common sense just to be a good wife."

That's the only thing I remember my folks ever telling me about being a good, submissive wife. Too bad I never heard that in a sermon.

Chapter Sixteen

Another thing about us Holiness Churches; Missionary Meeting is at ten o'clock in the morning on the second Tuesday of every month, forever and ever amen, no matter where in God's creation you may find yourself.

If we were parked at a church on a Missionary Meeting day, Merrilee and I were always invited. I suppose she enjoyed it; she never said otherwise. But me, I lived for it. There would be coffee in a big old-fashioned percolator, someone's fair-ribbon cake, gossipy prayer requests, someone to dote on Susannah. It was a little like being home again, knowing that I was doing the exact same thing I would have been doing if I were at Rose of Sharon.

But that day was still hard. I wanted to be home, for real, back at Rose of Sharon where Mom and Grandma Reenie and Grandma Daisy and the rest were all seated around a framed quilt-top, pieced with scraps from church dresses I could have identified almost as easily as I could name the aunts who'd worn them. A wave of homesick rolled in me like a rising tide, and I was afraid I'd get pulled under. I tried a deep, steadying breath but was cut short by a stabbing pain from my shoulder blade.

I hoped it would heal faster than my ribs had healed.

The morning's devotion was thoughts on the Apostle Paul's imprisonment in Philippi, i.e., *rejoice in your suffering*, and the missionary lesson was on the culture and customs of Papua, New Guinea. It did not ease my homesickness to think that the ladies back home at Rose of Sharon were studying the exact same lesson right then. Next came a potluck dinner, and the from-scratch macaroni and cheese and home-grown green beans tasted so familiar, I nearly came undone.

After lunch, I put Susannah down on a pallet of quilts next to two other napping babies and scooted a folding chair up to the quilt frame. I sat carefully, avoiding the hard metal chair back. If any of these good ladies had looked twice at me, they'd have thought I was very particular about my posture, or a little stiff from a bad mattress, that was all. If one of them had kindly remarked on how quiet I was, I would say truthfully how the quilting made me homesick. If anybody happened to note how often I reached for Kleenex and dabbed at my eyes or nose, well, there were always allergies to blame.

I prayed that nobody would talk to me. All I wanted was to sit and quilt.

I've known how to quilt since I was five or six, but once the initial pride and excitement of learning such a grown-up skill wore off, I found it tedious. I never could see what the women got out of it. I'd work long enough to feel big, but then I'd slide off Momma's lap and on to the floor, back under the quilt frame with my Betsy McCall paper dolls.

Now, I found a pure and soothing pleasure in mindlessly lining up thousands of tiny stitches, following the pattern someone else has laid out for me, hypnotizing myself with the up-and-down, up-and-down rhythm of a needle popping in and out of the layers, barely listening, yet still contributing. Belonging. I wonder if quilting was invented as a means of soothing consciences, a way of avoiding the sin of idleness, an excuse to sit down with your sisters and aunts on a sunny morning in the last days of summer when you could as well be out in the garden, working.

The familiar talk about show hogs and bridal showers and school shoes and zucchini recipes flowed around me and fluttered downward into hushed tones, a lazy, cozy, just-us-girls softness. The children too old for naps played outside in the sunshine, noises from their tag game drifting in to us. This was familiar. This was how I knew the world to be arranged. This was a place to get a foothold, some traction. Something deep inside me picked itself up, dusted itself off, and plucked out the sandburs. *So you got throwed*, Grandpa Pake would have said to me right then, if he could have seen me. *You gonna let some old cuss of a critter best you like that?*

No, Sir, I would have answered. No, Sir, I will not.

At five o'clock we were all at the doorstep of the parsonage. Old Rev knocked and the pastor's wife, already dressed for church, bustled us in. "Come in, come in," she greeted us. "I know you wanted a lighter supper before the service, but Joanna Everson brought over meatloaf with mashed potatoes and hot rolls." As we filed into her kitchen, thanking her profusely, I noted her current but neat hairstyle, sensible shoes and small gold cross on a dainty gold chain. Wedding band with no diamond, no pierced ears. That meant for the service, over our pastel lavender polyester dresses, Merrilee and I would wear a sheer drape with one brooch and no sequins or earrings. Merrilee would wear her dressy watch. We would both wear low heels. I was getting good at this game.

The pastor's wife pointed to the counter where everything was laid out buffet-style.

"Irvin and the boys just got back from helping the Kellermans put up some hay. Benton's been in the hospital, you know, and they are cleaning up now, so will it be alright if I let you fend for yourselves? I still need to iron Timothy's shirt." She handed us each a plate and we assured her that we would be fine, we understood, go on and get the men dressed, and so on. When she turned to hand me my plate, though, she said, "Oh! I'm not used to thinking about babies! I'll have one of boys run over to the church kitchen and get the high chair."

"Oh, no!" I protested "No need, we'll be fine. Really."

She looked doubtfully at the crowded dinette set and straight-back chairs. "You can't hold her and eat at the same time. Will she let me hold her?"

"No, you go on. JW and I will take turns holding her and eating." I said as I switched a wiggly Susannah to my other hip and bit back a gasp of pain. "Really. It's fine. We do it all the time." All the time? Maybe twice, is what I meant.

Convinced that we were well cared for, she turned to the laundry room. "Make yourself at home!" She said over her shoulder.

With one hand, I made up a plate for Susannah and me. "How about I take this to the bus and we'll eat there?" I asked JW. "She can sit in her booster seat at the table, then I can go ahead and wash her off and start getting us ready for church."

JW thought that sounded fine because Joanna Everson makes one fine meatloaf and he was going to be busy for a little while with that.

Susannah fussed to get down and walk across the yard when we got outside, but even though it hurt my shoulder to carry her, I didn't have time for her to amble along. I gripped her tighter and struggled to get us and the full dinner plate over to the bus. Once inside, I set the plate on the table, dumped Susannah on the floor and handed her the dinner roll. I went straight to the back of the bus where Merrilee and Old Rev's bed was, got down on my hands and knees, opened the door to the storage space under the bed and pulled out a lock box. I spun the combination to the numbers one-nine-two-six for 1926, the year that Old Rev was born and gave it a nudge. Nope, not it. I tried again, this time, 1936, my best guess for Merrilee's year. No. Of course not, it wouldn't be that. I did some calculating and tried 1955, for the year they got married. No luck. I tried 1957 for Billy Sunday, and 1959 for JW. The lock still wouldn't open. *Be smart. Think like a Jasper. Think like Old Rev.*

Of course.

For the love of money is the root of all evil. I Timothy 6:10. I dialed one-six-one-zero, the lock snapped, and the lid slid back to reveal neat stacks of bills, rolls of coins and several small colorful football-shaped rubber coin purses stuffed with loose change. I shuffled the bills aside and, sure enough, there, under the bus title, was my Greyhound ticket. I knew they wouldn't have wasted it; the ticket still had cash value until Labor Day. I itched to take it and run, but instead I put the box back exactly as I found it. The bus ticket, or any money, would certainly be noticed when Old Rev and Merrilee put tonight's love offering away, and I didn't have a plan yet. I didn't know how far I was from a bus station or even where the closest town was. I would have to bide my time. But — and I said quick thanks to Jesus for this — at least I still had a ticket home.

After the service, I lay awake wondering how to get to a bus station. There had to be a way, but I was not seeing it. I tossed and fretted and schemed. The later it got, the wilder and more far-fetched my ideas became. When I realized I was seriously considering strapping Susannah to my back, stealing a tractor and driving to the nearest town, I decided it was time to clear my head. Noiselessly, I slipped from my bunk and closed the curtain behind me. One peek confirmed that Susannah was sleeping deeply and I could tell by the breathing from across the aisle that JW was doing the same. The Jasper's bedroom door was closed, so surely they were asleep as well, but to ease my mind I hid the bus keys in the refrigerator anyway. Wasting no time looking for shoes, I tiptoed off the bus, gathered up the ruffled hem of my long nightgown and dashed across the churchyard.

Once inside the building, I ransacked the Sunday School rooms. In the juniors' class, I found a plastic globe bank filled with change for missions, but there was no way to get the coins out without breaking it. I am ashamed to say how long I held that globe and did not once think about hungry, lost children across the ocean. In the young adults' classroom, I took some packets of sugar and creamer, although I had no need for them. The pastor's office, with any really useful items, like stamps or maps or cash or a phone, was locked. In the kitchen, a drawer full of nothing but knives — carving knives, butcher knives, steak knives, bread and butter knives, plastic knives — made me shaky and dizzy when I looked at it too long. I slammed it shut again and backed away.

My reflection in the foyer mirror spooked me even more. What I saw there was a sad, scared little ghost in an old-fashioned nightgown, haunting the darkened House of God while all the good, upright members slept peacefully in their beds. I hurried past with a shudder.

In the sanctuary, I meandered up and down the rows of pews until, finally exhausted, I stretched out on one near a window. My shoulder was still too tender to lie on my back, so I rolled to my belly and considered my next move. I couldn't sleep here and it would be daylight soon, but I didn't want to go back to the bus yet.

I sighed. Alright, fine then. What else do you do in an empty church?

"God?" I asked aloud.

I didn't expect an answer; I wasn't that crazy yet. It was more like testing the line, seeing if the channel was clear. Sort of a "Breaker, breaker for heaven," prayer.

"God, I don't know what to do. I can't keep going on like this." I felt a sob threaten, but the pain in my shoulder cut it short. "God? Do you hear me? Do you even care?"

The silence in the church didn't answer, exactly, but maybe it did change a little, turn warmer, softer. Less lonesome.

Because I wasn't alone. Someone was pushing open the sanctuary door, letting in the pre-dawn light. Old Rev and Merrilee! I pretended to be asleep. If they found me, I could say I had gotten up early to come pray and had fallen asleep. Nobody would quibble with that.

But Merrilee and Old Rev weren't looking for me at all. They didn't even come down the middle aisle, but went straight to the altar. I heard their knees hit the carpeted floor, their clothes rustle. Old Rev cleared his throat.

"Almighty God, Heavenly Father, we approach Thee at

thy Throne of Grace," his sing-song prayer voice rolled over the empty room.

"Hear our prayers, the cries of your faithful servants," Merrilee's soothing voice added the perfect balance.

Dadgummit! They were getting a head start on their own morning prayers. I should have known. I can't get up now and interrupt them. Now I'm stuck! Dang, dang, dang. They could be at it an hour or more. Suddenly I had a desperate need to pee. I gritted my teeth.

Old Rev and Merrilee worked their way through the usual prayer list, taking turns sentence by sentence in a back-and forth, call and response. It was quite musical, really, listening to them. His sure baritone, her soft murmurs. Old Rev prayed for the lost of the world, paused, Merrilee prayed for world leaders. Old Rev prayed for the church we just left, Merilee for the service tonight and so on.

After covering all the major issues of the day, they moved closer to home, praying for friends and prayer-partners by name. Pastors they knew. Mrs. Gibley. I was not surprised when Merrilee prayed specifically for me — that happened all the time — but I was shocked at the sincerity in it. "Dear Lord, we ask for our daughter Ruby, that she will find the grace and peace and strength she needs," Merrilee prayed. "Bless her labors as she mothers and serves her child and her husband."

Before I could sort out my feelings about that, Old Rev spoke. "I thank you for my *one* faithful son, John Wesley, and his loyalty to our ministry. He has *ever been* my devoted companion in this lonely endeavor You hath set before our family. Thank you for sending me *one* trustworthy son."

He had barely finished when Merrilee added, more

loudly than before, "And bless our loving son Billy Sunday; remember his many kindnesses to me in my hours of pain, and reward Billy Sunday for honoring his mother so cheerfully."

Old Rev broke in, his voice rising and falling even more dramatically, "Lord, we know that you *reward* the faithful and *punish* the unfaithful. You have *no place* in your kingdom for those who would *abandon their work* for the shiny false amusements of this world. We trust in *your* perfect wisdom that you will *deal justly* with those soldiers who would *desert* the field of battle in this dark and desperate hour."

Merrilee's prayers were now ringing with the same force as Old Rev's. "And we know that you desire *mercy* more than sacrifice, and we thank you for welcoming prodigals home with *open* arms."

Old Rev shouted, "You reward the righteous, and say 'depart from me, ye faithless!"

Merrilee countered shrilly, "Luke 15:24 says 'For this my son was dead and is alive again; he was lost and is found, and they began to celebrate.' And we claim Your Holy word as Truth!"

Old Rev roared, "If your son or your daughter or your cherished wife entices you to serve other gods your eye shall not pity him nor shall you conceal or spare him! Deuteronomy 13, Deuteronomy 13! Thirteen!" He pounded his fists on the altar rail until he collapsed into a wrenching, weeping grief. "O Absalom, Absalom! My son, my son! Would that I had died, my son, Absalom," he babbled. Old Rev choked and gasped and sobbed while Merrilee said soothing, humming words too low to be heard. She shushed and tsked and made rhythmic rustlings that sounded as though she were rocking him.

An eternity seemed to pass before Old Rev finally quieted and Merrilee picked up the prayer again.

"Oh, Lord," she prayed, "I thank you for hearing the prayers of this lost young girl, many years ago, when you heard my desperate cries and sent this man, my Reverend Husband, to bring me out of my loneliness and despair and into your kingdom. I will serve him and you with gratitude and obedience all the days of my life."

Old Rev, his voice quivering, added, "In the words of Boaz, The Lord Bless you my daughter, for you have not run after younger men, whether rich or poor."

Merrilee finished with, "For such blessings, we give thanks."

Old Rev sniffed once more. "Amen," he said.

In the almost-silence that followed, I squirmed miserably when I realized I was hearing Old Rev give Merrilee a kiss.

I don't know. I guess every marriage has its moments.

Chapter Seventeen

It was our last night here. We were all loaded up to leave right after the service for Colorado, and I couldn't wait. I wanted to hit the road as soon as the last sinner got back to his feet.

At this church, we limited ourselves to the piano, organ, and marimba. No guitars. Some churches won't allow guitars on the altar because guitars are secular and might remind people of bars and night clubs. I'd never been to either one, so I couldn't speak to that.

As I held my mic and looked out over the congregation, keeping my eyes bright and my free hand welcoming, I noticed a woman seated alone, near the back. She looked familiar. I knew I had seen her somewhere, but I didn't think we'd ever been to this church before. I turned slightly, the way I always do, including everyone in the audience, making eye contact, letting everyone see the twinkle in my eye. I knew that beside me, JW was turning in the opposite direction, doing the same.

But during the second verse, as I scanned back over the

crowd, my eyes met hers again, and she gave me the tiniest wave. *How do I know her?*

It bugged me all through the service. I tried to place her. Every time I got up to sing, I sneaked more looks at her. She seemed about my mother's age and was wearing a Sunday-morning-kind-of dress, not a casual summer shift like the rest of the women wore. Her clothes were careful, but not extravagant. As if she weren't sure what to wear but wanted to play it safe and not stand out. She smiled at me every chance she could. Who was she?

After the service (two re-dedications, no conversions) I gathered up my purse and Bible and cut through the milling crowd to collect Susannah from the nursery. Someone touched my arm to get my attention, and I turned around to face my mystery woman.

"Ruby Fae?" she asked, "You've never met me, but I know all about you." Her voice wasn't familiar, but her drawl was. She had to be from around home. And her face — of course!

"You're Carol! Mom's friend from youth camp! I know you from your Christmas cards!" I am not usually a stranger-hugger, but she held out her arms and I fell into them. "Do you live here? Have you been here all week? I wish I'd known!" I babbled. This woman was a connection to home, and I hugged the poor lady for dear life.

Carol pulled back to look at me while keeping her arms around me. "No, no; we pastor at Bemidji, First. This is the first night I've been here. I'm so sorry I didn't get here sooner, but we've been on vacation. We got home last night. Your Momma said she'd been calling and calling, but, well, never mind that. I got here as soon as I could." She looked in my eyes and smoothed a strand of hair behind my ear. She lowered her voice. "I promised Mary Grace that I would look you over good."

I hesitated, aware of the church building around me emptying out. JW was almost done packing up our merchandise table, Old Rev was doing a little last-minute crowd-working, and Merrilee had disappeared. I should be cautious about what I say. But Carol is Mom's friend! She can call Mom!

"You talked to Mom?" I asked.

"Oh, yes, she called and—"

Carol paused to look around the church, and, with one arm still around me, began walking, steering me past the Reverends and out the sanctuary door, talking all the while. "You look so much like Mary Grace did at your age! I'd love to see her again. And you have a little girl of your own now, what is her name again?"

Once we were alone in the hallway, I stopped Carol. "If I give you a message for Mom, you'll give it to her for me? Just to her? And nobody else?" I asked. Carol looked at me with a sharp eye. She didn't want niceties, She wanted the truth.

"Of course I will, Ruby. Is there some reason you haven't called or written to her yourself? Your mama's worried about you."

You're in this far, Ruby. Go on.

"They won't let me," I whispered. "The Jaspers. They won't let me write or call home without them being right there. And I have to talk to Mom. I have to." I clutched at her arm.

"Oh, no. I was afraid of this," she said. "How bad is it?"

"Bad," I said. My eyes stung, but there was no time to cry. I grabbed for a tissue from my purse but froze when I saw the babysitter from the nursery walking down the hall, empty-handed.

"Where's Susannah?" I asked.

"Oh, your mother-in-law picked her up for you. She got the diaper bag, too. Susannah is such a good baby. She was already asleep."

Susannah! They got her on the bus already!

Ruby Fae, you fool! You piddled around and let them get Susannah on the bus without you. Carol could have helped you get home, but not now! You'll never get your baby off that bus. Never.

"I have to go." I pulled away from Carol and ran down the hall toward the back door. I banged it open and saw the bus warmed up, the lights on and the engine running.

Carol followed after me calling my name, but I charged across the parking lot and didn't look back.

Blessedly, the bus doors opened for me. I lunged up the stairs and didn't slow down until I was standing by Susannah's crib, watching as her blankie rose and fell with her sleeping breaths.

Would they really have done it? Left me? Driven off into the night with my baby? Was I going to have to do this forever, always in fear of losing her, never relaxing, never letting her out of my reach? Never blinking? Could I live like that?

Oh, God. What should I do?

I stood right there in the aisle, keeping watch as we rode through the night in our smooth-rolling coach. Old Rev and Merrilee went back to their room, so the only noise was the traveling hum and the only light, the reflection on JW's face from the dashboard dials. I finally turned away from the crib to get ready for bed when JW held up his hand to motion me to him. I came closer. He looked up at me in the wide rearview mirror and asked, "What were you talking about with that woman?"

I rolled my eyes. "Oh, man! You know how it goes, that lady would have kept me there, talking all night." I marveled at my effortless lying.

"You were awful upset, it looked like."

"Yeah, her story was...really sad."

He adjusted his back cushion. "What was it?" I almost had him, so I lied on.

"Well..." I hesitated for effect. "I should probably keep her confidences, it being between a man and wife and all..." That should do it. Shock him good.

It did. "Seriously? And him, such a respected pastor? I think he's even the assistant District Superintendent for this region! Wow. You'd think he'd do a better job of looking to his own household than that," JW shook his head and reached over to eject a cassette. "Just goes to show," he said wisely, "that you never know what goes on in other people's homes."

Chapter Eighteen

JW didn't talk on the CB much the next day; he only "read the mail." That's CB talk for "Just listening in." None of the usual chatter seemed to interest him until a little after lunch, a trucker came on with "Watch out, neighbors. Cute little Hippy Chickie right around yardstick 217. I'd pick her up, but I promised my Better Half I'd drive solo. Worried about the Little Bit, though, it's awful hot out there. Come on back?"

JW picked up the microphone and held down the button. "Break for Bible Boy here; we're in a big ol' Stage Coach, we'll get her. Plenty of room, and I got my Better Half and my family riding shotgun with me, so it's all on the up-and-up."

We picked up hitchhikers all the time, and I had mixed feelings about this since we had Susannah to worry about. They could have been crazy or dangerous. But on the other hand, picking up strangers did break up the road monotony because most hitchhikers understood that a little entertaining conversation was the price of their ticket. We also found your average hitchhiker to be more musical than the general population. One cold wanderer we picked up in Montana was so amazing with his harmonica and had such an agreeable demeanor, Old Rev invited him to join us onstage for the next service. The hitchhiker seemed to be on board with that idea, too, but I think we lost him when Old Rev got all excited and started planning this poor sinner's big moment during the altar call where he'd publicly confess all his sins. "They don't even have to be really your sins," Old Rev had explained, "but it's best if they're big ones. Know anything about prison? That always plays well." The hitchhiker assured us that he could provide a real fancy confession, but when we stopped for gas, he and his harmonica ended up on a semi bound for Reno.

JW slowed the bus and rolled onto the shoulder. The doors whooshed open, and a young woman in cut-offs carrying a guitar case and a trash bag trotted over to the steps and hopped in.

"Hi," she said. "And thanks. It was a long hot day out there." I caught her look of surprise when her eyes lit on JW's handsome face. She was trying to decide if his good looks were familiar because he was famous, or if his face had a sort of general-purpose perfection you might recognize from the "after" picture in an acne commercial.

JW gave her a friendly but impersonal smile and didn't even look at her long enough to register the tanned legs, the over-filled tube top, and the long mess of permed, bleached hair spilling around her bare shoulders. He turned his eyes back to the highway.

"Where you headed?" He asked.

"San Diego, eventually," she answered. "I got a job waiting for me out there, but there's no hurry. Wherever you're going is fine with me." She stood uncertainly, not sure where to sit.

Old Rev said to her, in his kindly-old-saint voice, "Welcome, sister! We extend to thee the right hand of hospitality. Welcome to our home. We have plenty of room for a fellow troubadour." Merrilee invited the girl to join her on the couch, but she saw Susannah and me playing on my bunk and waved at JW's empty one across from us. I nodded. "Sure, that's fine. There's a little room underneath for your stuff, if you want."

"Thanks," she said and stashed her trash sack under JW's bed. She held her guitar case for a moment, then decided to set it on its side on the bunk between her and the window.

"I don't know what a troubadour is, but I'll be one, if it gets me a nice ride like this," she said as she kicked off her flip-flops and stretched out beside her guitar case. "This is a luxury ride."

I pointed to her guitar case. "A troubadour is a traveling entertainer, like a wandering story-teller or musician. Do you play for a living, or for fun?"

"Huh? Oh. That. No. I'm, uhm, just learning."

"Stick with it." I told her. "Have your fingers healed over yet, or are they still sore? That's when most people want to quit, before they get callouses built up."

"What? You mean it hurts to play the guitar?"

"At first." She obviously hadn't learned much yet about the guitar.

The hitchhiker pointed to Susannah. "Is that your baby?"

"Yes." I said. "Her name's Susannah. I'm Ruby."

"I'm Starla." She said it thoughtfully, as though she had come to that conclusion after a considerable amount of thought. "How old are you, anyway? You look too young for a baby."

Yeah, I know. "I'm twenty."

"Huh. I'm older than you. I'm twenty-five already, but you are the one with the baby. Huh."

I had no answer for that, so I asked Starla if she'd like anything to eat or drink. She laughed.

"What I'd like is a beer, but I guess the bar's not open yet on this flight?"

Like magic, Merrilee appeared in the bus aisle with a cold can of Coke to offer, and I swear I actually saw Old Rev's ears perk up when Starla mentioned beer. Beer is a sin with a capitol S. Old Rev loved nothing more than a captive sinner, and here we had ourselves a live one. Fully alert now, he would bide his time until the perfect moment to pounce. I tried to think of a conversational topic that would stall him a little. At least until I could get Susannah fed and down for her nap.

"So, you travel a lot?" I asked.

"That's my life," she answered easily. "I live on the road. Looks like you do, too."

"Yeah, we do," I agreed. And before I thought much about it, I asked, "Do you miss TV? I really miss TV."

Starla flopped back on the cushions and rolled from side to side. "Oh, god, yes! All my favorite shows," she said. "Sixty minutes! Face the Nation! 20/20!"

I stared at her, wondering if she was joking. All news? No Dallas, or Love Boat? Not even Days of Our Lives? Suddenly I felt very silly and young.

"So...you like to keep up with the news?" I asked.

"Yes! Love it. Can't get enough of it. I mean, on the road, I do hear it all on the radio, but it's not the same. I miss seeing Walter Cronkite every night. And I love Dan

Rather sooooo much. I hope he gets the desk when Walter retires."

Well. Just goes to show. The book, not the cover, and all that.

"So what did you think about the Hearst release?" Starla asked me, as if she were asking about the latest celebrity gossip. "Do you believe her? Do you think she was an innocent victim, or should she do the time? Personally, I think Carter took a real political risk that he couldn't afford right now. I suppose a commutation was less risky than an outright pardon, but still damn humane of him, though, don't you think?"

"I, uh, am not sure what I think," I said. "Tell me the details again?"

She looked at me with disappointment. "Been traveling awhile, huh? You know she was kidnapped, right? And then she was with her kidnappers when she robbed that bank?"

I nodded. This sounded vaguely familiar.

"But her defense was something called the Stockholm Syndrome. It means you get so wrapped up in the little world of the people who kidnapped you that you forget who you were in the first place." Starla took a long drink of her Coke, then sighed luxuriously. "Almost as good as a cold Coors," she said.

That did it for Old Rev. He was on his feet, headed for us.

"Begging your pardon, Miss, you are new to our group, so we wouldn't expect you to understand. But alcoholic spirits are of no use to us. We fortify ourselves with the Holy Spirit. We do not drink from the dregs of the world's wineskins, but from the Well of Living Water."

Starla looked to me for interpretation.

"We don't drink," I shrugged.

"Ever?"

I shook my head.

Old Rev lowered himself onto a spare spot beside me on my bunk so that he was eye-level across from Starla. Dang! Now I was trapped. I stifled a sigh and settled in for a revival, to go. Susannah crawled up onto my lap, away from him, and began tugging at my shirt, but I didn't want to breastfeed her with Old Rev sitting ride beside me. I pulled out all the toys I could reach to distract her. Old Rev, however, was focused on Starla.

"Sister," he said in a surprisingly gentle tone, "may I ask if you've ever had hard times? Lonely times? Nights filled with fears, days where you are lost? Hungry, lean times filled with want and longing?" That was the magic, right there. His money-maker voice. His hypnotic shtick. I could tell already; he'd made a sale.

She shifted uncomfortably and looked down at the fringe on her cut-off jeans. She pulled at a thread. "Yeah. Some." Old Rev sat in encouraging silence. This was one of his most effective methods. Start a dialogue, then back out. Refuse to carry your share of the talking. People would say anything to avoid the silence, being left alone in their heads with their own thoughts. I'd seen it work a thousand times. Old Rev looking at you, with those soulful, eerie blue eyes. Going once.

It took less than a minute. Starla sniffed, then asked in a small voice, "But doesn't everybody feel like that?"

Going twice.

Old Rev nodded encouragingly. "Yes, of course, sometimes. There is no end to the darkness in this world. But it doesn't have to live inside you. There is a way, a way to live in this darkness without letting it overtake you."

She went still.

"There's an awful lot of darkness out there," she said without looking up.

"But it doesn't have to be in here." Old Rev tapped his chest.

She still didn't look up, but a hand sneaked to her face and wiped something away. "How?" she asked. "How do I get this darkness out of me?"

Sold! To the lady in the raggedy shorts.

I couldn't believe it, but even I was moved. Even now, despite everything, I am still always amazed at how powerful this moment is. I say that proves God exists, right there; if crazy, cold-hearted, mean old sons-of-bitches like Reverend Lemuel T. Jasper can herd people to Jesus, then there has to be Somebody Else on the other side, roping them in.

Patiently, patiently, Old Rev listened to the torrent of misery and sin this girl had lived with, sins committed both by and against her. She had stories of sins enough to last through half of North Dakota, but no one interrupted her. At some point, Merrilee materialized on the bunk beside her, holding her when she sobbed, handing her tissues, until her storm passed.

Old Rev moved over to Starla's side, so I stretched out on my bunk, pulled the curtain and settled in with Susannah for a naptime. I listened to the murmur of voices, Starla's growing calmer and steadier, the Jasper's, full of concern and encouragement. I was so confused. How could Old Rev be so empathetic, so intuitive, so unbearably gentle and understanding with complete strangers, but a tyrant to the people he lived with? I didn't get it. I couldn't understand any of it. Susannah dropped off to sleep. I lay back on my bunk and watched out my window, but we were on the interstate, and there was nothing much to see.

Susannah was napping soundly now, so I decided to get up and visit with Starla some more. But as soon as I'd re-adjusted my shirt and opened my bunk curtain, our bus stopped and I watched as Starla gathered the trash bag from under the bed. She said, "Well, this is where I get off."

"Here? What's here?" I asked, looking out the window. We were at a Howard Johnson's truck stop. She pointed to a decal on the diner door. The Greyhound logo. "I can catch a bus from here," she said. "I'm going home to Oregon, to my Grandma." Her eyes glistened. "Your father-in-law gave me a ticket." She waved my ticket in front of her. My *ticket*. "He's such a good man. You are so lucky to marry into such a wonderful family."

I wanted to punch her.

I was so angry, it made me nauseous. *A bus ticket home.* I wanted to scream. *My ticket!*

I stared at the girl, speechless.

"Hey, look," Starla said to me in a lowered voice as she pointed to her guitar case. "That, ah, isn't exactly mine, but it doesn't really belong to anybody else, now, either. I never used it, I swear, I don't even know how. And I never intended to. I thought I could maybe pawn it for money or something, but I don't know anything about 'em. So, you guys can have it, maybe do something with it. As a thanks from me, OK?"

"Thanks." I was short with her. I knew my problems weren't her fault, but still! "I don't need any more guitars, I have two."

"No, no. You keep it," she insisted. She slung her garbage bag onto her shoulder. "Bye, and, well, God bless.

I should say things like that now, shouldn't I?" She turned to go. Merrilee hugged her and JW shook her hand. I watched, dumb with envy and misery, as Old Rev followed her off the bus. Through the window, I saw Old Rev peel off a wad of bills and give them to Starla. She hugged him too, and we were back on the highway in minutes.

See how easy that was? To send a girl back home, where she belongs?

The rest of the day, I relied on auto-pilot to get me safely through the red haze of my fury. And since I couldn't unleash it on the Jaspers, I let God have it. To be honest, I don't remember what-all I did say to Him in my mind that day, but I can attest none of it was very nice.

Finally, finally, it was bedtime, and I settled in to ignore everyone for the night. But I couldn't sleep. Seething, I turned over on my bunk, punching at my pillow, yanking on my sheet. I tossed. I picked at a piece of rubber around my window frame. I watched the lights of the traffic on the interstate. I gave God another piece of my mind, then I rehearsed scathing, rebellious speeches I'd never say aloud. I groaned. I desperately needed to sleep, but I was still too angry. It was two, then three o'clock in the morning and my head still throbbed with my anger. My entire body shook with it. I had to calm down, for Susannah's sake. She would be awake by six or seven at the latest, and I'd be damned if I let a Jasper take care of her while I slept in.

I did some quick math, then reached under the corner of my mattress. From the silver foil card, I popped one pink capsule, stuck it in my mouth and chewed quickly. The horrible bitter taste soon flooded my mouth. Good. It matched my mood.

In no time, I was drifting, surrendering, to a pink

Benadryl haze, while JW drove on through the night toward Colorado, toward the High Plains. Toward home.

Even in my deepest sleep, I knew when we passed the dry line. I could feel it, the crackly air, the rusty earth, the brassy wind. I didn't have to be awake to know it; my open-range soul recognized its home without being told. Oh, we were too far north still, it was too cool and too high, but even so, I was almost back where I belonged, back where I could see, where I could breathe. Back on the plains. Even in my deepest sleep, I could tell because I started dreaming of home. I dreamed about Grandpa Pake. I dreamed I was riding in front of him on his horse like I did as a little girl. In my dream, Grandpa Pake was younger and stronger than I'd ever known him. He was the handsome cowboy I recognized from the old photos. We were riding in the upper west quarter, at the foot of the flat-topped red hills that underlined an empty sky. "Little Ruby Red," he said to me, "It's time we start back. Your old daddy will be out looking for you, directly. You know the way, don't you?" I told him I did. "Sure you do." He agreed. "You'd know it with your eyes closed."

Chapter
Nineteen

We weren't any closer to home, though. Sure, we were further west, but not in eastern Colorado. We were *too* far west, in fact, past the plains and into mountain country. And we were way, way too far north. I could tell that much, even though I had no idea where we were. No one else seemed to know, either, but they wouldn't admit it.

We wandered around back roads all day, following Old Rev's directions. He had a map and an idea, but that was all. We'd planned to spend our layover day in Colorado, and Merrilee looked like she wanted to ask Old Rev about that, but of course, she didn't. JW acted like this was the plan all along, like he had it all under control, of course he knew where to turn, but I was not fooled. We were lost.

Late in the day, we wandered into a blink of a place in southwestern Montana snugged up against the mountains. But not mountains I'd ever heard of before. Old Rev said they were the Tobacco Root Mountains. A state-issued road sign claimed this was a town named Pony, but it seemed to me the Montana Highway Department was overly-generous with their signs if they called this place a town. Pony was one narrow street of disappearing pavement running the length of town and a couple of dirt roads with houses, a few that even looked lived-in, breaking off at random intervals. Two pick-up trucks were angle parked in front of a building at the far end of the block, but the only other vehicle in sight was parked in an empty lot and had a small tree growing out of the rear window. A fat dachshund without a collar trotted purposefully down the middle of the street, dragging his belly as fast as he could.

"Here's good," Old Rev said, and JW rolled the bus to a stop in front of a boarded-up two-story brick building on a corner lot. Stern letters molded into the concrete over the arched doorway labeled it as the BANK, but it was clear that the prosperity in this town had long since fled. The only going concerns left in Pony seemed to be the tiny Post Office, a neat white square church with a good belfry and the building down the block with a neon Coors sign in the window. That was where the pickups were parked and the dog was headed.

Without a word, Old Rev hopped off the bus and disappeared. Merrilee looked like this was exactly what was on today's schedule and pulled out a fresh batch of proofreading work. JW stretched, visited the bathroom, then collapsed on the couch. Nobody seemed bothered about Susannah and me. It figured. The first time in over a year that we've been allowed out on our own, and it was in a ghost town.

I turned to my baby. "What do you say, Susannah, shall we hit the town?"

Susannah had no reasonable objection to that, so off we went.

I looked up and down the street, if you could call it that,

a street. There was probably a phone in the bar, but it would take more than my life was worth for me to chance getting caught in any bar. It was almost six o'clock, but maybe the lobby to the post office was open. Maybe they had a stamp machine. I set off with more purpose now, the change I'd found back in the car seat in Minnesota tucked in my jeans pocket. I stepped over cracks and roots in the sidewalk, gawked at the boarded-up storefronts, looking casual as I eased toward the post office. Susannah waddled along beside me.

The post office was a new little metal building the size of a lawn mower shed. *Please, God, let something work out right for me.* I tried the lobby door. It opened, but there was no stamp machine. Nothing but twenty or thirty tiny PO box doors and a bulletin board with old wanted posters. Disappointed, I backed out onto the sidewalk, closing the door behind us.

I decided to try the church next but changed my mind when I spotted Old Rev on the parsonage porch, talking to a woman in hair rollers. She shook her head and pointed down the street, toward the bar. Old Rev nodded and turned to leave, and I instinctively looked around for a place to duck and hide with Susannah. I don't know why, I wasn't doing anything wrong, but there was no need. Old Rev didn't even look our way.

Susannah and I fooled around, kicking at dandelions. Next to an abandoned school building, we found a well-cared for patch of grass with a set of wooden teeter-totters and a picnic table, and I got the idea that Susannah might like eating a picnic supper there, if Old Rev wasn't in a hurry to leave town. I picked up Susannah and headed back to the bus.

The sandwiches were made and the Fritos, Oreos and

cans of Shasta pop packed in the stroller by the time Old Rev got back. He readily agreed to my supper plans and bent over JW, waking him up. "Rise and shine," he said, not unkindly. "Supper will perk you right up. We've got a little driving ahead of us tonight." JW shook himself awake and stood. I put back one can of orange Shasta and got two cans of Coke instead. He'd need to start on the caffeine right away.

Seated at the table in the Pony City Park with our picnic in front of us, we all turned to Old Rev, waiting for his blessing. He cleared his throat.

"Before we bless the food, I want to share something with you." He looked at all of us, including everyone, but it was clear he really wanted JW's attention. Merrilee and I glanced at each other. For once, she let me read her own baffled expression.

"My father barely remembered his father. He left when my father was a small child, and my father only spoke of it to me once. When he was drunk. He told me the name of this town, where Pa—" Old Rev cleared his throat again, "—my father, thought his own father was born and raised. He also mentioned that somehow, he'd got in his head that his father, my grandfather, had been orphaned. That wouldn't be out of line; this town was a rough place back in the day. Miners and saloons and the like. That's what I gathered, anyway." Old Rev looked down at his plate. "I should have come here sooner. Seems there was an old maiden aunt, a younger sister of my grandfather, but she died last year. The barkeeper said she died alone. Had no people. I'm sure she would have liked to have known there was some family left. I should have come sooner."

No one spoke. I handed Fritos to Susannah under the table to keep her quiet. Old Rev continued, his voice growing stronger. "The Bible says that the sins of the father are visited on the sons, even unto the third and fourth generations. Third and fourth, JW. Understand?" He held up four fingers. He folded them down, one by one, as he ticked them off. "My grandfather. My father. Me. You." His fist closed. He pointed at it. "That's four. Four generations. Me, I was three, so that's not a given. Third *or* fourth, see? But you, you JW, are the fourth. The last one, for sure. People think that verse means God punishes us for our father's sins, but no, that's not what it means. It means that he visits the sins themselves, those same sins, they keep showing up, over and over. I tried to shake it, I tried, but I couldn't. I still lost Billy Sunday. You, though JW, you are the generation of change, the one who ends it. The last in the line of bad fathers, fathers who can't keep their families together." He pointed at JW. Old Rev's voice quivered. 'Whatever you have to do, whatever it takes. You, JW, will end this."

There was a long silence, finally broken when Old Rev said, "Merrilee, dear, would you mind saying the blessing?"

Merrilee recovered nicely from the shock of being asked to take over such a fatherly duty and said a very fine, yet succinct, table blessing. We were glad to put food in our mouths because we didn't know what words would be right for this occasion.

After our supper, none of us knew what to do. Old Rev seemed in no hurry to leave Pony, so we sat, listlessly, in the "city" park. I watched Susannah cruise around the benches of the picnic table and thought about picnic suppers back home. On a night like this, we should be waiting for lightning bugs to come out, but Montana was too cold for lightning bugs. Also, the colors here were all wrong. These greens were a dark, piney color instead of the soft pastel plains green, and the sunset was thoroughly unexceptional. The sun just sort of dropped down behind the mountain and disappeared, no big to-do about it. Very anti-climactic. A sunset over the red hills of Oklahoma, though, now, that is a daily glory. Grandpa Pake used to say, "God is everywhere, but the Great Plains are where He lays down of an evening. It's the only place He can get a good night's sleep. And this here draw is where He rests His head, because not even God wants to miss a western Oklahoma sunset."

"Hey, Ruby Fae," JW broke into my thoughts. "Did you look at the guitar Starla left us? Is it any good? What is it? Can you use it?"

"Oh! I forgot all about it. I doubt it's worth much, or somebody else would have already got it, don't you think?"

"You never know. Could be a treasure in there. Maybe some priceless Fender or something. Bring it out here, let's look at it."

"It belongs to The Lord," said Old Rev, sounding like himself again. "Whatever is in it was an offering."

JW said hastily, "Oh, of course. I didn't mean otherwise. I thought, if it would be something we could use in a service, Ruby could make good use of it. It would belong to The Ministry, obviously."

While we had all been busy talking about it, Merrilee had slipped into the bus, brought the case out and laid it on the picnic table in front of us.

"Well, open it, see what it is," JW said to me, as though it were a Christmas present.

To play along with him, I made a big production of it. I stood at the head of the table and turned the case towards me as I opened it.

I unlatched the case.

"Drumroll, please...." I said.

I propped the lid open a few inches and peeked inside.

"Oh!" No, I did not expect that! I dropped the lid back down, then opened it again toward me. "Oh! It's just like my mom's!" I said.

"I didn't know your mom played the guitar," JW said, as he tipped the lid back for a look.

No, Mom can't play, but she sure can shoot. It wasn't a guitar, at all. It was a gun.

JW yelped.

"We shouldn't have that! We need to take it to the police! We don't know anything about that girl. This could be a murder weapon!"

Old Rev and I both laughed at him. "That's no murder weapon!" we said in unison.

"It's a bunny gun!" I said. "To shoot skunks and stuff."

"A girlie gun." Old Rev said. "For women and children."

For once, he and I agreed. It was an old Winchester pump-action .22 short-barrel. All the farm women back home have a .22 like this one by the back door, handy to grab when you need to guard your home or hens from snakes and coons and what-not. I'd shot one like this a million times, rooting around for gophers with my brothers, shooting at home-made targets with Dad. He always told me not to say anything to the boys, but I was the best shot in the family, next to Mom.

"Geez, a .22 is one step above a BB gun." I told JW dismissively.

That was a grave sin, scoffing at a husband, but surprisingly, nobody called me on it, not even Old Rev. Instead, he reached for the gun. "I wanted one like that so bad I could taste it, when I was a kid," he said, almost tenderly. "Oh, how I prayed for one, when I was out hunting jack rabbits with nothing but a sling shot." He held it up, sighted an imaginary bird in flight, and then abruptly, unbelievably, handed the gun to me. Clearly, it held no happy memories for him. "Praise the Lord, I can eat better now, without having to stalk my dinner and slaughter and skin it first."

I walked away from the table, the gun cradled in my hands. I ran my hands over the wooden forestock, feeling the well-worn ridges. I pumped it once, then turned it on its side to see if it was loaded. It was. Both chambers. Without thinking, I turned to the empty pasture behind us. Swift and smooth, I fitted the gun to my shoulder and sighted a sunflower, its outline barely visible in the fading light. In less time than it took to blink at it, I squeezed the trigger and blew the petals right off that blasted daisy. I had to smile.

How about that, Daddy? I am still the best shot in the family.

Chapter Twenty

I woke up sharp and fast when we rolled into a state park near Hasty, Colorado. Four o'clock in the morning and my mouth was as dry as a dust storm. That's how I always feel when allergy medicine wears off. Old Rev and Merrilee were asleep, and JW dangerously close to it when he finally tumbled out of his driver's seat and into the bus bathroom. But I was wide awake, excited to be here. And I was glad it was still dark out. That way, I couldn't see the mountains looming in the distance over my left shoulder, but I could feel the wide-open night around us. Everyone talks about Eastern Colorado the same way they do the Oklahoma Panhandle, like it's a gauntlet of boredom you have to fight your way through best as you can to get to your reward of the Rockies. Even the state troopers will tell speeders, "All the way to Holt? Aw, go on. Just watch out for deer." Nobody even gives this country a good look. It's all about the mountains. People go on and on about the majesty, the beauty, of the Rockies, how they feel so close to God there, and all that.

Not me. I hate mountains.

I'm boxed in and claustrophobic when I'm beside the mountains, woozy and cold on top. They block off the sunlight by four in the afternoon. How are you supposed to even *see* anything? Everywhere you look, it's nothing but the ground all pushed up in your face, covering up the sky. It's no better than downtown Kansas City, as far as I'm concerned. Give me the plains, any day.

I pulled on jeans and a sweatshirt, stuffed my feet in my sneakers, grabbed my shower bag and told JW that I was going to the park facilities. He was so exhausted from driving, he barely acknowledged me, crashing onto his bunk, fully dressed, already asleep.

I opened the bus door and scrambled down the steps. It was too cold for August and the air was thinner than I'm used to, but the star-spangled black emptiness looked like home, sweet, sweet home to me.

I took a long, decadent, steamy-hot shower. Showering on the bus was nothing but business, no luxuriating involved. Even if I weren't claustrophobic, we had a limited water supply, and I couldn't very well relax all naked and wet, inches from Old Rev and Merrilee. But campgrounds had bottomless hot water tanks, it seemed, and the ones in state parks, at least, were free. Some private campgrounds, you had to put quarters in the slot, which meant I had to beg bath money off JW. I found that beyond humiliating

I figured Susannah would sleep until at least six or later, so I took advantage of it. I shaved my legs, shampooed and blow-dried my hair. I warmed up under the hand dryer before I dressed. I plucked my eyebrows and trimmed my toenails. When I couldn't think of any more excuses to linger, I moseyed outside.

I found the information center, a big wooden signpost with a little rooftop over it and covered with plastic bins full of pamphlets like, "Your Colorado State Park System Safety Guide" and "Nature Fun for the Whole Family." I found the one I wanted, a map of Colorado, and snatched it quickly, looking over my shoulder. You'd think I was shoplifting, as jumpy as I was. But even though I was ninety-nine percent positive that no Jasper was awake right now, I still felt sneaky and nervous.

I took the map over to a picnic table where there was enough light spilling from the lighted parking lot and opened it. We would be in Eastern Colorado for one week, at a small town called Spring City. I'd heard of Spring City before. It was less than three hundred miles from home. Our next booking was in Idaho. No telling when we'd be this close to Oklahoma again.

I stared at the map, slowly tracing the highway before me.

Please, God. Help me get home.

Chapter
Twenty-one

Another laundry day, but it was the most inconvenient laundry day imaginable. The laundromat was on the street right behind our church. So close we could walk, Old Rev and JW pointed out. Isn't that handy?

Yes, it was handy, if hauling seven loads of laundry, a box of Tide, a toddler, and a diaper bag along with you on your morning stroll is what you call "handy." But we were the Queen and Crown Princess of Make-Do, Merrilee and I, and so we dug the stroller out of the cargo hold under the bus, piled it with laundry, strapped Susannah to my back and shuffled, hobo-like, down the sidewalk and across the street.

Merrilee and I sorted all the washables into machines, then I walked up the row with the detergent and Merrilee followed me, feeding quarters into each machine. The clinking sound of her change purse, fat with the "tips" from our last service, usually rankled me. I always wished I could ask her for some; after all, I helped earn it. But this time, I had my seventy-nine cents of seat-cushion money in my pocket. Lucky strike number two for me was a pay phone, right there on the laundromat wall. All I needed now was the right timing.

Susannah jabbered alongside me, holding onto the bar across the legs of a rolling laundry basket cart and using it as her walker. I always talked to her as though she would answer me.

"How do you like Colorado, Susannah?" I asked her as I poured the Tide and slam-closed a machine lid.

"Ba-ba-ba-da-da."

"Oh, I think so, too," I agreed with her as we both moved to the next machine. Pour. Slam. Next machine.

"Buh-buh-buh?"

"Yes, it is a dry year here. I imagine all the ponds are low."

"Pblpblpbl." She spit thoughtfully.

"Most likely." I responded. Pour. Slam.

Through the plate glass windows, I watched JW hop off the bus. He stood for a moment surveying the street, then set off down the block. I went to the window and guessed his destination, a lumberyard and hardware store at the far end of Main Street. He would be out of my way for an hour or more at least, browsing there. I looked back at Merrilee, but she was poring over a stack of proofreading, her pencil skittering across the page. Old Rev, I knew, was seated at the dinette on the bus with his Smith-Corona typewriter banging out a new sermon series. I spread a quilt on the floor a few steps from the pay phone. Near enough to reach Susannah, but not so close that my interest in the phone was obvious. I set Susannah on the quilt, knelt down beside her and dug some of her favorite toys out of the diaper bag. We got right down to the business of pushing yellow plastic stars and circles into the red Tupperware ball together while I worked up some courage.

"Oh, Dear."

I looked up, surprised to see Merrilee rummaging through the papers. Merrilee never "rummaged" through anything. She always had every item of her life organized, collated, clipped and filed. I watched her fret, flicking through this file and that. Without explanation, she set down her papers and scurried back to the bus. Meanwhile, I rejoiced, lunged for the pay phone and fed a quarter into the slot.

The line was busy. Shit. I'd never said that word aloud before and I was surprised to find how helpful a word it was. I counted to ten and checked the coin return slot. My quarter wasn't in it, but I didn't have time to wait. Who knew how long Merrilee would be gone? I inserted another quarter and dialed again.

Still busy. Shit, shit, shit. Three "shits" in a row, but under my breath. I counted to ten again, but before I put my quarter in, I remembered it was Tuesday. That time, I yelled the "shit" as I banged the receiver down hard. Mom and Dad were still on a party line, and Tuesday mornings were when Aunt Jannie always called everyone to ask for news for her Woods County News column. Depending upon who won last week's Rook Club high and low prize or how many pullets Mrs. Eulah Riggings had dressed out, Aunt Jannie could tie up the phone all morning. I had no idea how long I'd be alone with this phone. And I still wasn't getting my quarters back.

Tearfully, I asked God for this one little favor here, and fed my last quarter into the phone.

It rang once.

"McKeever's."

Dad! I was knocked speechless. Dad hates answering the phone. And he's never in the house before noon, anyway. He should be out feeding cattle. Dad. Oh, Daddy. I swallowed hard.

"Hello," I squeaked out. "Hi, Dad."

"Ruby Fae, is that you?" His voice was hard. Unfamiliar. What? Was he still angry with me? He couldn't be. That's not how we are. My chest felt mule-kicked.

"Yes. It's me." My heart was pounding. "Dad, I'm sorry. I'm so sorry I didn't listen to you. I'm so sorry about saying all those terrible things to you," I was babbling, but he cut me short.

"Ruby Fae, I don't want to hear it, I want to know why you haven't called. Your mother is worried sick about you. I ought to turn you over my knee. Where are you?"

Then four things all happened at the same time.

Aunt Jannie picked up the phone. "Oh, Harvell! Is that you on the line? I'm sorry, I'll let you have it."

Clyde Shoemaker, Dad's old bachelor neighbor who never, ever, used the phone also picked up on the line, "Whoops, sorry there, Jannie; I can call Willet later."

I said, "Colorado, Dad. Spring City. Please, come get me."

But I doubted he heard that, because the fourth thing that happened in that same moment, while the party line was overfilling with voices, was an earsplitting scream that exploded from Susannah. I twisted around and saw Merrilee, suddenly underfoot and holding her. What the heck? *How did she get in here so fast? Where did she come from?*

And my baby was screaming bloody murder.

"Ruby? What's going on? *Where are you?*"

Merrilee handed my frenzied, screaming baby to me, and the ear-piercing screams drowned out Dad's voice.

"Just a second, Dad—hang on," I turned back to Merrilee, "Please, please, hold her just a sec," I started to ask, but stopped short. Merrilee was holding the limp, soggy, Bunny-Wunny away from my wild baby lunging at it from my arms.

What? Are you kidding me? Merrilee has to do that right this minute? Why now—

No.

I was already too late. That fast, Merrilee's fingers, so light and so nimble, flicked across the cradle. With the very same invisible sleight-of-hand she used to turn the pages of her hymnal at the piano, she had cut my phone call off.

I yelled into the receiver. "Dad? Dad! Daddy!" I jiggled the lever and punched the buttons, ignoring the dial tone. I jammed my fingers in the coin return slot as I heard the internal clink, clink, clink of Ma Bell digesting my coins. A sticker on the phone warned me No Change Given.

Merrilee couldn't apologize enough for her clumsiness, she claimed. I burned with fury, but I kept my voice and my face flat. I said to her, "It's fine. No worries. We were leaving, anyhow." Turning to Susannah, I said, "Let's walk down the street and meet your Daddy, how about that?" And, because I was feeling peevish, I made a production out of returning Bunny-Wunny to her.

I felt Merrilee's eyes on us but refused to look up at her until she cleared her throat.

"Ruby," she said, in that stubbornly, infuriatingly, soft way of hers, "This may be an inconvenient moment, but perhaps you might wish to read this."

"What?" I spluttered in disbelief.

She held out to me a typewritten sheet which I instantly recognized as a proofreading page from Old Rev's sermons. I didn't even try to hide the acid in my voice. "Merrilee, I am not in the mood to read a sermon right now, thank you." I shoved the page back at her.

Meek as lamb made of solid iron, she folded the paper into quarters, then put it back into my hand, wrapping my fingers around it. "You can keep this," she murmured. "I have made two copies."

To get her out of my way, I shoved the page into my front jeans pocket with one hand, and with Susannah clamped to my hip with the other, I stormed out the door and thundered down the street toward the Spring City Lumber and Supply Company. Of course, I was barely halfway down the block when I regretted not grabbing the stroller or baby back-pack first. Susannah can get heavy fast these days, and I was in no mood to amble along with her walking at her own sweet pace. But not for a million dollars was I turning around and going back. That would have seemed like a defeat, retracing my steps. So, fine. I would just suffer.

I joggled Susannah as I stomped past the Dairy-Dog Drive-in and the Colorado Cuties Cut'n'Curl. In front of the T, G. & Y store, I shifted her to my other hip and heard Merrilee's paper crinkle in my pocket. I fumed all the way past the Farmer's National Bank and two empty store fronts while Susannah grew heavier and heavier. Finally, in front of the Rex-All Drug I stopped, set her down and let her walk.

With one hand Susannah guided me down the sidewalk on a whack-a-doodle course, careering from side to side. Our lazy progress, the sluggish afternoon heat and Susannah's idle baby-chit-chat opened a slow-release valve on my temper until I gradually began forming more complete thoughts. A recurrent one — Merrilee's odd behavior — looped through my head. What was that all about? I must have asked that out loud, because Susannah looked up at me and confidently answered, "Mum-mum-mum-mum."

"Beats me, Susannah. I don't ever know why your Grandma Jasper does what she does. As a matter of fact, I don't know much about your Grandma Jasper at all."

I know one story about Merrilee. One. And I had to beg JW for that much, even. I thought we should have it. You know, for Susannah one day. After all, she is her family.

All I know about Merrilee is that she was raised in an Indian Boarding School in South Dakota. She wasn't taken from her home by the government, or sent by a tribe, or anything like that. She may not even be Indian. She turned up there, sometime toward the end of the Depression. Just sort of appeared, according to JW.

"You mean she was left on the doorstep? Like 'Annie'?"

"Not that she ever told me about. I only know about it because once we stopped at a church near there, and an old lady who used to be a cook at the Indian school remembered Mom and told me the story."

One evening in the early fall, about the time of year children stop fighting their sweaters, the dinner bell rang and a noisy, raggedy mob of black-eyed children fell into one silent, neat line in the school yard. They tromped in, one by one, wordlessly knocked the mud off their shoes at the doorstep, hung their threadbare jackets on rows of hooks, and held out their hands as the soap and washrag passed down the line. They scrubbed their hands and faces, then, still in one straight, silent, row, trooped into the dining room. They lined the walls and bowed their heads without being told. Someone said a blessing, then the children, like little tin soldiers, filed onto their benches around the table.

It was then that a bigger boy, the last in line, spoke up. "There's not enough bowls!" he protested in Ojibwa. "Where's mine?"

Some shouting, some scuffling, some shoving and blaming broke out, but the house parents quickly snuffed it with threats of belts and no supper, followed up with extra slaps all around as a reminder to speak English. Whether or not that boy got any soup is a story some other family may be telling now.

After supper, each silent child picked up a task, a dust rag, a broom, a dish towel. Then, at the sound of a bell, they scattered to their sleeping rooms. Again, there was an outcry, this time from a small girl. Her nightgown was missing. She was spanked soundly then put to bed, shivering in her under-drawers.

At breakfast the next morning, the children were short one biscuit. In the school room, the children searched for one more pencil and a lost McGuffey's reader.

It wasn't until halfway through the day that the cause of all this misplacing and miscounting was discovered. The teacher for the primaries didn't live at the school. She was a real teacher, employed by the county, grateful for her job and conscientious in her duties.

"Who is the new little first-grader?" She asked the housemother during afternoon recess. "I don't have any information on her. I need to get her properly enrolled. Did she come yesterday?"

"What? Who do you mean? We haven't had anybody new all month," the housemother answered. She didn't care for the teacher much and relished the idea of catching her in a mistake.

"Yes, the new little one. She was too shy to tell me her name, poor little thing. She's so tiny, too. She doesn't look old enough to be in first grade, but I think she can read already. And she's so clever with music. Watch this."

The teacher called over a small group of children and told them to bring the new little one with them.

The children ran eagerly toward the teacher but skidded to a halt when they saw the house mother standing beside her. Glancing at each other uneasily, they inched forward in a tight little group. But the house mother ignored the bigger ones. She cocked her head. Come to think of it, who *was* that little scrap of a thing? She wasn't one of the Wanatabee girls, was she? She looked more like those Creeks that had come up from somewheres down south last year. But weren't they all bigger than that now? The housemother opened her mouth to ask the girl her name but shut it again when she realized the teacher might not approve of what the housemother liked to call her "business-like mothering system."

"Children, will you sing for Mrs. Crouch? Just do it like you did this morning. It was so lovely."

A timid "Row, Row, Row Your Boat," began unremarkably, but was suddenly transformed into something special and lovely. While the rest of the children doggedly concentrated on the three-part round, a strong, clear voice soared in a high counter-melody above them, the tune new and sweet and unfamiliar, but pitched in perfect harmony. "Merrily, merrily, merrily," were the only words the little girl sang.

"Isn't that the cleverest child? What's her name?" the teacher asked.

"Merrily," snapped the housemother. "Her name is Merrily." Great, the housemother thought. The last thing I need around here is another clever child.

That's it. All the story I have about Merrilee. There should have been more, but nobody seemed willing to share it. There should be the part about Old Rev holding a revival near the Indian school and Merrilee up and running off with him. She would have been about seventeen and he must have been a good ten years older, but I'm sure he was the prettiest thing she'd ever seen, what with that Jasper smile and charm. I bet his life of travel and adventure sounded so glamorous to anonymous, orphaned, maybe-or-maybe-not-an-Indian Merrilee. You'd think that part would be a story, too, but nobody seemed to have a word to say about it.

"Did your mom have to sneak off, or was she allowed to go? Did your dad sweep her off her feet, or was she just anxious to leave the school? Did they have a wedding? Where did they get married? What do you mean you never asked?" I pestered JW. "How can you not be curious? Your parents *eloped*! How romantic! This is your *history*! I can't believe you aren't even interested!"

He'd only shrugged. "I dunno. They never said much about it."

I thought about Merrilee's story and it wore on me until I finally broke down, gave in and pulled the paper she had given me out of my pocket. She had been acting weirdly out of character, almost pushy, so she must have felt very strongly that I needed to read it. I gave in. I unfolded it and the first thing I noticed was the handwritten note at the top. *For tonight*, it said, in Old Rev's hand. *S has to be ready 7:25. M brings her in after R sits — don't forget rabbit.*

What in the world?

I read the first paragraph, re-read it, grasped its meaning, and was afraid I was going to be sick.

I grabbed Susannah with both hands, swung her back up onto my hip and ran toward the lumber yard.

I had to get JW to stop this. I had to make him see sense. I had to get him to take us home.

Tonight.

Chapter
Twenty-two

I found JW in the hardware store, piddling up and down the aisles, carefully considering every last nut and bolt. "Hi, Sweethearts," he said to us. "How's my girls?" He was always happiest in a hardware store. Susannah, sensing my more dangerous mood, decided to lean away from me and held her arms out to JW. Flattered that she was preferring him for once, he held out his hands and she scrambled into them. I ignored their angelic, identical grins, planted my feet in front of JW and waved the sermon notes in front of his face.

"Do you know about this?" I demanded.

He was taken aback. I never talked to him like that. "What? What are you talking about?" He didn't even look at the paper in my hands. He looked, thoroughly befuddled, at me instead. "What do you mean?"

I pinched my mouth together and held the page up in his face. "This!" I jabbed at the words. "This right here. Did you know about this? Did you approve of this?" Please say no, JW, I silently begged. Please say no, of course not, you'd never agree to your daughter being used like this.

Please say you knew nothing about it, but you'll go take care of it Right This Minute. Please say that. Please.

He glanced at the writing; his confusion disappeared, and his cheeks flushed pink. His eyes darted away from me.

Oh, Dear God.

JW already knew about it. He was going along with it. Even though he knew better, he was going along with it because that's what Old Rev told him to do. "Ruby Fae..." he put one tentative hand on my arm.

"What?" I hissed. "What are you going to say that could possibly justify this treatment of your own daughter?" Susannah's little brow wrinkled in confusion. She'd never seen me so angry, poor baby.

"It's not like it's going to hurt her. And she's so little, she won't understand what's going on, or even remember it." JW said.

"For now!" I snapped. "But what about later, when she is old enough?"

"Oh, I doubt we will be still doing it then. You know how Dad likes to keep things fresh. He'll be on to the next trick before she even understands what's going on. Really, it's not that big of a deal."

"*Not that big a deal?*" I exploded, flinging my arms into a shelf of spray paint and sending them clattering all over the aisle.

Susannah shrieked in terror and buried her face in JW's shoulder. "Pick that mess up, Ruby," JW snarled as he turned on his heel and ducked into the rows of the storm door display.

"You alright over there?" the clerk at the cash register and the customer he was helping both turned to look at me.

"Oh, I'm fine! I'm so sorry, I'll get this picked right up."

"No, no; just leave it. Are you sure you're alright?"

I assured him I was alright, he assured me he was glad I was alright, his customer assured us he was in no hurry, alright, and I finally convinced them both to continue their transaction while I got down on my knees and considered the differences between "Green," "Hunter Green," and "Pine Green." Over by the storm doors, I heard JW playing a world-class game of peek-a-boo with Susannah. Her belly laugh steadied me; maybe I hadn't permanently traumatized her. Yet. As I began lining the cans of paint in precise rows, my mind returned to my real dilemma — how to prevent Susannah from beginning her new role as BORN TO SIN: EXHIBIT A.

I had to get her out of this. Out of here. Home.

How?

Every little town has a bus stop somewhere, I reminded myself. Can you get on a bus without a ticket and get someone to pay for it on the other end? Like you're a collect call or a COD package? I'd never heard of anything like that, but then again, I wasn't up on a lot of things in the world.

While I mourned the loss of the sixty dollars from mom and my bus ticket as a fresh, sharp grief, something from the exchange at the counter reached my ear.

"You wouldn't happen to have a counter check from Guymon, would you?" the customer asked.

"Guymon," the clerk said. "That's a little out of our territory, but I think maybe I've got one. You from there?" He brought the counter-top sorting rack over in front of him and rifled through the variously-colored pads of promotional checks from dozens of different banks.

A counter check. I never thought of that. I'd seen

counter-checks from Salt Fork State by the register as far away as Wichita and Oklahoma City. If they had one from a Guymon, Oklahoma, bank all the way up in Colorado, maybe, maybe, they also had one from the Salt Fork bank, a measly hundred and fifty miles on past Guymon. It was a long shot, but, still.

"Yep, from Guymon," said the customer. "My sister lives here, though. Her husband is in the hospital, and I came up here to help her out a little. I want to get a ramp built today before he gets home tomorrow."

"You're not talking about Huey Randall, are you? Your sister married to him?" The clerk asked as he tossed a light pink check pad to him. "Here you go. I thought I might have seen one. Sometimes when the Wheaties come through here on harvest they need supplies, so I never throw these things away."

"Thank you," the customer said and began printing his bank account number in the box along the bottom edge of the check. "Yep, Huey's my brother-in-law. Terrible, terrible accident. And that seed-wheat outfit is trying not to pay them a dime." He shook his head, filled out the amount and date on the check and asked, "You need a phone number or address or anything on this?"

"Oh, no, no. If you're kin to Huey, you're fine," the clerk assured him. "You need any help building that ramp? It's slow today. I can send Eb out there, you'd get 'er did in no time with an extra hand. He's loafing, as it is." He jabbed his thumb over his shoulder, indicating the teenaged boy outside loading what must be the lumber for Huey's new wheel-chair ramp into a half-ton Ford pickup. While the two men made arrangements for unsuspecting Eb's day, JW came alongside me. He handed Susannah back to me, picked up a bottle of wood glue, and went to the counter.

I followed, hoping to get a peek at the selection of counter checks.

The newly-injured Huey Randall's helpful and honest-looking brother-in-law left, and JW and I stepped up with his purchases, a handful of various scrap woods, a package of fine grit sandpaper, and wood glue. When it was all rung up, he pulled his checkbook out of his back pocket. He probably had plenty of cash on him, but anything that could possibly be claimed as a ministry expense was paid for through the tax-free ministry checking account.

"Do you have some ID on you, son?" the man behind the counter asked him. JW pulled his driver's license out of his wallet. "How about your Federal Tax ID number? You got any paperwork to prove that's valid? You have that on you?" His tone was pleasant, but his message was firm; you and your check look shady to me.

JW fished another card out of his wallet. The counterman placed it beside the driver's license and studied it as well. He copied JW's address and license number on the memo line of the check. Meanwhile, to pass the time and fill his hands with something, JW reached for Susannah.

"Hey, Sweetie," he said to her. "Wanna come back to Daddy?" I swear, he could sound so normal sometimes.

"So, you folks are from Iowa, then?" the counterman asked JW personally. JW looked startled for a second, as though he were caught in a lie. Yes, JW's legal address is Mrs. Gibley's house in Iowa City. But where he's from? That's a good question.

"Uh, yes. Yes, we are. We are the revival team at Prairie View Holiness all this week."

The counterman was still holding JW's check. "How about a phone number?" he asked.

"We don't have a phone. We live in a bus." JW said.

This was not the correct answer. The counterman scratched behind his ear. "So you're down at the Holiness church, then? Reverend Baker will vouch for you?"

"Yes," JW assured him. "We would love for you to come to a service, if you've got a few free hours. Starts at seven." The clerk finally put the check in the till, but clearly, he still had his doubts. Amazing. One man strolls in here, no ID, no address or phone number, and writes an IOU for fifty dollars on a paper that is really nothing more than an advertisement from an out-of-state bank, and it's as good as cash. But JW, a minister of the cloth, with a pre-printed business check, a local pastor for a reference, a federal tax number and commercial driver's license can hardly spend six bucks. Are some people gifted with a super-power that enables them to determine a person's level of integrity at a glance?

Or was it that JW's character flaws were stupendously obvious to everyone but me?

JW passed Susannah back to me and picked up his bagged purchases, but Susannah decided Daddy was where she wanted to ride and leaned back over to him. Thinking of the long walk back to the bus, I didn't argue but instead traded Susannah for the bag.

"Thanks," the counterman said. "I appreciate the invite. I'll ask the wife if she's got plans for me tonight. You know how that goes."

JW smiled and nodded in an "aren't-we-a-couple-a-good-ol-boys way", as though he had the vaguest notion of the kind of marriage this guy was talking about.

We smiled and waved our way out the door.

Neither of us talked as we walked past the IGA, the town hall, and the one-room City Library. JW had nothing to say because he considered our fight over. He'd declared himself the winner, of course. I had nothing to say because I was trying to figure out how to get Susannah out of town before church started that night. We were more than halfway back when JW suddenly stopped. "Oh, shoot! My driver's license!"

We stopped and both looked at the long walk back to the hardware store. Then we both looked at our beautiful baby, sweet, solid and heavy in her sleep.

And I knew. Here it was. My chance. I calculated the risk.

And decided to take it.

"JW, she is going to get so heavy. Why don't you go on to the bus and put her down? I'll run back and get your license. It'll only take me a sec."

JW hesitated, looked up and down the street. "I hate to leave you all alone in a strange place." Oh, honestly. What was going to happen to me here? I might get side-swiped by a tumbleweed. "Well, I guess it would be alright," he said, reluctantly.

"Of course it will. I'll be fine." I said, and, for good measure, stood on tip-toe to kiss his cheek. "Go put Susannah in her bed. I'll be right back." I hooked the bag of wood scraps around his finger.

The kiss did it. He relented, kissed me twice more, warned me to watch for traffic, looked once more to see no one was watching, patted me on the behind, and finally, finally, turned to leave. I made for the lumber yard, trying to walk at precisely the right pace. I didn't turn to look, but I was certain he stopped and turned to watch me at least twice before I got to the lumber yard.

At the hardware store, the door closed behind me and

the jangly string of bells hanging from it sounded as sweet as the peals of the Liberty Bell to me.

The clerk saw me and smiled. He reached under the counter and handed me JW's license and tax ID card. "I thought you'd be back." He said. "Sorry I asked so many questions before. I'm in the habit of being extra-cautious. You never know, these days."

I smiled and said something pleasant, then I asked, all cool and nonchalant, "Do you have any more counter checks from Oklahoma? My husband is from Iowa, but I'm from Salt Fork."

The suspicious look came back. "Well, I don't know, Salt Fork, where is that? In the Panhandle?"

"Oh, I wasn't going to write it to you. I need to mail it. I want to order my husband a birthday present from the catalog, but I ran out of my own checks. Will Montgomery Ward still take a counter check?" I shone an innocent smile on him.

It worked. "Oh, yeah, sure. The wife trades with Monkey Ward all the time, and she uses a counter check." Apparently, he felt that Monkey Ward could fend for themselves when it came to check fraud crimes. He spun the rack around toward me and I looked through it. Sure enough, Guymon was the closest bank. I knew it was a long shot.

I thanked him and turned to leave, but he said, "Wait a second. Let me look under here. I forgot this handful of old ones." He dipped down under the counter and came up with a shoe-box lid filled with a rainbow of loose checks. I flipped through them, praying; and oh, Heavenly Day! There it was! The familiar little black diamond logo on the harvest-gold background of Salt Fork State's free checks. Thank you, Jesus and Salt Fork State!

Outside on the sidewalk again, I looked both ways, sprinted back down the street to the bank and skidded to a stop inside the big brass-edged double doors.

I had been in a lot of different banks in a lot of different cities, tagging along on JW's errands. Most of them were all gleaming steel, glass, and tile with modern, airy designs that crooned, *don't worry, sophisticated customer! We are current in style and practice! We are modern! We are on top of things!*

Not this bank. Here, the counter was worn, the floor was scuffed, and the dim globed lights hung from ancient, lazy ceiling fans. The dark wood planks halfway up the wall met a giant, dusty, bigger-than-life mural of a cattle round-up and next to the door, a row of wire loops mounted on a sign reading Stetson — Made to Last a Lifetime (Rack provided for your convenience, courtesy Morton Bros Tack & Supply) held two straw hats. This bank's style didn't soothe; it barked. *What? You want fancy, or you want solid? We're not going anywhere, and neither is your money. Sit down. How's your folks?*

I stepped up to a teller window where the name plate read Midge Fulton and, as I filled out my check with the chained-down ink pen, told Midge, oh-so-casually, "I'd like to cash a check, please."

Midge had a squinchy-nosed smile that was probably cute one, and only the one, time, so she was stuck with it now. Her facial die had been cast, and this was the smile she had been dealt. "Are you a customer here?" She chirped.

"No, but I thought maybe you could do something...it really is an emergency situation."

I handed Midge the check, written on my Dad's

account, for one hundred dollars. I'd pay him back, somehow, when I got home.

"Well, there is, possibly, but it would take a few days, until it's cleared."

"A few days?"

"Maybe a week to ten days, in some circumstances."

"Oh, No! No, that's too long! Ten days? I can't wait ten days!" My pitch rose. I was already in trouble. I had about ten minutes left, tops, before JW came looking for me. "It has to be today! Now!"

Squinching the central features of her face still smaller, Midge said, "Let me see what I can do." She stepped out from behind the counter and entered the largest glass office where a sturdy man with a gray handlebar mustache sat behind a desk reading a local newspaper.

I watched anxiously as she showed him my check, said something, and they both looked at me. He waved me in.

"Sit down, sit down, Miss Jasper." He pointed to a seat and I obeyed. I started to correct him that it's Mrs., not Miss, but I stopped. I had no ID on me except JW's. What if he wanted me to get JW to vouch for me? Sweat began collecting under my shirt sleeve. I was on borrowed time, and this was a stupid idea in the first place. "You want a Coke?" he asked.

Hoping to appear relaxed, I said, "Yes, please, thanks."

He waved my thanks away. "Get us Cokes, Midge."

Midge skittered to the door, but stopped to ask me, "What kind of Coke do you want?"

"Do you have 7-UP?" I asked. In my head, I ticked off the seconds and imagined JW watching for my return.

She assured me she did, indeed, have 7-Up and retreated on clickety heels. A desk nameplate said Butch

Wilberton, Bank President, belonged in this office, so I assumed this man across from me was Mr. Wilberton.

"Well, now, Miss Jasper," he said, "You can appreciate my position; I need to make sure everything is in order. That's what the shareholders give me my peanuts for. So don't take this personal, but I'll need to make a phone call, then we can get you on your way."

He pulled open a drawer in his desk and brought out a flat red Prince Albert tobacco can. He shook out a pile of business cards onto his blotter, shuffled them like dominoes, then settled on a particularly worn and frayed one. He adjusted it to an angle that told me he damned well did not need reading glasses, no matter how much the girls nagged him about it, then grunted and pulled his black desk phone closer. He picked up the receiver and dialed, watching me, unsmiling.

Midge appeared and set a tray on the desk between us. Two icy bottles, one a Dr. Pepper, the other a 7-Up, both opened, flanked one sweaty glass of ice. I wasn't sure what to do, so I waited. Besides, I didn't want them to see my hands shake.

Someone on the other end of the phone must have answered, because Mr. Wilberton rumbled, "Yeah. Let me talk to that land-thief in the corner office, if he's not too busy."

Pause.

"Tell him it's Butch, in Spring City."

Pause. He allowed a begrudging "Thanks. You're a good girl."

Longer pause. He looked at me and motioned that I should take the glass of ice. He picked up the bottle of Dr. Pepper and rocked back in his chair. I care-ful-ly began pouring my pop into the glass.

"Yeah, it's me. You too busy screwing widows and skinning orphans to talk to me?"

Pause.

"When hell freezes over. Now listen, I got a young lady here in my bank who wants to write a counter check on your outfit, so I wanted to make sure it's good. I know you clowns can barely keep your asses out of jail as it is, and I don't want you dragging me in on it."

Pause.

"Account number's 04-339-15, name's Ruby Fae Jasper."

I waved wildly, shaking my head, holding my ring finger up, "McKeever!" I interrupted. "Jasper's my married name! They know me by McKeever!"

"Hold up!" he said into the phone, "Hold up, says her maiden name is McKeever. That name any good to you?"

Long pause. Mr. Wilberton raked his eyes over me, from the top of my head down to my shoes and back up again to my eyes. "Uh-huh," he said to the phone, "Kinda red, yeah." He lowered the receiver an inch to talk to me. "What's your daddy's brand?"

"Walking K!" I shot back at him. I saw a flicker of something good happen with his face and hope began to stir.

Mr. Wilberton repeated my answer into the phone, paused, then said, "Oh, you are a hardass if ever I saw one! You think she got ahold of a County Cattlemen's Association Directory from three hundred miles away, memorized the names and brands?" Pause. "What the hell?" Pause. "Oh, alright, already." The hope shriveled again as Mr. Wilberton concluded his phone call with, "Yeah, you, too, ya son-of-a-bitch. Yeah, it's been too long." Pause. "You oughta come up here and see me instead, if your Momma'll let you outta the house." Pause.

"You're not a bad hand yourself, but don't repeat that." He hung the phone up, giving it one last fond look.

He looked up at me now — but wait! Was that a smile fighting out from under his handlebar? "Sorry about that, but you understand. Mr. Radford at Salt Fork State has his responsibilities, too. He wanted me to ask you one more question to verify your identity, though." He waited.

"Of course. Of course, I understand." It was going to work! He was talking to red-faced Jimmy Radford's dad, who must've said told him they'd cover my check! Thank you, thank you, Jesus!

"Mr. Radford said to ask you how Jimmy likes his steak."

Everybody in town knows this one. "Chicken fried, smothered and covered."

Mr. Wilburton smiled for real then, all bluster and growl gone, and said, "That's the right answer." He held the check up and nodded to Midge, who had been watching us through the window. While she scurried in to us, he said to me, "Is a hundred enough? Radford said to take care of you, make sure you had whatever you needed."

"Yes! Thanks! Thanks! That's all the money I need! Everything is going to be fine now!" I considered hugging Mr. Wilburton but settled for giving him fifteen or sixteen "thank-yous" instead.

He waved them off. "Nah, Sis, if Radford says you're good for it, it's good enough for me. Are you sure you're alright, though? If you don't mind me saying, you look mighty young to be so far from home and in need of money. You in touch with your folks? They know where you are?"

"Now that you mention it, if it's not too much trouble, could I possibly use your phone? I'll call collect. I promise they'll accept."

He pushed the phone across the desk to me. "Call direct. My shareholders are decent Christians, every one of them; they won't likely begrudge one little prodigal girl's call back home to her daddy." He pushed back his chair and put his hands on the armrests. "I'll give you some privacy."

I shook my head. "No, thanks; this will only take a second. I need to tell them when to meet the bus, is all." I was grinning from ear to ear as I dialed. "Oh," I remembered to ask Mr.Wilberton as I waited for the call to go through, "Do you know where and when the bus stops in this town?"

The phone was ringing. I couldn't wait to talk to the folks.

Mr. Wilburton looked both pleased and relieved. "Leaves from the old Texaco, the one across from the Dairy-Dog, every evening around eight."

Perfect. "Thanks," I mouthed, as the phone rang for the fifth time. In a second, I'd be telling Mom I'm on my way!

But no one answered. I let it ring and ring. I was a little disappointed, but not worried. Mom may be in the field, or maybe she and Dad went to town together, or any number of places. Really, it wasn't a big deal. Mr. Wilburton, however, looked concerned. "It's OK," I reassured him, "I'll be home by morning." I jumped up to leave, still thanking him.

Chapter
Twenty-three

I ran the length of Main Street and braked to a stop when I reached the church's sidewalk. Catching my breath, I straightened my buttoned-down cotton shirt and tucked the tail of it into my jeans. Smoothed a stray hair. There we go. Nothing out of place. I looked up and down the street. Still deserted. I checked my posture, my facial expression, aiming for agreeable, neutral. *Feels about right.* Ok; ready, set, go. I strolled around the corner of the building toward the back parking lot, casual as any pleasure-walker who ever lolly-gagged down a small-town street, maybe petting every stray kitty and admiring every blooming Zinnia.

I even hummed a little *What a Friend We Have in Jesus* as I looked in the window of the bus door. I didn't see JW anywhere, but Old Rev was still seated at the dinette with his typewriter, banging away. I didn't want to interrupt him, but I was surprised that Susannah could sleep through the noise. I wanted to peek at her, and then I'd get her diaper bag ready. Old Rev wouldn't pay any attention to me fiddling with her baby stuff. I could pack right under his nose. For a fleeting moment, I imagined yanking the crumpled sermon page from my pocket and telling Old Rev exactly what I thought of his little "object lesson," but there was no need to push things. Not anymore.

I swung up the bus steps and Old Rev didn't even look up as I passed. Stopping at the bunks, the first thing I noticed was that JW hadn't latched the rails back. How irresponsible! If Susannah rolled into the bars and fell, she'd have a four-foot drop to the floor! The next thing I noticed was her blanket, flat and empty on her mattress.

I jerked the blanket out so fast that it whipped up a breeze big enough to disturb Old Rev's papers.

"Where is Susannah?" I demanded. "Where is she? Where is my baby?" I flapped the blanket again and the rest of the pages went flying. My voice cracked and shrilled. "*Where is my baby?*"

Old Rev stared at me, motionless, his eyes narrowed but the rest of him unchanged. I lunged for his table, possibly with the plan of throwing his Smith-Corona at him, but he put one hand up to halt me, saying, "Ruby, she is fine. She's with JW, in the church. He's setting up the sound for tonight. You left her with her father, or did you forget? Did you think you'd misplaced your child?"

A slow hiss of air escaped from me like a punctured tire. "Oh. I, uhm, No. I'm, well, very sorry. I didn't mean to interrupt your writing." *What is wrong with you Ruby Fae? You are so, so close; the bus leaves in a few hours. Don't blow it now!* My hand, unbidden, skimmed over the curved stitching of the front pocket of my Levi's and I was comforted by the thought of the bus money. Only a few hours. Steady yourself, girl.

I looked down at Old Rev's papers scattered all over the bus floor.

"I'm so sorry," I said meekly as I knelt to gather them. "I'll put them all back together for you."

Old Rev said nothing, merely got up and came around the table to help me. We worked together for several minutes, picking them all up and stacking them loosely. We got a little system going, me, picking them and reading the page numbers, him putting them in order. He was surprisingly cooperative. When I thought we had them all, I got back to my feet beside him and waited for him to finish counting and move out of the aisle.

"Thank you for your help, Ruby Fae," he said. "But wait, I don't see page forty. Do you see it anywhere?" He looked around. I did, too, but I didn't see it.

"Oh! There!" Old Rev pointed behind me. "It flew in there. Can you step in there and get it for me?" he asked. Eager to please him and get on with things, I turned around and stepped into the bathroom to look for the missing page.

He closed the door behind me.

Funny, how I saw it on the reflection of my face in the mirror, actually watched as the fear blanched my face white; it's funny how my body knew before my brain interpreted the sound that my ears had sent to it, the sound of Old Rev flipping the traveling latch in place, locking me in the bathroom.

"Reverend Jasper?" I asked, making the words sound timid, polite, and submissive. Nausea, vertigo, and panic threatened to overwhelm me. I screwed my eyes shut tight, tapped on the door. "Reverend? Sir? The door seems to have locked? Sir? Can you, please, help me?"

No answer. Footsteps. The whoosh of the bus door releasing. Closing again. He was gone. I was alone, locked in this windowless closet of a bathroom.

I'm trapped. I can't breathe. I will suffocate.

My vision went fuzzy around the edges, I could only see the glaring white walls pressing in on me, closer and closer until they scraped on my eyeballs.

I can't breathe. I'm choking. No, I'm not; I'm panicking. No; I really am, I'm really choking on something. My own terror, it's a real thing, a hard thing; it's a big clay dirt clod, lodged in my throat.

I heaved, was sick, didn't come close to hitting the tiny bowl of the sink. The stuffy air was now also filled with the smell of my own vomit. I heaved again and again until my guts ached. My breaths came shallow and fast. *I'm suffocating. This isn't even a room, it's a slippery, white, upright coffin.* My shaky legs gave out, and I slid down, landing halfway on the toilet lid. I rested my face against the slick plastic wall and gave in to the dizziness, the blackness closing in on me. I was grateful for this gift. Thank you God, for letting me faint, was my last rational thought.

I was hysterical when I came to. I pounded and yelled, pounded and yelled. I rattled the door, jiggled the latch, slammed at it with my body. No response. I worried about the air supply. Be logical, I thought. The Silver Eagle company wouldn't build a space that is meant to be a room, a bathroom, that is meant to be used with the door closed, that was air tight, would they? They wouldn't expect you to shower in a refrigerator shell. Then why couldn't I breathe? I pounded and yelled some more. I'm running out of air; no, I can't be. I tried to reason, but my thinking was muddled. Darkness fell behind my eyes again.

I surfaced again, tried the door, and screamed for help, my voice hoarse, my mouth foul. No sound, no movement from the bus. Where is everyone? What if something happened, an emergency? A car wreck? Would anyone think to look for me here? Wilder thoughts than that come to me. A tornado, and the bus has been carried miles away, where no one can find it. The bus was repossessed, and I'm stuck on a used bus lot. The rapture. Looks like the last joke's on me. I never was born in the first place; this is the in-between world. I'm already dead. I smelled like it, anyway; probably I am, already. Dead. Already Dead.

No. I will not faint again. I won't. I closed my eyes and instantly felt better.

But it reeks in here. I gagged on the thick, putrid air.

My eyes still closed, I slapped around the wall until I found a towel hanging from a hook and wrapped it lightly around my head. That helped. I considered opening my eyes again, but thought about it and decided not to. I plunked back down on the toilet lid to wait, listening hard to the silent bus.

I thought about Jonah, stuck in the belly of the whale for three days. This was better than whale innards, right? I thought about some old-time McKeever, was it Great-Great-Grandpa Jack's father? He was a nine-year-old orphan stowaway from Dublin who cut holes in a steamer trunk and rode to America in it. I wondered how much of that story is true. I thought about Pop Fletch assuring me that no, Santa was not afraid to go down all those chimneys, he slides through so fast there's no time to get stuck. I thought about the time I fainted in an elevator, and how Dad had rubbed my back, saying, "You weren't meant to be holed up, that's all. You're a flatland girl, born and bred for the High Plains. You like to see what's coming at you, and plenty of room to meet it. No shame in that."

I listened hard. Is someone out there?

Yes. There was. I knocked. Not crazy-wild knocking, but normal, tap-tap-tap knocking. I slipped the towel off my mouth and it fell somewhere down in the mess on the floor. The smell rushed back. "Hello?" I croaked. I cleared my throat and tried again. "I seem to be stuck. Can you help me?" I jiggled the door handle up and down. "Hello?"

They were out there! I could hear them all, even Susannah! I pounded on the door, and Susannah cried "Mama." Scuffles, murmurs, Susannah crying.

"JW! Let me out! Let me out!" I hollered and pounded.

"John Wesley, can you get control of your family, or will I have to do it for you?" Old Rev thundered.

Susannah was in a high-pitched frenzy and I was wild with fear. I had to get to her. "Let me out!" I shrieked, rattling and pounding. Susannah screamed for me. I screamed and pounded back.

Lunging at the door, I threw my body at it, howling with rage. The hinges creaked, the flimsy wood door cracked, but before I could get enough momentum to break through it, JW leaned back against me, on the other side of the door. "You're scaring Susannah," he bellowed at me. "You have to calm down. She needs a mother who will be a good example for her, a meek and quiet spirit, not some hysterical shrew. Listen to her! See what you're teaching her?"

My eyes still clamped shut, I walked my feet up the opposite wall, wedged my legs against it and pushed away, against the door with all my strength. Susannah was screaming. So was I. I bowed my back against the door, against JW, against the world. But on the other side of the door, JW propped his leg against the refrigerator across the aisle and easily counterbalanced me.

"You really wanna do it this way, Ruby Fae? Huh? You think you are stronger than me?"

OK, ok, ok, be calm, Ruby. He's right. Think. You're not stronger than JW, not strong like that, anyway.

I dropped my legs and leaned away from the door, listening.

Easy, Ruby. And do not open your eyes. I counted to three, in-out, in-out, in-out. I heard Merrilee trying to comfort Susannah. "Jesus loves the little chil-dren; all the children of the world," she sang softly. Some more murmuring, some sounds of movement, things being shuffled around. Susannah's volume gradually decreased.

JW continued. "Is this how you want your daughter behaving? Really, Ruby? You're a terrible example of gentleness and womanhood."

I tried to make my voice sound serene, calm. "Yes, yes. You're right. I've been terrible. But I'll be a good example from now on. You'll see. Please. Let me out. I'll be so good. I will." If I waited for JW to move, I could try to break the door again. It's a flimsy camper door. I'd already cracked it. I had to get the timing right and I was sure I could bust it down.

JW tapped the door with his fingers, drumming a light rhythm, considering. "Perhaps. We'll see. Maybe after you've both composed yourselves." JW leaned very close to the crack in the door, trying not to be overheard. "You really upset Dad," he whined. "You got all crazy on him for no reason. You frightened him. And you interrupted his writing!"

Then he moved back "Thanks," he said to someone else. Then the door shuddered, like JW was slamming something against it.

"Stand away from the door, Ruby. I mean it." That voice. When he used that voice, it was bad.

Shaking with fear, I scrambled back, away from the door and against the outside wall of the bus. Two fast hammer blows rang out and the whole bus rocked from the force. A pause. Two more blows. I forced open my eyes and saw the points of nails coming through the wall on either side of the door jamb. Nails. He was nailing me in. Nails.

He nailed me in.

Like a dead woman in a coffin.

I vomited again. And again.

I retched one more ugly, noisy dry heave and JW's footsteps beat a hasty retreat. He can't handle illness or bodily messes. The bus door whooshed open and closed again as he fled, but I heard Old Rev and Merrilee still on the bus, moving, talking, sounding ho-hum, another-day normal.

I pulled my feet up, hugged my knees, dropped my head and made my body into a tight little knot.

Oh God, Oh God, Oh God. Help me. Oh God, Oh God, Oh God. Help me.

I rocked and whispered. Help me.

I rocked and prayed my repetitious little chant until it became a monotonous, hypnotic, droning. I heard the words hum in my throat. Felt my breathing become a steady rhythm that fell into timing with my rocking. Heard the soft hiss of air in and out my nose.

I lost track of time.

Gradually I became aware again of the sounds on the other side of the door. Merrilee, whisking an iron across cloth. Old Rev, crinkling a newspaper. Susannah, settling down with her toys. I will not cry out again as long as she is still on the bus, I vowed. I didn't want her hearing me and crying for me. I also resolved not to black out again. Or open my eyes. I unfolded my legs, testing them. I could stand. I groped for the shower head and snapped it out of its bracket. Pulling the hose down to the direction of the smell, I turned on the water and blindly washed down the walls and sink. I stripped off my shirt and sprayed water over my face and down my chest, soaking my bra but stopping at my jeans when I remembered the money in the front pocket. I didn't want it to get wet. I still stank, but a slightly less powerful stink. I rinsed my mouth out and tried to drink, but the water didn't sit well on my empty stomach. On the other side of the wall, I heard Old Rev and Merrilee converse in pleasant tones. I could make out what they're talking about. Ordinary, everyday church stuff. Susannah clomped around in the aisle of the bus banging a toy. I ached for her, but I refused to make a noise. The stench in the bathroom was nearly unbearable. I made a filter out of toilet paper and held it to my nose.

I can do this. I can do this. Just keep my eyes closed and wait them out. They have to let me out eventually, right?

I have to be strong, that's all.

I opened one eye, just a sliver, as a test.

Nope. I squeezed it back shut, against the dizzying whiteness.

I'll have to amuse myself with my mind.

God, help me.

A memory comes to me. A class field trip, to the Gloss Mountains. I was, maybe, ten. It was before the state cleared a path and built the stairs to the top. Mom had gone with us as a parent sponsor. Leland was there too, because both of our grades had gone.

In my mind, I replayed the trip in detail. How we first

glimpsed on the horizon the Martian landscape of the barren red dirt cliffs, salted with glittering shards of selenite that dazzled like the finest chandelier when the morning sun hit the perfect angle and the busload of children said, "Ohhhhh." How could it be that this jewel of immeasurable size and worth had existed, all along, not fifty miles as the crow flies, from our own familiar, flat, dusty home?

In this bus, here, now, I heard Merrilee ask Old Rev if the water was hooked up, or were we still using what's left in the reserve?

"No, the hose won't reach." Old Rev said loudly. "And I was thinking, anyway, that maybe this would be a good time to clean out the tank. I haven't in quite a while. I'll go drain all the water in a minute, so I can get that done."

He's only trying to scare you, Ruby, I hoped. To be safe, though, I blindly slapped around in the sink to make sure it was clean, popped in the plug and filled the sink with clear water. Susannah sang a little tune, whumped her little hands against the bathroom door, then scuffled away. She'd already forgotten I was in there. Tears welled up in my eyes. *Don't! Don't you cry, Ruby Fae McKeever. Don't you do it. You'll dehydrate. Stop it.*

Gloss Mountains, Gloss Mountains. The first time I saw Gloss Mountains. Think about that.

We climbed up the side, clawing in the red dirt. Which, up close, didn't look quite as glittery, but you could still find some good-sized glass-like slivers. Up close, you could also see that the ground wasn't really barren at all but teeming with life; red ants had established intricate systems of well-traveled highways, thousands of miles of tiny trails webbing out for their secret, important insect purposes that were none of our human business. Horny toads defended clumps of dirt, bluffing to the death with their puffed-up bodies and blood-spitting eyeballs. In front of their twig nests, tucked in crevices and crags, Rock Wrens tidied pebbles and shaped their little front porches.

As we kids grabbed at clods and clumps and outcroppings on the hillside, scrambling for footholds and leaving our handprints, we kept a sharp lookout for a cactus, a scorpion, a beer can or a snake hole; anything dangerous enough to be interesting. And then, when at last we had clambered our way to the top, that was where we knew, where we discovered our true destination, the real reason for this trip. As our reward for reading twenty-five books, our teachers had brought us to Heaven.

Gloss Mountains are puny by Colorado-lovers' standards, not even real mountains. They are mesas, really. They don't come to a peak, they lop off into an infinite, native-grass-covered plateau. But that's OK, you don't go there for the mountains. You go for the sky.

The sky, the sky, the sky; that's what I'm trying to remember right now, that's what I'm trying to wrap up around me. If I can just concentrate on the sky, I'll be ok. I won't suffocate. I won't panic. I won't wither and die. I have to remember the sky. *O! The land of a cloudless day! O! The land of an unclouded sky!*

That endless afternoon on Gloss Mountain, I lay back in the Buffalo Grass and watched the shimmery smoke of a blackbird flock waft across the sky above me. I tracked a lone hawk as it soared. I turned my head north and south and east and west and saw nothing but sky. First Leland and then Mom wandered into my quiet world I'd staked and dropped, silent, to the ground beside me. I wondered if they, too, noticed that the blue was not simply one shade but delicately graded with each degree up from the horizon. I didn't ask. Eventually, Leland spoke. He said, "I like it here. There's nothing between you and God. Nothing He can hide behind."

This time, when I remembered that I was still locked in a closet, I don't think I passed out, I think I just fell asleep.

Chapter
Twenty-four

I woke up stiff-muscled but with a clearer head. Still furious. Still stinky. Ferociously thirsty. But I was alive, and I was thinking, which was better than I had hoped for the last time I checked. I unfolded my body while straining my ears for sound. The bus seemed empty, but I wasn't certain. Splashing some tepid water from the sink onto my face, I tested the faucet. There was still water, that liar. When I cupped my hands under it and brought the fresh water into my mouth, it didn't come back up, but I still kept my eyes closed. Somewhere under my feet in the guts of the bus the electric water pump switched on, then off again. Another noise, a motor-hum, one that had been in the background for a while whirred softly. It was the bathroom vent fan. That shows you how panicked I was earlier; I didn't even think to hit the switch, right there, by the door, for more air. How stupid of me.

Wait a minute.

I didn't think to hit the switch.

Then who did?

While I was passed out, somebody had opened the door, flipped on the switch, and then closed the door again.

How thoughtful. How Jasper-branded, backhanded, self-righteous, almighty thoughtful.

Wait a minute.

Lightly skimming my fingers along the wall by the door frame, I discovered two jagged holes. I opened my eyes. The nails. They were gone. I tried the door.

It wasn't locked.

Stumbling out into the aisle of the empty bus and gulping hard enough to pop my lungs, I lunged at the nearest window. It wouldn't open, but I could see out and that was enough. Through the window, I could see the rest of Jasper family. Starched and pressed, bathed in the glow of a late-day sun, their golden heads crowning them like the holy family in an old masters' painting, the Jaspers strolled, hand-in-hand with my baby between them, up the walk to the church steps. Picture perfect, right off the cover of my childhood Sunday School Quarterlies. You'd never know they were crazy by looking at them.

The kitchen clock mounted over the stovetop showed six o'clock. I had been locked in the bathroom for almost four hours. Well, I had been *in* the bathroom for that long, and for some of that time it was locked.

Wasn't it?

Locked? It was locked, Right? I didn't just imagine it was locked, did I?

Was I the crazy one here?

No, there's the nail holes. See? I'm not crazy.

Through the window I watched the Jaspers disappear into the church.

Never mind them. What mattered was that I still could make the evening bus. I would get ready, collect Susannah from the nursery, and slip away. Then, like Roy Clark sings it, Thank God and Greyhound, I'm Gone.

I propped the bathroom door open with the diaper bag and hesitated. The thought of going back in there was almost too much, but the smell of my own sweat and vomit left me little choice. I sprayed the bathroom down with cleanser, rinsed it off with the hand-held shower nozzle, then stripped down. Tossing my clothes in a rank heap on the bus floor, I jumped into the shower. But I scrubbed fast, leaving the bathroom door wide open and one foot in the hall all the while.

I was getting out, wrapping a towel around me when JW popped in. He was all bouncy, cheery. "Are you alright?" he asked, concerned. "I turned the fan on for you, so you could have some air while you napped."

What? While *I* *napped?* Napped? Did he actually say while I "napped?" I was incredulous, but I bit my tongue. You mean, while I was buried alive and passed out from lack of oxygen, I wanted to say. But I didn't. Instead I said, "Yes. I am fine. Just fine."

He was watching me dry off and put on underwear, but I wouldn't meet his eye.

He lounged against the refrigerator, watching me open the closet, take out my dress, lay it on the bed. "Is Merrilee wearing the flowered scarf tonight?" I asked him as I plucked a pair of panty hose out of my drawer. Of course he didn't know which scarf, so he offered to go check with Merrilee and report back to me. First, though, he grabbed my wrist and gently pulled me closer to him. He turned me this way, then that, poring over my goose-pimply bare skin. His brow furrowed and he traced a fading bruise below my hipbone. "This isn't good stewardship on my part," he said with a deadpan sincerity. "I saw this, while you were napping, and I realized I should be ashamed of myself for not taking better care of my belongings." He pulled my hand to him, kissed my palm, then turned to leave. I stared after him. I was so stunned; it took a second to comprehend he had just admitted that he'd been a bad boy who hadn't put his plaything, *me*, away when he was done with it. Even more outrageous is the fact that while I was passed out in the bathroom, covered in vomit, he'd unzipped my jeans to look at me.

My hands shook as I sat on my bed to put on my panty hose. *Stick to the plan, Ruby.* Go ahead and dress for church, that way no one would think twice when I dropped into the nursery a second before the service to look in on Susannah. I checked the diaper bag. Plenty of diapers, two juice bottles, a sleeve of saltines and a jar of peanut butter, as well as an extra change of clothes for me. I looked around the bus and realized there was nothing else here I wanted. I picked my jeans up off the floor and reached into the front pocket.

It was empty.

I checked the other pocket. Nope. Not there, either. Desperately, stupidly, I pulled the pockets out, again and again. Nothing! Not even the sermon notes! Where did my hundred-dollar bill go? It was right here! I had come straight from the bank and felt it in pocket, seconds before I got locked in. Now I was holding my jeans, and the money wasn't in them. What had happened to it? Who even–

JW.

While I was "napping", JW had handled me, had unzipped my jeans, had plundered my pockets. *He took my money.* Enraged, I turned the jeans inside-out. I balled them up and hurled them at the bathroom. I made noises, grunting, snarling, frustrated animal noises as I pounded on my mattress. I had to get on that Greyhound. I had to get Susannah. We had to get out of this evening's service.

I smacked the pillow one more time before thinking of the money box.

After a quick check out the window, I dropped to the floor, scurried back to Old Rev's bed and pulled out the money box. I dialed in the numbers on the lock. Is this stealing? I mean, bad stealing, beyond my usual Benadryl borrowing? Maybe. Probably. Definitely. The box slid open.

No cash. Not even change. Old Rev must have made a deposit today.

"No!" I slammed the lid shut, pounded my fist on it, "No! No! No!" I hefted the box in an overhanded pitch, flinging it toward the back wall of the bus, but it was too heavy to make a satisfying amount of damage. It fell harmlessly to the bed. I looked up to see Merrilee standing in the entrance of the bus.

"What?" I demanded. "What?"

Merilee paused, checked her watch, told me we were on in ten minutes and confirmed that, yes, I was correct, we were wearing the floral scarf tonight. She looked at me a second longer than required before she left.

With one stupid idea and my last shred of hope to guide me, I crawled to the front of the bus, picked up the CB microphone and clicked the button. "Breaker, breaker for Itty-Bitty Betty. Itty-Bitty Betty, this is Bunny-Wunny. Come in." I paused. "Breaker, breaker for Itty-Bitty Betty. Over." Nothing. "Betty, come on." The frequency was silent.

Slowly, slowly I rose from the floor and pulled my dress down over my head. I shoved my feet into my strappy heels, shook out my half-dried hair and swiped a lipstick across my mouth.

Fine. I will go to church like a good girl. I won't fight anymore. I'll be a good, submissive wife. They beat me.

They won.

Chapter
Twenty-five

Somebody was getting saved that night, and it was gonna be a doozy. I could tell. It was in the air. That Heaviness of the Spirit, it hovered over the sanctuary, the building, the whole end of town. The elderly saints, arriving early, they seemed to draw strength from the extra warmth. Their steps had a certainty that heartened their kids, made them wonder if maybe the old folks weren't failing so fast, after all. But the rest of us, we felt unsettled, listless, overheated. It wasn't an unpleasant sensation, exactly; not dread, not like waiting in a dentist's office. More like watching thunderheads to the west, waiting, praying they'll break over your own thirsty land but also praying it will be rain, only rain, and not another one of those life-shattering storms.

Usually, on big nights, our energy ran high, the singing was outstanding and we were on straight adrenaline. Sometimes, and this sounds bad, I know, but sometimes I even played a little game of guess-the-sinner as I looked out over the crowd. I hit about 60%, I think, but JW was terrible. He never got them right.

But not tonight. Tonight I was as enthused as a fencepost. Oh, I went through all the motions, I hit my marks. I kept my place in the order of service. Merrilee played. Old Rev talked. JW and I sang. JW talked. I sang. JW and I sang. I sang again. I smiled. A lot. But inside me, where there should have been a fire blazing, there were ashes, cold and blowing.

After my solo, JW escorted me to my station on Wife's Row. I watched my hands tweak his tie. He handed me my Bible and leaned in to kiss my cheek. "Guess what I found?" he whispered in my ear. "They have a bride's room, too." He winked and turned back to his work, skipping the middle step as he leaped back up to the altar. I didn't respond. I had nothing to answer him with.

I stared straight ahead at Old Rev. I knew what was coming, and I should have stopped it, but I couldn't. I was stuck in my pew. My body was made of concrete, my mind rusted shut.

Back in Pony, Old Rev had said that it's God's Will for JW to keep his family together, no matter what. Whatever it takes, that's what God wants from him. That's what Old Rev had said. Maybe he was right. Maybe God was on their side, after all, because it seemed like no matter what I tried, it didn't work. There was nothing I could do. I couldn't very well fight God. And what about Susannah? Who knows? Maybe they were right about her, too.

Right on cue, Merrilee appeared with Susannah in her in her arms. She was in a quiet, watchful mood; her bright eyes dancing across the crowded sanctuary, taking it in, Bunny-Wunny clamped in her teeth. Merrilee rushed past my pew so Susannah wouldn't see me and carried her up front on stage where she held her sweet, trusting arms out to JW. A soft "aw" noise rolled over the congregation.

My stomach lurched, but I didn't move. I tried to rationalize what was coming. It's not like they were hurting her, a voice buzzed in my head. And she would forget all about it in about five minutes.

But it's wrong, Ruby.

Is it? I didn't know anymore what was right or wrong.

"Did you ever see anything so beautiful? So pure and unblemished? So innocent?" Old Rev asked in a warm, gooey voice. Susannah, in an unexpected moment of shyness, laid her head against her father's lapel and smiled faintly. The congregation's sighs of approval grew louder. It was the most darling thing anyone had ever seen, it seemed.

"Surely there can be nothing evil here. No sin could possibly be lurking behind this precious, guileless smile, could it?" JW looked down at his daughter with a nervous grin. His eyes flicked toward me, then to Susannah, and finally rested on a spot on the carpet.

He can't even look a one-year-old in the eye, I thought. Even JW was ashamed of what he was about to do.

But no matter. Old Rev was in charge here.

"No selfishness. No stubbornness. No disobedience, no willfulness." Old Rev shook his head as he paced. "Not in my precious grandchild!" he said in mock disbelief, and everyone chuckled, recognizing themselves. He continued pacing, musing, "...and yet, I wonder..."

He stopped right beside JW, smiled broadly, and snatched Bunny-Wunny right out of Susannah's mouth.

A screech of outrage pierced the room.

Everyone laughed, but there was an uneasiness it. *Yeah, so, what is he getting at here? Teasing a baby? Seems a little unnecessary, doesn't it?*

He let Susannah get a little more worked up, then dangled Bunny-Wunny in front of her.

"Susannah, I need this. I need it desperately. May I have it?"

She screamed louder than ever and lunged for Bunny-Wunny, but Old Rev held it further from her and the congregation went very still. "Susannah, you are to give this to me, and stop crying," Old Rev said firmly but calmly. Of course she ignored him. Her screams turned frantic, painful. "Susannah, Jesus needs this. Can you let Jesus have it?" No, Jesus most certainly cannot have my toy, Susannah informed him.

Susannah's face was red, tears and snot ran down her face. She was angry. She banged on JW's chest with her little hands, then lunged so wildly toward Bunny-Wunny that JW had to scramble to keep her from back flipping out of his arms. She was confused and scared. Why was her grandfather teasing her? Why wouldn't her daddy help her? Where was she, and where was her mommy?

Her mommy was sitting not ten feet away, frozen. Numb. Helpless and defeated. Useless.

Eventually, Old Rev shook his head sadly, held Bunny-Wunny out to Susannah and released it to her grasp.

Peace instantly descended and Old Rev dejectedly addressed the congregation, "Selfishness," he sighed. "Disobedience. Willfulness. Rebellion. Yes, even in this dear little one here, we see an unwillingness to submit, to put others first, to share our worldly goods. And we weren't surprised, were we? We predicted she would react this way, didn't we? Why is that, I wonder?"

Merrilee slipped up alongside them, cradled Susannah in her arms and carried her back down the aisle to the nursery. She arranged Susannah so that her face was turned away from me as they walked past, but even so, I could hear her snuffling breaths, her fierce sucking at Bunny-Wunny's cloth ear.

My heart pumped like it was full of mud. My beautiful, beautiful baby girl. I tried. I did. I tried to save you from all this, but I couldn't do it. Maybe it really was for the best. Maybe you'd be better off if you grew up like this, in a world oozing with the fear of sin. Maybe, if it were all you ever knew, you'd make a better Jasper than me. A better Christian. Me, I still remembered how it felt when God seemed glad to see me every morning, when He was more concerned with the rain and the wind and the sun and the crops than He was with the length of my dress and the sass in my eyes. I didn't do so well with the sin-handlers, but maybe you will. I'm sorry, Baby. I tried to save you from them. I tried.

Old Rev was still talking. "We expected Our Little Susannah to sin. We knew she would behave in a self-centered, evil manner, because, yes, we know that even Our Dear, Sweet, Little Susannah was born to transgression. It breaks my heart to say it, but it's true. And it's true of you, and it's true of me. We all are born in a desperate state of wickedness and depravity."

Old Rev had everyone's attention now, after using my baby as a stage prop, and so he launched into his usual spiel, an impassioned plea for repentance. I couldn't look at him.

Merrilee was at the piano already. *Why should we tarry, when Jesus is pleading? Pleading for you, and for me. See? On the portals, he's waiting and watching. Watching for you, and for me.* I stepped up to take the microphone from JW, but I didn't look at him, either. My eyes swept over the congregation. I supposed these people were all sinners. I should have been praying for their souls as I sang, *Oh! For the wonderful love he has promised! Promised for you, and for me!* JW and Old Rev were standing two steps below me. I could see, through the matching slicked-back hair on the backs of their matching heads, patches of skin where matching bald spots were beginning to take hold. *Though we have sinned, He has mercy and pardon, pardon for you, and for me.*

Like first drops of rain on the porch roof, the soft whispered prayers, the gentle hiss of *Yes, Jesus,* pitter-pattered throughout the room. Here came a ruffling breeze of motions — this woman dropped her head in her hands, that man put an arm around his wife, another turned to kneel at his seat. The wind picked up force; the singing grew louder. A hymnal was dropped and no one turned to look. On the back row, a hand raised skyward, then another on the third row. Two neighbors came forward to kneel at the altar and conduct their business with Jesus. A teenage girl edged past her friends and out of her pew, crossed the aisle to her mother and put her arms around her. The low rumble of thunder, a deacon's baritone *Praise the Lord,* rolled out. The storm broke. The drought was over. The blessings rained down.

But for me, everything was drier than dust.

Oh, I forgot. I was supposed to be praying for the lost. Who were they tonight? *Come home! Come home! Ye who are weary, come home!* The young couple over there, the ones expecting a baby any time now? Were they the lost? That lady there, most likely Baca County's top Avon Saleswoman, sitting by herself? *Earnestly, tenderly, Jesus is calling.* The unhappy teenaged boy, slouched over in the corner of his pew? Or this couple — I saw them through the window in silhouette, backlit by the foyer light, his cowboy hat in his hand, her purse clutched close, coming through the outer door and into the foyer. They must have been lost for real because they were an hour and a half late. While I sang, I watched them peek through the windows of the sanctuary doors wondering whether or not they could slip in without disrupting the service. The doors opened and in the lighting of the sanctuary, I saw them clearly.

It was Mom and Dad.

Chapter
Twenty-six

With a startled cry, I dropped my microphone on the floor and ran down the aisle. I flew at them both and they caught me, knotting all our arms together into an unbreakable hug. Mom stroked my back and we shook with silent tears while Dad's big, calloused hand crushed my head to his shoulder.

A few people turned to gawk, and of course, the Jaspers had seen my defection, but Merrilee played harder and Old Rev cranked up the "Praise the Lords" and the floodwaters of the service rose and swirled around and past us. We were only one reunion of one kind happening here. Prayers of reconciliation and healing were being heard and answered all around. God would do whatever he came here to do tonight; the service would run its course, the storm would follow its path and play itself out without any help from me.

"Will you take me home?" I asked Mom and Dad. "Me and Susannah? Please? Take us home?" Dad's voice had an unfamiliar hard edge to it. "That's why we came," he said, his words coming short and clipped. "Get the baby, and let's go." His hand on my elbow pointed me firmly toward the door.

"Oh, Mom, wait 'til you see her!" I gushed as we walked. "You'll love Susannah!" Mom gave a shaky laugh. "I peeked in the nursery first thing," she confessed. "I couldn't stand it one more second. I had to at least look at her."

But before we reached the door, a thunderbolt of repentance struck the front of the church and the biggest sinner yet crashed noisily to his knees, weeping, wailing, bawling out, "Oh, God, Oh, God, please forgive me! Forgive me, God, I am the worst of sinners! I am a hypocrite! I am a fraud! I am unworthy to be called by Your name! Oh, God! Oh God, Oh God!" He dissolved into great, bellowing sobs. I heard the sound of his big fists against his own chest, thumping against his lungs like giant hollow gourds.

My blood froze. I didn't have to turn around, I already knew. It was JW.

"Ruby," Dad said, in the same voice he once used to warn me of a Diamondback rattler underfoot. "Just keep walking. Don't even look back."

But I couldn't. I had to stop. I had to look. Like Lot's wife, I had to look back, one last time, to see my old life go up in flames.

"Praise the Lord," intoned Old Rev, arms open wide, rushing over to JW, "He forgets not his own! He chastises him, whom he loveth, and casteth down even the proud and the mighty!" He knelt down to put his arms around his son, but JW shook him off, leapt the two steps off the altar, and sprinted down the aisle toward us. I felt Dad stiffen and Mom reach behind my back to put a warning hand on his arm. "Harvell," she murmured, "we're in church."

JW tore through the crowd and reached for me, but Mom and Dad, one on either side of me, edged a foot each between us. JW's hand hovered, then landed on Dad's shoulder the way a man suffering a heart spell grabs the nearest wall, like he could barely stand.

"Ruby Fae, please! Please, I was, I've been — No! I am! I *am*! I am a terrible husband. I know that. I don't deserve you." He gripped Dad's shoulder hard and the three of us watched him without speaking. "I don't blame you if you hate me. But please, please, don't leave yet. Not like this. Ruby. I love you. I have loved you for as long as I can remember. I will love you forever. Don't go like this. Please."

The muscles in Dad's arm tensed and Mom shifted her weight, but they said nothing. I had seen JW cry hundreds of times, but I had never seen him like this before. He was a mess. His suit sleeves were soggy and disgusting where he'd rubbed them across his face. His hair, full of Bryl-cream and sweat, stood out all over his head, as though he'd tried to yank it from its roots. He sniffled and gulped so hard, it came out as snorts through his red nose, and his streaked, swollen face was the most miserable thing I'd ever seen. Should I feel pity for him? Or hatred? Fear? I felt none of that. The most definite emotion I could name was a mild curiosity. What if this was for real? What if he meant it, if he really wanted to change? Then what?

"JW," I said, "I am going home."

Mom and Dad both relaxed their shoulders, and I did, too. I suddenly felt thousands of pounds lighter and a hundred degrees warmer.

Dad's big hand came down on top of JW's and squeezed

it, as if maybe he could risk a little compassion now, for a man whose wife was leaving him. JW gulped twice and nodded. "OK," he said. He nodded again. "I know. You need to go home. You do." Another sniffle. He looked at the floor. "But," he hesitated. "Can I come home with you?"

Mom and I gasped. Dad gave a surprised grunt and pulled back so fast that JW was thrown off-balance.

"Home? To Oklahoma?" I asked. "You mean you'd leave? With us?" I did not see that one coming. I couldn't fit it into my head. I didn't know what to do with it.

JW nodded. "Yes. Can I?"

"You'd leave Old Rev, I mean, your dad? He'd never let you go! You know he won't!"

JW's chin went up a notch. "What's he going to do? Spank me? You are my family, now, Ruby. You and Susannah."

Wasn't this what I had wanted? Our little family, together? Back home, in Oklahoma, away from his parents, off the road, out of this traveling salvation road show business? In a real, honest-to-goodness, always-stays-put house?

Suddenly, I didn't know.

JW looked so pathetic, so broken. He looked like Susannah, when she can't find Bunny-Wunny.

"Ruby," he said, his voice hoarse, "please, you promised, 'for as long as we both shall live.' Before God. You promised."

Yes. I did. I did promise. 'Til death do us part.'

Everyone looked to me for an answer, and I didn't know what that answer was.

Finally, Mom said, "Look, kids, this is a big decision. You need a minute. And Ruby Fae, you look like you are about to fall over! Have you eaten anything today?" I admitted to her that I couldn't remember when I last ate. "Well, then, I think what we all need, first, is some food. We can all think clearer once we've eaten," she declared.

Oh, Momma, your trusty food cure. You're right. My brain was as empty as my belly.

"Does that drive-in down the street have a place to sit, do you think? I bet it does." As she talked, she nudged us along, down the aisle and toward the sanctuary doors. "This service is about to wind down, so why don't you and Dad and I get Susannah and go order some hamburgers for everybody? JW, you stay here and tell your parents to meet us after they're finished. We'll all be more sensible after we've had some protein. And then we can have a nice long talk about what to do next."

Dad and JW both looked doubtful. Dad would rather punch his son-in-law, JW thought his life was over, and neither one believed the Dairy-Dog Drive-in would fix it. But if they were waiting on some word from me, I didn't have it, and supper, at least, was something for everyone to do while I tried to think.

Picking up Susannah was a noisy, tearful affair for all of us. She had been away from me all afternoon, so she squealed and squawked to get at me as soon as she saw me. Mom cried openly at the sight of the two of us together in arms' reach of her, at last. Even Dad had to blow his nose several times and couldn't talk.

After a few moments of more group hugging and crying, I remembered to thank Cassie, the thirteen-year-old who had watched her during church. Cassie eagerly offered to sit with her again tomorrow night, but I told her that wouldn't be necessary because we wouldn't be there. Tomorrow night, we'd be home.

Chapter
Twenty-seven

The giant flat-pattied hamburger on a soft bun with a crisp-grilled edge was the best thing I'd ever eaten in my life. Except for maybe the over-salted, hand-cut fries in their greasy, waxed-paper lined plastic basket. Or maybe the strawberry shake. I was so hungry, I took three bites before I remembered to pull the fancy curly-colored toothpick out of the middle of the burger. You're right; I did need some protein, Mom.

By the time the Jaspers joined us at the picnic table outside the walk-up window at the Dairy-Dog, Susannah had already decided Mom was her new best friend. She straddled Mom's lap, facing her, opening her mouth like a baby bird while Mom popped ketchup-loaded fries into it. I wondered if that registered with Merrilee. Susannah would sometimes go for days without allowing Merrilee to hold her.

Though it killed him to do it, Dad nodded once to Old Rev. "Lem," he said.

Old Rev met Dad's gaze. "Harvell," he answered.

Dad nodded at JW, who said nothing, then looked at

Merrilee and touched the brim of his hat. "Merrilee," he greeted solemnly, then he crossed his arms on the table in front of him. Maybe Mom wanted this to go as smoothly and graciously as possible, but Dad had no such ambitions. He wanted it over with and wasn't pretending otherwise.

Mom waved a generous arm across the table and the plastic trays filled with Dairy-Dog baskets. "Please, sit down! You must be half-starved," she said. "Merrilee, how good to see you again. You're looking fine. Lemuel, I gather the service went well."

As the Jaspers sat down on the bench across from us, Mom apologized for not waiting for them, and I realized she was apologizing only for me; she and Dad had waited. I swallowed my mouthful and set my burger down. Mom handed the rest of the hamburger baskets out to Old Rev and Merrilee and JW, then, same as she would if she were presiding over her own dining table back home, Mom looked to Old Rev and asked, "Would you like to bless our dinner, Reverend?"

Old Rev looked skyward for a moment, as if asking God whether or not he should proceed, then bowed his head. The rest of us bowed, too.

"Gracious Heavenly Father, giver of all good gifts, we thank Thee for thy bountiful provision. Bless the hands that prepared this meal, and grant us all, if it be Thy will, a good night's rest tonight and traveling mercies for those who will be on the highways and byways tomorrow. Amen."

Mom made a few stabs at chit-chat while we ate, but as Susannah was monopolizing her attention and no one else was in the small-talk mood, her efforts didn't net much. We ate carefully, sneaking looks at each other around the table, sizing each other up. JW was too restless to eat at all.

He poked at his food, squirmed and fidgeted until, finally, he announced. "Dad, I have something to tell you."

Old Rev seemed unperturbed. "Alright, Son." He held up his burger, ready to take another bite. "What do you need to say?"

"I'm going, too."

"Going to what?" Old Rev asked.

"Go home, with Ruby Fae and Susannah."

Old Rev nodded. He acted as though he had been expecting this very thing, all along. "Home, to Iowa?"

"No, Dad. Not the home office, I mean home. Oklahoma."

Merrilee looked up quickly, her eyes darting from her husband to her son and back again, but she said nothing. I suddenly remembered Billy Sunday and the beautiful grandson she'd never seen. Merrilee had given up her firstborn son for Old Rev's ministry, and I wondered if she was prepared to sacrifice her last son as well.

"If that's what you think best for your family, John Wesley," Old Rev said neutrally, as though it didn't matter to him one way or the other. "Of course, if you're not traveling with us, you'll lose our financial support."

"I know. But I'll make a little money from the parsonage remodeling." No one asked any details about that, about Reverend Dixon's offer. I suddenly realized that everyone already knew all about it. JW had told his folks, of course, but Mom and Dad must have known about the letter before it was even sent. How was it that everyone had been in on that discussion about my future except for me?

JW went on. "We'll need a place to live eventually, after I finish the church job, but we'll figure something out, won't we, Ruby?" He risked a tiny grin in my direction.

"We don't need much room, do we? We're used to a small home."

Dad couldn't stand it any longer. He put a hand up. "Hold up a minute, here! Ruby is coming home with us; that's a done deal. But whether or not JW is coming along, well, that's up to her. Maybe that wasn't her plan, I don't know. I need to hear it from you, Ruby Fae. Do you want JW to come home with us? If you do, fine; your mom and I will do everything we can to help set the three of you up. But if you don't want JW to come with us, well, frankly, that's more than fine with me. But it's your call. Yours. Not mine, or your mom's, or theirs," he pointed to the Jaspers, "and especially not his." He jabbed a finger toward JW who clutched his chest as though Dad's finger had shot him.

Everyone, even Susannah, turned and waited for me to speak.

I looked at my husband sitting across the table and thought about the beautiful boy I'd loved and the beautiful baby we'd made together. I remembered all the secret moments we'd shared, the wild exhilaration of discovering each other's bodies. The look on his face when he watched me sing. The way his arm fit around my shoulder. The way he smelled, fresh from the shower. Our 'til-death-do-us-part vows.

The cracked rib. The ache in my shoulder.

An airless, claustrophobic death inside the bus.

"I'm taking Susannah, and I'm going home with Mom and Dad," I said. "JW can ride back to Oklahoma with us if he wants, but I don't want to live with him. I'm going to stay at Mom and Dad's for a while, and he can live wherever he wants. But not with me. Not now." I looked at JW and saw his hopeful face. "I don't know, okay?" I snapped at him. "We'll see about later. I don't know right now. Don't ask."

And just like that, I'd made all my problems go away. It was that simple. Poof. A few words from me, and they had dissolved into dust. I couldn't believe it! I was going home!

We finished eating, but JW was feeling better, hopeful, even, so he finished his basket and ordered a second hamburger and another vanilla shake. We all walked back to the church where Dad and JW started loading things into the trunk of the car. We wouldn't be able to take everything because some things, like Susannah's stroller, took up a lot of room. I worried aloud whether or not we should have had a car safety seat for Susannah, since it was such a long drive, but there was nothing to be done about that now.

Surprisingly, Old Rev and Merrilee weren't fighting us leaving, not one bit. They even helped JW go through the cargo hold, sorting out what we needed to take with us. Go figure. I would have sworn the Jaspers would have done anything to keep JW with them, but there Merrilee was, working through the closet, emptying out every last thing we owned, and Old Rev helpfully piling our belongings in space-efficient stacks.

Mom and I kept telling them that we didn't need to get everything right this minute, that they could ship some of it or even pitch it; we couldn't fit it all in the car. But the Jaspers were on a mission, and JW hopped around as excited as a kid packing for Disneyland. Dad, though was quiet and antsy, itching to get us on the road and away from here. But Mom pulled him aside and told him that this seemed to be important to the Jaspers, this long-drawn-out process of packing and parting. "Maybe it will help everybody let go," she said. "We'll give them another thirty minutes. After all, this is sudden."

It was late. Susannah was cranky and tired, so while Mom and Dad packed, I took her on the bus to put her in jammies. But she was still so fussy, I decided to lay down with her and feed her for a few minutes. She should drop right off to sleep about the time we were ready to leave.

I went to crawl into my bunk with Susannah, for the last time. But I was still dehydrated from my nausea that afternoon. The vanilla Dairy-Dog shake that JW got me was on the table, so I wriggled away from Susannah long enough to grab it. She protested loudly, so I gulped it down fast, dribbling some of it down the front of my yellow Georgette dress. That stain probably won't come out — a thought that gave me a childish pleasure as I kicked off my heels and settled back in the bunk with Susannah. I wrestled the top of my dress open and my bra up so she could reach me and she latched on. I lay still, willing her to hurry up and get to sleep. I softly sang a quick-made lullaby. *Grammy and Grampa are almost ready, sweetie! Go to sleep now! You'll wake up in Oklahoooooooma!*

Susannah's fretting gradually subsided, and the comfort of this sweet, maternal ritual washed over both of us. Our weary, tensed bodies loosened and warmed to each other as I rolled onto my side and curled around her. I watched Susannah's eyelids flutter and heard her ragged breath slowing and smoothing. My big little girl. My panty hose and half-slip were twisted and digging into my waist, so I wiggled and tugged at them, but my movement disturbed Susannah. Her eyes popped back open, she clamped her teeth harder, and let a shriek of disapproval out the side of her mouth. I settled back into position and decided that once we were home I'd give her a few weeks to settle in, and then wean her for good.

Feeding her always made me drowsy. I think I read somewhere it's the hormones.

I yawned and thought about weaning Susannah. That made me think of weaning calves. I closed my own eyes. I sure hoped Susannah wouldn't bawl as much as the weaning calves do. Those stupid calves can dang near break your heart, the way they'll cry themselves hoarse before it's over. They even sound like they're hollering "Ma-ma! Maaa-Maa!" I stretched my legs out and thought about the calves in the corral, how Chuck and Leland and I used to crawl up on it and perch there, watching Dad and Pop Fletch work cattle. I heard the thumping and packing going on around me, but behind my curtain, in my own little world, that seemed far away.

I heard the comforting murmur of Mom and Dad's voices.

I heard soft, steady breathing and wondered if it came from me. Susannah unloosed herself. A blanket was pulled up over me, covering my wet, naked breast. Somewhere, Mom said, "They're both all worn out."

She said something like "Motel."

"Over that way, a few blocks, by the highway."

Somebody said "Eight."

Was that Dad, saying "No; seven?"

What are they talking about? Why is Dad raising his voice? I should get up and see, but I'm just too sleepy. Mom can take care of it.

I think my husband said, "We'll be ready."

I was happy, but I didn't remember why.

I dreamed about Jesus, on the portals, waiting and watching. I don't know what portals are, for sure, but this one looked a lot like the dock Dad had built over our best fishing pond. Jesus was smiling and waving, big and friendly-like. "Come on! Come on home!" I'm rowing as fast and hard as I can toward Him, but my rowboat only drifts further away with each stroke. Jesus grew smaller, hopping up and down now, his robes billowing, his arms outstretched over his head, now his hands cupped around his mouth like a megaphone. "Come home!" he hollered. But it's beginning to drizzle, and puddles are forming at my feet. I'm cold. And rain is hitting the windows of my boat. I mean, my bus.

Chapter
Twenty-eight

Rain was hitting the windows of my bus.

My eyelids slammed open to a gray light. I jerked up to look out the window, and I knew that everything was all very, very wrong. I was cold. It was raining. And we were moving.

With a cry, I leapt out of bed and looked around the bus, trying to make sense out of this. Merrilee was sitting at the dinette, feeding Susannah a hamburger. JW was standing in the stairwell talking to Old Rev, who was driving.

They all looked so normal, so regular, every-day. With the exception of Old Rev and JW switching places, it could have been any old driving day.

"Where are we?" I rasped. Why did my tongue feel like sawdust? "Why are we driving?"

"Honey." JW took a step toward me, hands open. Eyes beseeching.

My mouth was so very dry. I tried to swallow, but my throat was made of velcro. "Where are we?" I repeated, looking around, but Merrilee looked down, wouldn't meet my eye. "JW? Answer me! Where are we?" I tore open the curtain over the stove and looked out to see a highway number sign, outlined in a maple leaf.

Canada!

I shrieked. I slammed my hands on the cabinet doors and howled, "No! No! No!"

What have they done? Why didn't I wake up? How could I have been so stupid? I was frantic. I glanced down at the pink stain on the front of my dress and I knew. Pink? My shake was vanilla. I plowed into my bunk, pulled up the mattress corner and searched wildly, but found nothing. The Benadryl was gone. All of it. I'm lucky I woke up at all.

I screamed and hurled my weight at JW, grabbed his shirt front, pounded on his chest.

"Take! Me! Home! Take me! Home! Right now!" I wailed. "You liar! Take me home!"

Susannah was screaming and JW was crying. "Sweetheart," he pleaded, "I had to! I had to keep you with me, don't you see? It's the way it's meant to be, us together. It's my job to keep us together, no matter what." I hit and shoved at him, but he grabbed my wrists. I broke free, and he grabbed again. We were an uneven match in strength, maybe, but this time, my fury far outweighed him.

While JW and I fought, Merrilee tried to hold Susannah. But she was scrambling and wriggling, wild with fear, so Merrilee gave up and shoved her into her bunk, locking the rail. Old Rev kept his hands on the wheel and the bus on the road, but he hollered encouragement to JW, "Hold fast, son! The heart is wicked and deceitful, above all else!"

JW wrenched my clawed hands from his biceps and flung me to the floor. As Old Rev jerked the bus to a stop on the shoulder, I was thrown under JW's bunk and my hand smacked hard against a guitar case. Starla's guitar case.

I lifted the latch, grabbed the .22, rolled back into the aisle and leapt to my feet.

I pointed the barrel at JW's chest.

"Take me home," I said.

JW froze, his hands held up in surrender.

"Get in the driver's seat and take me home. Now, please." My voice was steady. The only noise in the bus was Susannah's wailing that trailed off into a hard snuffling, gulping sound. It killed me to scare her like that, but what else could I do? If we disappeared into the Canadian frontier, we would be stuck on that bus forever.

Old Rev turned sideways in his driver's seat, twisting around to watch us. "John Wesley, get control of your wife now," he advised. "It'll only get worse, the longer you put it off."

But JW was shaking. *Come on, JW*, I silently pleaded to him. *Please! Take me home.*

"JW," I said, "You know Mom and Dad won't just let us go. They'll eventually find us, and I'll say you kidnapped me. I'll press charges. So help me, I will. And you know what else?" I lowered my gun but changed my mind and brought it up again, level with JW's chest. He gasped. His eyeballs nearly exploded out of their sockets, he was so scared.

Good. I wanted him terrified. I didn't want to shoot him; I'm not stupid. But I needed him to listen to me, to take me seriously. I raised the gun higher. He thought I was aiming for his head, but I wasn't. I was really sighting the American flag sticker on the sun visor behind his left ear. He looked like he was going to faint. I pressed him further. "JW, if you keep me here against my will, our marriage will be over, for good. Oh, I may still legally be your wife, but after this, we can never be happy again. I will never forgive this. Never."

Nobody moved.

Old Rev stood up beside JW. "Son, she's bluffing."

If I was bluffing, I was going to do it right. I pumped the gun once and a spent shell popped out, hitting the bus floor with a ping.

JW flinched, but Old Rev snorted. "Of course she'll forgive you. That's why we married Christian girls in the first place. They have to forgive us."

That's when I pulled the trigger.

Chapter
Twenty-nine

I shot him. I did. I won't lie about that. I, alone, am responsible for the bullet.

But where it hit? That's more complicated, isn't it? How did it happen like that? Was it on purpose? Did I, in a split second, reason that to stop evil, you have to get to the root? Or was it some left-over romantic impulse of mine? Maybe I looked into those desperate, trapped eyes and wanted to do them a mercy, an act of kindness. Was it all pre-ordained? The will of God?

Or, was it the discreet touch of a graceful hand, a hand whose fingers were so skilled and nimble and quick, fingers that could flash, almost unseen? Was that how the bullet missed Merrilee's son, but instead lodged itself in her husband's heart?

I'll never know for sure. I only know that as Old Rev slumped to the floor, Merrilee was standing beside me.

"I'm not losing another son," she said, her lovely, talented fingers on the barrel of my gun.

Had they been there all along?

The next part doesn't happen in a neat straight line for me. It's all jumbled together. Mostly, I remember Susannah's screaming. Also, JW, his anguished cries. Merrilee, silent and still, turned to stone. Blood, of course. One car, speeding past us, unconcerned, unaware.

"What have you done?" JW screamed at us as he tugged at his father's body, pulling it into his arms. "What have you done?"

"Ruby Fae!" Merrilee said, "Get that baby to your room. She shouldn't see this." Of course. She was right. I grabbed Susannah and pulled her into my bunk with me, shutting the curtain behind us. "JW, Help me get your father onto the bed," Merrilee told JW. "Get up! Now! Get his head."

They half-carried, half dragged Old Rev's body down the bus aisle and past my bunk. I pulled Susannah down beside me in bed and locked her in my arms. I thought about praying but didn't know where to start. Merrilee and JW both grunted, and I heard a soft whump on the mattress. JW was still crying, hard. "What will we do, Mom? What will we do?"

"You'll get me all the bedding you can find. And a bucket, that's what you'll do," Merrilee answered.

She was going to clean up her husband's blood.

"Merrilee," I called from my bunk, "Don't. I will do that. Come sit with Susannah."

"No!" she said. "You stay there. JW, fill this with water."

Susannah had found Bunny-Wunny and clamped his ear between her teeth. After soothing herself, she turned to me, patting my cheek and cooing. I watched her and wondered why I was shivering so hard. The rain came down faster, drumming on the roof of the bus, roaring in our ears, washing away the buckets of reddish water

JW splashed out the doorway, onto the muddy roadside, turning the wet earth dull red.

Finally, Merrilee said, "Ok, you can come out now."

I tumbled out and stood in the aisle of the bus. I didn't know where to look. Not behind me, at the closed door to Merrilee and Old Rev's room. Not at the front of the bus, still wet where it had been mopped clean. Especially not at JW, who had stripped out of his bloody clothes and was now sitting in his undershorts on his bare mattress, tugging at a clean t-shirt, turning it this way and that as if the process of putting it on confused him. So I looked at Merrilee.

I opened my mouth, to say, what? Sorry I shot your husband? I didn't mean to?

So I closed my mouth. Merrilee had changed out of the everyday dress she was wearing and into a clean, identical one. She had an additional crease down the middle of her forehead, and her lips were more tightly clamped than usual. But that was it. Nothing else was different. Except the fact that she was now a widow, as well as an accomplice to her husband's murder. She gave me one hard, searching look, then turned to JW and said, "Get dressed. We're taking your father home."

"Home to where?" JW asked.

"Oklahoma."

Chapter Thirty

Back home, when an unexpected winter storm blasts down on you, the old-timers will say, "Somebody left the north gate open." I caught the joke early on; even as a little kid, I understood that the "north gate" was imaginary and those Canadians couldn't really corral a blizzard. So when I saw a highway sign pointing toward "North Gate, North Dakota, United States" I got a fairy-tale-ish feeling, like the next sign might say, "Santa Claus Lane, 10 mi." The rain fizzled, the sun came out on one side of the bus, lighting the last flurries of sprinkles, casting prisms. On the other side of the bus, the sky was still threatening and gray.

What would happen at the border? I had been asleep when we'd crossed into Canada, so I didn't know what to expect. What if we had to stop and get out? Would they ask for our ID? Merrilee has never even had a driver's license or any ID at all, but that was the least of our troubles. Would they remember Old Rev, and ask about him? Would they board the bus? If they took us all to jail, what would happen to Susannah?

"What do I do? What do I do?" JW panicked. He was,

after all, transporting two kidnap victims and a dead preacher across an international border.

"You slow down," Merrilee said, her voice steady. "And get your driver's license out. Ruby, get back on your bed and keep that baby quiet. Wait—" She grabbed my arm and turned me toward her as the bus slowed to a roll. "Look me over good. Am I clean?" She held her hands and arms out toward me, turning them in and out.

Jesus, give me strength; she was asking if she got any blood on her.

I looked carefully, head to toe. No, I told her. Her hands were clean.

I crawled into my bunk with Susannah and pulled the curtain closed. For once, I was more scared of what was on the outside than I was of being stuck inside. No one spoke. Even Susannah was silent. The bus slowed, and I heard JW slide the driver's window open.

"Yes sir," I heard him tell someone, his voice high and thin. "Here you go." He must have handed over his driver's license. I heard Merrilee move up the aisle toward JW. The agent asked JW how long we'd been in Canada, because he truthfully answered, "About two hours."

This was not the correct answer. Now I could hear the agent clearly. "Sir, I'm going to have to ask you to pull over to the secondary inspection area. Please have identification for all passengers ready. Any explosives, alcohol, live plants, animals and firearms will need to be made available for inspection."

JW choked out an unintelligible reply, but Merrilee talked over him. "Is there a reason for this delay, officer?"

"Ma'am, your length of stay is highly unusual. If you would have your photo ID ready as you and all other passengers exit the vehicle, I'll begin my inspection."

I stifled a whimper.

Merilee's voice, however, never wavered. "'I'm sorry, but we really can't spare the time. We are On Mission." She said it exactly like that, like it had capital letters, like we were deployed military. That importantly.

"Ma'am, I can appreciate that, but as I've said, the time frame of your visit does raise some concerns."

If my life was ending, I was at least going to watch. I rolled away from Susannah and peeked through the curtains. I couldn't see out the driver's side, where the customs agent was standing, but I could see Merrilee, in her beige-striped belted house dress with her hands on her bony hips, her concrete-set chin and her hard-hat of Aqua-Netted hair. Her feet planted wide and solid. All she needed was a wooden staff and she'd be Moses, parting the Red Sea for us.

"We are ministers of the Gospel. We go where we feel the Lord leads us, but sometimes, we are mistaken," she said. "And this time we heard wrong. We don't belong here. We're going back home."

The agent tried to take that in. He needed a moment. To this day, I've never prayed so hard in my life.

Sometimes miracles float down from heaven on silken feathers of angels' wings. And sometimes, they roll in on a GMC wheat truck with an impatient, honking harvester at the wheel. His rigs, loaded with combines and headers, fourteen of them, including the cook house, sleeping wagons and his own family's quarters, are blocking the highway, he told the officer. And you can hear the wheat ripening up as we speak, so, is this going to take much longer?

"Aw, nuts," I heard the agent say to JW. "Just don't come back today, OK?"

Thirty seconds down the road, JW threatened to fall apart again, but Merrilee said, "JW, remember, you are not innocent here, either, so pull yourself together. Get us to Oklahoma, and at least we won't be kidnappers anymore."

Chapter Thirty-one

The next twenty hours took an eternity. We couldn't risk getting pulled over for speeding, so JW listened in on the CB to avoid troopers. Before long, though, he picked up chatter about "helping the bears for a change," and "kidnapped girl and her baby."

Me. That was me. Oh, why, why, couldn't we have been caught earlier, during Old Rev's wild midnight ride across the country? He had to have been driving over ninety most of the way, why couldn't we have been stopped then? But right now, a flashing red light was the last thing we wanted to see.

JW signed on and played dumb.

"Break one-nine, this is Backslider coming at you. What's the chatter?"

"Go ahead, Backslider, you're talking to Easy Money. There's bear traps all over the countryside today. Every Boy Scout and County Mountie they got is out looking for a traveling Bible-Mobile. You seen one?"

"You mean a church bus, over?"

"Negatory, more like a preaching star in a gussied-up

people-hauler. They say his cheese slipped off his crackers and he snatched up a nice little Okie girl and her baby. Her daddy reported 'em missing this morning. The last 10-20 on 'em was somewhere in the Colorado pancakes last night. Everybody's got their eyeballs peeled. A lot of us out here on the road are daddies ourselves, you copy?" said Mr. Easy Money.

I knew it. Mom and Dad wouldn't let me slip away like that. I knew they'd kick up a fuss. But how could they have imagined that would be the worst possible outcome for me, to be pulled over now?

JW sounded like a regular good ol' boy. "10-4 on that, good brother. I got a little curtain-climber of my own, safe and sound back at my stack of bricks. But tell me more about this Bible-beater. I saw something like that, early this morning. Sleek-lookin' movie-star bus with some kinda Jesus words on the side of it, an old geezer and a sweet thing? I even talked to her, she said she was from Oklahoma."

"For real, Good Buddy? What was the 10-20 on that?" Easy Money asked.

"You know that big new Eat'Em'Up at I-40 and I-80, east of Mormon Town?"

"10-4, know it well."

"That's where I saw them. They said they were headed for Dice City."

"Smokey Bear, got your ears on? Did you get that?" Easy Money asked the air waves.

A new voice broke in, no folksy chatter, all business. "10-4. This is North Dakota State Trooper Parker; Backslider, approximately what time was this encounter?"

JW fibbed with ease, "Around five, this AM."

"Can you describe the persons?"

"Yes, sir, an older, gray-headed man with a young woman, red-headed, pony-tail; she was short. She had some Oklahoma college t-shirt on."

"Backslider, did you see a baby?"

"No, but she mentioned one. I was trying to pick her up, thought she was a rental model, if you catch my drift, but she said something about the baby, and I saw the bus and felt like a regular fool."

"Understood. Can you describe the bus?"

Of course he could. "A Silver Eagle Coach, looked like Merle Haggard's. Said some churchy name on the side. Jagger? Jazzy? Jester? Like that. It's dark brown." He was satisfied with his almost-remembered-the-name-ploy. Lying comes easy to JW, when he's anonymous.

The trooper and the trucker both thanked and praised JW profusely and signed off, the trucker with all kinds of trucker blessings, like, "keep the shiny side up, and the greasy side down, Good Buddy."

JW's good-ol-boy act bought us a little breathing room, but we still had to listen for sightings and avoid the law. We sped when we could, took the back roads when we had to. We stopped for fuel, once, at a small gas station in Nebraska, which was brutal, because I had to go pay while JW fueled up. I was a nervous wreck at the counter, but fortunately, only one cranky old man was on duty and the phone rang during our transaction. Whoever was on the other end put him in an even fouler mood, so maybe he would forget about us. I threw bills at him and charged back to the bus. JW was exhausted out of his mind. He leaned against the side of the bus, asleep.

"Let me drive a while," I shook him awake. "It's gotta be easier than driving a twenty-year-old wheat truck."

To my great shock, he agreed.

After he finished fueling up, he crawled, zombie-like, into the bus. I was in the driver's seat, buckling up, getting oriented, as he lurched past me. "Sorry about all this," he mumbled to me. "I meant to be better." I had no reply. He flopped onto his bare mattress, and I fired up the bus.

I made sure the fuzz-buster was on, checked the CB, consulted the map once more, adjusted my mirrors and pulled out.

Finally, I was going home.

Chapter Thirty-two

Yes, I even have a story about Old Rev.

This story should go to Susannah one day, because of all the grandparents in it, but I'm not sure I can tell it to her. What other questions would it raise? I don't want to think about that. I admit it. I'm a coward.

But do I even have to tell her my story? Maybe not. After all, she's my daughter, a McKeever from Rose of Sharon in Woods County, Oklahoma. She'll grow up feeling the red dirt in her veins and she'll always sense how the land loves her like a second mother and she'll absorb the truth of it long before she has enough words to question it. She will never doubt, she'll always believe, always know *this is where I come from.*

So maybe I can put it down here, with the rest of my story, and then, as Grandpa Pake would say, I can "Forget it. Walk away and leave it for the buzzards."

Old Rev's story includes my Grandma Reenie, who once told it to me, and her good friend, Cora, who was my Grandma Daisy's mother. They both were, of course, members in good standing of the Rose of Sharon Church

International Pilgrim's Holiness Missionary Society, and the minutes filed with the IPHMS headquarters in Cleveland, Ohio reflect that at the August 1936 meeting, both of my grandmothers were present.

The minutes will also show that Mrs. Cecilia Hopper presented the lesson on Paul's Second Trip to Macedonia and the selected hymn, *Onward Christian Soldiers*, was led by Miss Maisy Cobbles and accompanied by Miss Daisy McKeever. Following the devotional time, the group voted to approve a charity food basket for a neighboring family (parents, non-members; one child, a boy, a member and regular Sunday School attendee, and two other children, names and ages unknown) to serve as both a prospect contact and member welfare activity. Two birds with one stone nearly always being in line with The Lord's Will in these times of drouth and need. In other items of business, the circle voted to authorize the purchase of two new spools of quilting thread — one white, one gray — from the treasury. A final vote, to save Mrs. Hetty Knowles' most excellent chocolate meat-dripping cake with boiled fudge frosting until coffee hour, after quilting, rather than eat it now, with the hobo-stew lunch, was unanimous. The weather that day was sunny and fair, the temperature only 93. The barometer was broken, so no pressure reading was available. The minutes would stand approved as read, with no corrections or additions. Little Libby Matherson, aged five, moved that the meeting be adjourned.

What the minutes did not reflect was the way the sweat trickled unnoticed into threadbare girdles and slips shoring up faded, but starched and pressed, feedsack dresses. Or how the dust-covered windows, clay-tinged and opaque, were open for the moment but once the quilt came out, would have to be slammed shut against the blowing dust.

The minutes make no mention that the spools of thread were to finish a scrap-work quilt in time to raffle it off at the county fair next month. It would not, as they had hoped, bring enough money to buy the County Home a new goat. They would be able to buy three pullet hens (two Rhode Island Reds and one Barred Rock) however, to donate instead. At least it was something.

The official meeting records will not show that the ladies always ate hobo stew at every meeting, every month, because even though times were hard, everybody should at least have a few potatoes or a mess of boiled okra they could contribute to the pot. And as for saving the dessert? Saving dessert always won out, with the excuse of prolonging the party as long as possible. But also, on the days when the hobo stew was especially thin and the saltines were politely rationed, it helped to fill everyone's bellies once more before going home. A woman could go a little lighter on her own supper that night if she had a hefty bowl of bread pudding and a cup of coffee filling her up at four o'clock. Which might mean a little extra food on the plate of a growing child or a plowing man, should you be so lucky to have those in the house.

Nobody ever came right out and said those things, because pride is a commodity to be stocked and hoarded as well. It was a silent understanding. Except that one meeting, during the terrible Winter of '35, when they'd all confessed to suffering from the same nightmares, the same recurring dreams of finding your last potatoes rotted or of dishing up food that evaporated on the plate; that unspeakable one of forgetting to feed your quietest child.

These things weren't included in the minutes.

Another detail missing was the name of the prospect/ welfare family to be visited, Sam and Josephine Jasper (non-members) and their boys, including nine-year-old Lemuel (regular Sunday School Attendee). That was an act of generosity in itself, because who among them wanted their names entered into the permanent record as being in need of handouts?

Cora and Reenie were chosen as the ones to go calling on the Jaspers. Reenie, on the grounds that she had so many boys of her own, she could maybe pass off a few pieces of clothes as hand-me-downs, rather than as outright charity. Cora, because the McKeevers were now the Jasper's nearest neighbors, since the Howes went bust and the McKeevers had bought their place from the bank. Cora could use the excuse of asking Lem to come haul buckets of water to her garden in exchange for supper on a regular basis and maybe the two littler boys, too, once in a while, could help weed or hoe, if she had enough supper to go around.

So one week later, Cora and Reenie drove over to the Jasper Place with the donations they'd gathered up from the Society members. It was a pitiful bounty; no one out here had extra food just piling up and getting in the way, not even the McKeevers. But everyone found a little something to give, even if it was only a jar of cactus jelly. Prickly Pear Cactus makes a good spread, and it doesn't really need much sugar at all.

Cora stopped her car in the yard. While she and Reenie waited for its wind-caught trail of dust to lie down, they looked through the gritty windshield and took stock of the place. "That hen house might save a chicken from a coyote if it fell on him."

"I don't see any chickens around, though. Or a garden, either. How do you think they've been eating?"

"I don't know. Maybe Sam or Lem hunts rattlers and jack rabbits? It would be hard to garden here, anyway, There's never been any good water on this place."

Without discussing it, they both removed their hats and gloves and left them in the car.

"Hello? Is anyone home?" Reenie called toward the dugout.

The wind swept over the roof of the dugout and caught a flap of tar paper. It waved at them, but nothing else gave notice. "Hello?"

Where the Jaspers lived couldn't rightly be called a house. Sam's pa had dug it the day after the Land Run and had promised Sam's ma that it was "only temporary, 'til things started lookin' up around here." Before he took off for good, he did at least board up the walls and the ceiling to block out some of the dirt. Then Sam's ma had died and left him the place, and pretty soon Sam was old enough to get some marrying ideas of his own. So he brought home Lucinda, and for a brief time, it looked as if things finally were looking up around the Jasper Homestead. Sam promised her a new house one day, but in the meantime he plastered up the walls, Lucinda sewed a few house-pretties, together they fixed up a bright clean corner for new little Lem and the dugout was almost homey. But after Lucinda died there trying to birth her dead baby girl, those cozy days were gone for good and that's when Sam brought in Josephine. For her, he'd added the lean-to kitchen out front, said he'd keep Lem from being too much underfoot and that was about all he'd promised her. So where the Jaspers lived couldn't rightly be called a house, but it couldn't rightly be called a home, either.

"Nobody's home." Reenie said. "But I wonder where they could be? They don't have a car that I know of. And there's their wagon. I don't see that old horse of theirs, I imagine Sam's on that, but where are Josephine and the boys?"

Something almost out of sight, behind the dugout, caught Cora's eye. Two small boys peeped out from behind an old caved-in outhouse. Cora took one step closer, slowly, the way you approach wild barn kitties. "Hello, there," she said. "You know me, I'm your neighbor down the road." She pointed toward her house. "We wanted to visit with your folks. Are they home?"

Over-big, sunken eyes stared out from under mops of ratty, black hair, expressionless and silent.

"Well, I came over because I was hoping somebody would eat these extra sugar cookies and bread and butter sandwiches I have in the car," Cora continued. "Do you boys know anyone who could help me with that? I have way too many, and it'd be too much trouble to throw them to my dogs."

The boys darted from their hiding place, made a wide circle around Cora and planted themselves behind the car as if they were playing freeze-tag and the car was base. Cora and Reenie looked at each other, shrugged, then unloaded two boxes from the car and set them on the table under the lean-to. Reaching under the old dish towel covering their box, they pulled out a paper sack with cookies and a Mason jar of cold milk and set them on the table.

In a flash, the boys were there, grabbing the jar, pulling off the lid and guzzling the milk, taking greedy, sloppy turns, spilling too much, both of them trying to drink from it at the same time.

"Why, they're thirsty!" Reenie said. She saw an empty jar on the lean-to shelf, held it up, made a face, and then wiped the jar out as best as she could. Prying the milk jar from their hands, she poured half of it into the empty jar as they grabbed for it. She gave them each their own jar, which they promptly drained.

"I think I have some water," Cora said as she went to look in the car. She always tried to keep a jar of water with her, in case there was car trouble and she was stranded on her way to town. Reenie showed the boys the cookies which they gobbled down before Cora was back. The sandwiches were next, but when the boys saw the water, they dropped their half-eaten bread on the ground and grabbed for it.

"Wait! Stop! You boys will get sick, you're eating and drinking so fast." Cora held the water above her head while they jumped for it. "You sit down on the bench, and I will give you all this water. But first you have to do what we say."

Miraculously, they followed her directions.

"You," Cora pointed to the slightly larger boy, dressed only in a pair of thin undershorts. "Can you tell me your name?" She poured a half-inch of water into an empty jar, ignoring the milky tinge, and handed it to Reenie.

"Delbert."

Reenie handed him the jar. He drained it and handed it back for more. The littler one's face screwed up, ready to cry.

"You? Tell me yours?" Cora asked quickly, pointing to him and pouring another serving.

"Otis," he answered, earning his drink.

Cora poured another serving and pointed to Delbert. "Where's your Ma?"

"She was sick."

Answer, drink. Otis's turn.

"Where's your Pa?"

Shrug. Drink. Delbert's turn.

"You know where your Pa is?"

Head shake. Drink. Otis.

"Where's Lem?

"Going to look for Pa."

Drink.

"Where?"

Shrug. Drink.

Reenie paused, handed her jar back to Cora, came around the table and sat beside the boys on the bench. Ever so kindly, she asked. "Boys, when your mother got sick, was she here, at home?" They nodded uneasily, wondering if the food and water part was over now. "Did anybody come help her? Anybody come see her?" Head shakes, no. Cora and Reenie looked at each other. "Have you two been outside all day?"

Nods.

"Lem told us when he woke us up yesterday not to go back in the house til he got back. Said there was a family of rattlers under the bed. So we stayed outside all day." Otis said. He held up two fingers. "Both days. Both days and the night of the one day." He added one more finger and was soon so busy counting and pondering the math involved with an extra finger that he lost track of the conversation, so Delbert took over. "I didn't believe him," he said. "I didn't hear no rattles, but Lem said they was asleep so that's why we had to sneak out so quiet and fast and not even look once at the bed or they'd wake up and git us. So we did."

Cora set down the water jars, came to the bench and

sat on the other side of the boys. "Boys, did your momma get better?" Puzzled looks. Shrugs. She stood back up and reached into the box for a fat, paper-wrapped square of cornbread and handed it to Reenie.

Reenie made a big production out of unwrapping the cornbread, dividing it and serving it while Cora edged to the door of the dugout. She didn't have to open it, she could hear the flies buzzing and see enough through the gap between the door and the jamb. Cora closed her eyes, leaned her forehead on the door, and tried to think of a little prayer for the departed soul of Josephine Jasper.

She turned back, caught Reenie's eyes and shook her head.

"Say, boys," Reenie said, too brightly, "I have a great idea. Why don't you two come over to my place and wait for Lem and your Pa there? I have a whole passel of little boys your size to play with. And we'll have catfish for supper. Would you boys like that?"

"OK." Otis said. The boys hopped off the bench and trotted toward the car. Delbert, though paused long enough to ask, "Will Lem know where we are?"

"I'll stay here to wait for him." Cora told him. "Reenie, you take my car, but stop and get Floyd. Send him over here." The boys were out of earshot now, already bouncing on the back seat, excited to be in a car. "It's gonna be dark in a few hours, somebody needs to hunt up Lem. And then there's— " she nodded toward the dugout.

"I'd best send Pake for the sheriff," Reenie said before she opened the car door, mindful of the little ears inside. "Who knows what happened here?"

Sheriff Cole saw no signs of a crime as a cause of death. "Least-wise, no crime on the books." He shook his head in disgust then turned his head to spit in the dirt. "And I bet we've seen the back of Sam Jasper for the last time." Pake, Cora, and Floyd all stood around the Jasper's yard in the early evening heat waiting for instructions from The Law. What to do about Josephine Jasper? "We ain't gonna find Sam. Word is, he's crosswise with that boot-leggin outfit up in Kansas right now, so he ain't gonna pop up for some time. That is if they ain't already caught him and put him down themselves. You all know anything about her people, where she come from?"

"Reenie heard her say once she was full-grown when she first came to Kansas. That's all I know," Cora said. "I don't know where she called home."

"I suppose I could make a call to the sheriff in Kiowa, but I'd have to drive all the way back to town for a phone," said Sheriff Cole, "and I doubt that'll turn up much, anyways. Anybody who knows anything about her won't likely be hospitable to a social call from The Law. So that means no next-of-kin immediately handy, and she becomes the responsibility of the county."

"You gonna bury her in the Potter's Field, then?" Pake asked.

"Well, now that's what we could do, yes. But here's what I'm thinking. She's been holed up in there for, what, two days? And it's been mighty hot. I'm not anxious to haul her in my car with me, and it don't seem quite right to put her in the trunk. Other choice is, I drive all the way back to town and get the undertaker to come back out here to fetch her. But as I was leaving town, I saw him puttin' gas in his 'hearst' on his way to pick up Claude Schute from clear over at the Cherokee hospital to bring him home to bury. So it'd be near midnight by the time he could get her, and somebody would have to wait with the, ah, remains til' then." Nobody looked eager to volunteer. Not that they were squeamish; but evening chores still had to be done, no disrespect intended.

"And even then, we'd put her in Potter's Field in the morning, and that's the end of her. No marker, no way to look her up, in case Sam ever does show up asking, or those little guys one day feel the need to decorate a grave. She was a mother, after all. And it is getting late."

"So what are you suggesting?" Cora asked.

"Ain't Sam's first wife and her newborn, and even his own ma, buried out here, somewheres on the place?"

Floyd pointed to a scrubby cedar tree about two hundred yards past the barn. "Right there. All of 'em, I remember. I helped him put Lucinda and a baby there, myself. That was a terrible sad day. Lem was such a little bitty guy, to lose his momma."

Pake saw where the sheriff was headed with this. "I have a pickaxe in my pickup right now, to bust up the ground with. We could have it all done in no time, if Floyd runs home for another shovel."

"What do you think, Mrs. McKeever?" asked the sheriff. It seemed prudent to have a woman weigh in here. These kinds of things required someone used to civilized thinking to remind menfolk how to act, and, after all, his position was an elected one. "I can take care of the death certificate when I get back to town, so's there's record of it at the court house."

"I'm thinking of those boys." Cora answered. "I know I would sure hate to come back one day and find my Momma's in a pauper's grave in town, lumped in with all kinds of unnamed, homeless peoples. At least here, she'd be at home. And whoever buys it back from the bank—" she glanced at Floyd, their eyes meeting, "could make sure it's noted in the deed, that there's graves in the northeast corner of the section."

Sheriff Cole nodded, relieved. "Sounds as Christian as we can manage, under the circumstances. I already got one shovel in my car. Let's git 'er did."

The boys went to the County Home, but weren't there for long. The littlest one — nobody could ever remember which one was which — was adopted out right away to a couple from Enid. The middle one died of appendicitis that first winter. And Lem kept running off. He would run off, the sheriff would round him up and take him back, and he'd run off again. Eventually, they got tired of looking for him, and nobody knew his whereabouts for some time. Neither his Pa nor his Ma's family ever did come around asking after him.

But a few years later, as a young man on leave from the army, Lem showed up at Salt Fork. He drove around the county in a borrowed car, looking things over. He dropped in on a Sunday Service at Rose of Sharon. People were real glad to see him, Grandma Reenie said, but even so, he didn't stay long.

Chapter Thirty-three

Susannah and Merrilee fell asleep somewhere south of Topeka, and I was all alone in the empty, dark, outer space of the high plains at night. Around two-thirty in the morning, I was getting a little sleepy myself, so I picked up the CB mic one more time. "Breaker one-nine for Itty Bitty Betty, this is Bunny-Wunny. Come in." I repeated it three or four times until a trucker finally replied.

"She's gone, Bunny-Wunny. Nobody's heard from her all week. You want her old business, you're welcome to set up shop now. Meet me on channel three?" I turned the unit off and said a little prayer for Betty.

I sang my way home. All the way to Wichita, I sang through the Rose of Sharon Hymnbook I keep in my head — the old red one, not the new tan one — then from Wichita to Oklahoma I sang all the old Swing-Singer songs. From the state line to our house took three John Denvers, and then I was home.

It was not yet daylight when I turned into the long driveway. Duke and Blue Dog must have heard us coming and woke everybody up with their barking. I saw the porch lights, first ours, then Chuck's flick on. By the time I got the bus to our yard, Mom and Dad were already on the porch. I cut the motor, grabbed Susannah out of her bed, and flew down the bus steps.

Dad, barefoot and bare-chested, held his shotgun in one hand as he reached for me. I noticed Mom's own .22 lying on the porch swing, handy. I loaded my sleeping daughter into her arms.

Merilee had roused herself and now she stood in the stairwell of the bus, with JW nothing but a shadow behind her. Merrilee waited for us to greet each other and then called to Dad. "Harvell? Could I see you on the bus for a moment?" She could have been asking him for help with a stuck jar lid, she was that composed.

Someone else had joined us in the yard. Chuck! I threw myself around his neck, and he grabbed me up with one arm. The other held his rifle away from us as he swung me around. "Sis!" he hollered. "Why don't you come and see me sometime!"

Dad hopped off the bus. "Chuck," he said, as he hustled toward the house, "Is the dozer still loaded on the trailer?"

Chuck told him it was.

"Go get it and meet me down at the new pond. Hurry, we have to beat the rain."

"What on earth?" Mom tried to ask, but Dad ignored her as he ran into the house.

"Is everything alright? Do I need to see to Merrilee?" Mom asked.

"No. She's fine." I said and grabbed her arm to stop her.

"Do I need to make some breakfast for everybody then? At least some meat and biscuits," she asked. And I laughed. So help me, I did.

"Yes, Ma'am. We need meat and biscuits."

Dad came out of the house, a twenty-pound sack of builder's lime slung over his shoulder.

"What are you doing with that?" Mom demanded, mystified. "I bought that for my pickles."

He didn't answer. Instead, he got on the bus, closed the door, and turned over the engine.

'What in the Sam Hill does he need lime for?" Mom asked again.

I knew, but I wouldn't tell her. Maybe it would come to her eventually, how the lime burns your skin until you wash it off. How it eats through the soft flesh of the cucumbers.

Dad backed up the bus and turned it around in the barn yard. Over by his house, Chuck started up the tractor that would pull the dozer down to the new pond, the pond that was all dug and ready, waiting for the rain to fill it. The new pond that Dad finally got around to building down by the old dugout — on the quarter section of land that everybody still calls The Jasper Place.

This was Old Rev's homecoming, too.

Shortly after sunup, Dad and Chuck came back to the house. "Merrilee and JW left." Dad said. "They're going to Mexico to join Billy Sunday. I'll tell the sheriff to call off the search, that you're home, safe. They shouldn't have any trouble getting down there." We sat down to a breakfast of steak and eggs, biscuits and gravy. Leslie and the baby came down to the house and joined us. We said Grace. We remembered to include Leland. Outside, lightning slammed to the ground. "Looks like God is sending us a good rain," Mom said. She put on more coffee. "Always does," Dad said between bites. Thunder rattled the windows. It would rain all that day and half the next. This dry spell was over.

We hope you enjoyed *The Red Dirt Hymnbook*.

You can help support this book and its author by leaving an honest review at your favorite book review site.

We wish we could leave five-star reviews for all our readers!

Thanks for reading,

Roxie

Fine Dog Press

ACKNOWLEDGEMENTS

Blame this all on Dr. Ken Hada and his best-kept literary secret, the Scissortail Writing Festival. It was there he first said, "Are you going to write, or not? Either do it, or don't. Put something on paper and let's see what you got." Thank you, thank you, Ken, for bossing me around as any self-respecting big cousin should.

Then, straight from heaven came help from award-winning author Anna Myers. You made me believe, Anna, and for that, I am grateful.

God bless my earliest beta readers Carol Noble — AKA World's best BFF — and John Noble, an author himself, gracious with his time and far from my target audience. Brett Kirk, my first editor, I should have paid you more. Lauren Kirk, Alex Rivera and Candace Morey, I should have let you read it sooner. But none of you laughed at the idea, and that was enough. Kim Davis, you never even blinked when I told you what I was scheming, so you also deserve extra-friend credit. There were many more readers — poet and encourager Gary Worth Moody, my sister Dixie, and others too numerous to mention. To all of you, the gift of your time is treasured.

To Brenda Copeland, my final editor, you polished

Ruby's story to the finest sheen. Thank you for your generous expertise.

Lauren Spieller, you can't know what it meant to me that you believed in Ruby and Roxie. You worked so hard, and all you ever got out of it was a jar of wild honey. I will forever be grateful to you.

At its heart, this story is about the love of parents for their children. Mom, thank you for teaching me how and Rebekah, Silas, and Eli (and now Drew!) thanks for being mine to love. Always, everything, it's all been for you.

As for you, Terry, I'm not thanking you here. Because of all there is in this big beautiful life to see and do and be and know, only one thing — your love — has ever left me truly speechless.

Reader's Guide

1. A major theme in *Red Dirt Hymnbook* is the relationship between parents and children. How would you characterize the relationship between Ruby and each of her parents? Ruby and Susannah? JW and each of his parents?

2. An early working title for this book was *The Parables of Ruby*. How is Ruby's story a mirror of the beloved parable of The Prodigal Son? How does it differ?

3. When Ruby looks back on her teenage years, she hints at the contrast between her home life and her school life. Can you relate to this? Can you see how it might have played a role in her decision to leave college and marry JW?

4. For much of the book, Ruby is in denial about the true nature of her relationship with JW. Can you see certain places in the story where she is looking at her marriage realistically? Do you see this as a realistic portrayal of domestic abuse?

5. How would you characterize Ruby's spiritual life, i.e. her relationship to God? Does it change over time?

6. Two key characters, Merrilee and Susannah, have the least to say of anyone, yet are very strong

personalities. How do they express themselves without words?

7. What role does music play in Ruby's story?

8. What would your CB handle be?

9. Where do you see Ruby now? And Susannah? JW? How about Itty Bitty Betty?

10. Is there a particular landscape or geography that calls to you the way the Great Plains call to Ruby? Describe it, and how it affects you.

Roxie Faulkner Kirk is available to Skype with book clubs and would love to hear your questions and comments. You can contact her at www.roxiefaulknerkirk.com. Thanks for reading!